Into the Heart of Life

Henry Miller
at One Hundred

HENRY MILLER TITLES AVAILABLE FROM NEW DIRECTIONS

The Air-Conditioned Nightmare

Aller Retour New York
(Introduction by George Wickes)

Big Sur and the Oranges of Hieronymus Bosch

The Books in My Life

The Colossus of Maroussi

The Cosmological Eye

The Durrell-Miller Letters, 1935–80
(Edited by Ian S. MacNiven)

From Your Capricorn Friend:
Henry Miller & the *Stroker* 1978–80

Henry Miller on Writing

The Henry Miller Reader
(Introduction by Lawrence Durrell)

Into the Heart of Life: Henry Miller at One Hundred
(Edited by Frederick Turner)

Just Wild About Harry (Play)

Letters to Emil
(Edited by George Wickes)

The Nightmare Notebook
(Limited Edition Facsimile)

Remember to Remember

The Smile at the Foot of the Ladder

Stand Still Like the Hummingbird

The Time of the Assassins

The Wisdom of the Heart

Into the Heart of Life

Henry Miller at One Hundred

EDITED BY FREDERICK TURNER

A NEW DIRECTIONS BOOK

Manufactured in the United States of America
New Directions Books are printed on acid-free paper
Published in Canada by Penguin Books Canada Limited

Library of Congress Cataloging in Publication Data

Into the heart of life : Henry Miller at one hundred / edited by Frederick
Turner.
p. cm.
ISBN 0–8112–1185–1 (pbk.) : $10.95
1. Miller, Henry, 1891–   —Criticism and interpretation.
I. Miller, Henry, 1891–   .   Turner, Frederick W., 1937–   .
PS3525.I5454Z699 1991
818'.5209—dc20

91—29996
CIP

New Directions Books are published for James Laughlin
by New Directions Publishing Corporation,
80 Eighth Avenue, New York 10011

CONTENTS

EDITOR'S INTRODUCTION

On March 4, 1930, a boat train from England chugged into Paris, and Henry Miller descended into the streets of the most cosmopolitan city in the Western world. He put up at the Hotel St. Germain-des-Près, unpacked his bags, placed his copy of *Leaves of Grass* next to the manuscripts of his two unpublished novels, and then to hearten himself went out for a stroll and a meal. At the restaurant he discovered he had forgotten the French for "green beans"; and with this his flimsy knowledge of French collapsed, leaving him mute in this city of strangers. If he was to get along here, he would have to learn to speak anew.

During those first weeks in Paris Miller maintained an air of cheerfulness in the long letters he wrote his boyhood friend, Emil Schnellock. Schnellock had himself been to Paris, and Miller now took some pleasure in describing for Schnellock scenes he had known. Back in New York he had poured over Schnellock's map of Paris, pestering his friend to point out various locales. Now he was in the wondrous place himself and equipped with maps of his own to explore the city's rich literary history. He was still having trouble making himself understood, he told Schnellock: stumbling about on the Right Bank after midnight his pronunciation of the "Seine" got him nowhere closer to it, and "when I want to say 'drunk' I say 'fuck'. . . . Imagine telling a waitress that you were well fucked last night." But language difficulties were only a temporary inconvenience compared with his grand opportunity here: he was in Paris indefinitely, away from the nightmare New York City had become for him, and he could see stretched before him endless days free for writing. And that was the problem. It was put up or shut up time for Henry Miller as a writer, and none knew it better than he.

It is not wise to trust everything Miller has said about his life. He was a compulsive fabulist, and as he grew older and more aware of himself as a work of art his autobiographical inventions became more pronounced and pervasive. Still, there is good reason to listen to him when he says that from "early manhood on my whole activity revolved about, or was motivated by, the fact that I thought of myself, first potentially, then embryonically, and finally manifestly, as a writer." Yet the Henry Miller who regarded his Paris stint as the opportunity of a lifetime really had little more idea of what becoming a writer might mean than the Henry Miller who some years earlier had hauled a giant mahogany table from his father's tailor shop to the house he shared with his first wife Beatrice and installed it smack in the middle of the living room. That had been an almost desperate statement of his literary ambitions, but when it came to composing at the table, Miller had found himself to be a stammerer with nothing worth articulating. As he regarded the experiences of his life thus far—the German immigrant background, the boyhood in the gamy streets of Brooklyn, his ranch hand experiences in the West, his job with Western Union—it all looked so prosaic, so formlessly sprawling, so thoroughly working-class American that he was struck dumb with mingled fear and rage: what the hell did all this mean, and how could he, "a poor slob of a Brooklynite" (as he once put it), discover what meaning there might be in it? Nor was his voracious and unsystematic consumption of the world's literature of any apparent help: Boccaccio, Petronius, Rabelais, the great American Romantics (Emerson, Thoreau, and especially Whitman), Nietzsche, Dostoyevsky, Lawrence, Knut Hamsun. He read them all and more, searching through their pages for the formula that once possessed would allow him to join their company.

In 1923 in New York, Miller had met a taxi dancer named June Edith Smith (a.k.a. June Edith Mansfield). Here for the first time was someone who believed Miller was destined to write, whereas his family and Beatrice had derided this peculiar ambition. Whatever else she may have been—and much about her remains mysterious—June was the first member of the Miller cult, and she was determined that through her efforts Miller would come to greatness. Miller left Beatrice for June, and together the couple descended into a shadowy world of marginal work, frequent forced changes of address, and numerous get-rich-quick-without-really-working schemes in the New York of the 1920s. But as far as Miller's literary career was concerned, all their efforts came to nothing. He had peddled some literary sketches door to door, written a gallery of portraits of Americans warped by the Horatio Alger legend; a novel he was calling *Moloch* and which he had brought with him to Paris; and yet another, still unfinished, telling the tangled, murky story of his life with June. None of these had yet found a publisher, and Miller was beginning to admit to himself that perhaps they never would. June herself, for all the vitality of her belief in him, had begun to wonder if she had been mistaken. At last she had almost deported him to Europe, buying his steamer ticket with money provided by one of her many "admirers" and all but pushing him penniless out the door of their apartment. He'd had to borrow ten dollars from Schnellock to take ship with.

"I can't understand my failure," he wrote Schnellock from Paris. "Somewhere there must be an audience waiting for my words. Where?" Why, he wondered in the same letter, "does nobody want what I write? Jesus, when I think of being 38, and poor, and unknown, I get furious. I refuse to live this way forever. There must be a way out." This was the real condition of the Henry Miller who dropped his bags at the Hotel St. Germain-des-Près and faced the daunting prospect of his freedom there.

Dependent on the uncertain arrivals of money from June, Miller soon enough discovered that like the anonymous hero of Knut Hamsun's *Hunger,* his freedom included the freedom to starve in public. Each day he would go to the American Express office, hoping to hear from June. Most days there was nothing; at best he might find a cable telling him to hold on, that money would arrive soon. Meanwhile, he entered on the dreary business of seeking ever cheaper hotels, then avoiding the baleful glances of the proprietors as his bills mounted.

In September, June arrived for the first of the four wrenching visits she would make before asking for a divorce. But she had little money herself and so joined her husband in the hunt for affordable lodging. A month later she left, and Miller felt more than ever on his own. The illusion of marriage was slipping away along with his hopes of ever seeing his novels published, though he continued to slash and revise the one about June with a sort of self-slaughtering despair. There was, he felt, something fundamentally wrong with the book, what precisely, he didn't quite know. "What I must do," he wrote Schnellock, "before blowing out my brains is to write a few simple confessions in plain Milleresque language." The suicidal reference was not all melodrama, for at some level he had contemplated it, once seeking out the hotel where Strindberg had thought of ending his own struggles, even going up to view the shabby, empty room.

As 1930 turned into 1931, he drifted lower, glancing now into countless rank hotels, occasionally sleeping in the open, gradually acquiring the appearance of a *clochard*, so that "people everywhere nudge one another and point me out." For a time a friend let him sleep on the floor of the airless office of the Cinema Vanves where each morning Miller heard the rumble of a cart and the keening chant of its unseen operator. Everything now began to drop away from him—pounds, clothing, literary pretensions, even his heroes like D. H. Lawrence and Thomas Mann whose work now seemed inadequate compared to the bottommost truth of life as he had come to know it. Neither Lawrence nor Mann nor indeed many of the other masters he had once so esteemed had known real hunger—when, as Hamsun had described it, your intestines curled inside you like snakes. They had not known the dread of winter when the sharpening winds sent you into the cafes "to breathe the sour breath of stale, smoked bodies bombinating in the void." He felt like a frontiersman moving along the border between order and insanity, forced to the expedient of sitting in the same place in the same cafe each day as a way of simulating a structured existence. By the spring of the year he believed he had hit absolute bottom. There was nowhere farther down he could go, except to the bottom of the Seine.

Yet, looking up at down (as the old blues line had it), he displayed a curious resiliency, even a kind of tough bounciness, like a ball of India rubber that cannot quite be flattened. "If I were told tomorrow that I must hang," he wrote, "I would say O.K. I've seen the show. And fuck you, Jack!" Then, from these depths, he wrote Schnellock on August 24th, "I start tomorrow on the Paris book: first person, uncensored, formless—fuck everything!"

The uncensored, formless, first person book was *Tropic of Cancer*, published in Paris in 1934. Fittingly, it bore a preface by Anaïs Nin, Miller's mentor, patronness, and lover, then as unknown herself as Miller was. It was she who had taken over where June left off, similarly sure that Miller had literary greatness in him, but convinced that he would never come to it until he shed much of his intellectual baggage (including his preciously gathered literary preconceptions) and stripped himself down to the raw, ineradicable Henry Miller. In essence, she told Miller, he was already too old to write effectively; he would have to become young again, make a truly new start. Since his life thus far had been pretty much a failure—two marriages, numerous jobs, two botched novels—and his prospects barren, Miller must have felt he had nothing to lose by trying to make this new beginning, by tackling the work of writing armed only with his bare hands. And in any case, his Paris months had already so much reduced him that he had left about him little actual or metaphysical avoirdupois. But there was something else as well that prepared him to assent to Nin's message, and this was his cultural heritage as an American.

On the face of it this seems strange since no major American writer has been more consistently critical of his native culture. Indeed, his existence in Paris, whatever its initial motivations, had become in part a furious denial of his nationality. Looking at the whole of his work, however, it is clear there are few more radically American writers of the twentieth century, and at some point in the writing of his first major book Miller himself evidently came to appreciate the artery that stretched from him back through Whitman and Thoreau to Emerson and beyond Emerson to the making of the American nation. *Tropic of Cancer* contains some telling references to Whitman and for its inscription Miller cited Emerson: "These novels will give way, by and by, to diaries or autobiographies—captivating books, if only a man knew how to choose among what he calls his experiences that which is truly his experience, and how to record truth truly."

Emerson's subject in the passage is ostensibly the future content of American literature, but as Miller knew in using it there was something else in here as well, and this was Emerson's interest in the process of spiritual debridement and reconstitution that he saw as fundamental to the national experiment: the unprecedented way in which individuals in America were invited by its history and geography to create themselves anew, just as the nation had invented itself out of the deadness of monarchy and colonialism. For Emerson, as for his heirs Thoreau and Whitman (and now Miller) the discovery of the New World was both the central spiritual fact and the governing metaphor of the American experiment and forever proof against all the tragic and silly mistakes that had since been made: out of the old and outworn and dead, the new thing.

In his own life Emerson knew the process was actual. In his thirties he had shaken off ill-health, feelings of inadequacy, and the brooding ghost of the Puritan past to make the lightning claim that the individual must look inward to find his guides. Finding them, he must have the courage to follow wherever they might lead. In his instance, by shifting his attention from society's expectations inward to his own spiritual drama, Emerson had successfully reinvented himself as the cosmic optimist and sage who sparked off the American Romantic movement. In his words was the first adequate expression of that anarchical American lust for renewal that had already by Emerson's time manifested itself in a persistent strain of antinomial thought and behavior; a successful revolution; several thwarted rebellions; frontier lawlessness; splinter sects; utopian efforts; and that crowd he styled "Madmen, madwomen . . . Dunkers, Muggletonians, Come-outers, Groaners, Agrarians, Seventh-day Baptists, Quakers, Abolitionists," and other uncontrollable types that made up part of the reform movement of the pre-Civil War decades—a crowd from which Emerson took some pains to distinguish himself.

Thus Emerson was prepared to instantly appreciate Whitman's achievement in the 1855 *Leaves of Grass*. Here was a man who had listened to Emerson and then to himself; here was another who had reinvented himself, emerging in the mid 1850s as a barbaric, autobiographical singer; here was one who had broken all of prosody's rules and had written an American epic. And if later the master would become uneasy, even appalled when he saw the direction in which Whitman's autobiographical revelations were leading his poetry, still the great breakthrough had been made for all time to come.

Made for Henry Miller, too, who echoed Whitman in the opening passage of *Tropic of Cancer* as he commenced in mid-life his own "Song of Myself": "To sing you must first open your mouth. You must have a pair of lungs, and a little knowledge of music. It is not necessary to have an accordion, or a guitar. The essential thing is to *want* to sing. This then is a song. I am singing."

And such a song as there began American letters had not known before and may never again. Whitman had said that the great writers were to be known "by the absence in them of tricks and by the justification of perfect personal candor." The latter quality, he thought, was so important that all a writer's other faults might be forgiven if only he were perfectly candid. The writer who so startlingly announced himself in *Tropic of Cancer* and who sustained his own "barbaric yawp" over the next three decades was distinguished both by his apparent lack of artifice and by his scabrous candor. Discovering that there was nothing else to be done short of completely remaking himself as a writer, he junked all the literary conventions so laboriously learned in his reading and attacked his subjects in a deliberately ham-handed way, allowing impulse to rule over design and artifice, flinging his books together in such a way that the reader often is left with a sense of wonder: how did all this get jammed between two covers, and where did it begin and end?

At the top of his form, Miller is unlike any of his contemporaries, his language rushing forth in a great imaginative torrent and sweeping the reader along on a wild dizzying ride. Images and effects lesser writers would have shed heart's blood to achieve are tossed off and flung aside as Miller races to keep up with his vision. William Gass has said that Miller's best writing conveys the impression of being *talked* rather than written, as if one were in the presence of some superbly gifted barroom monologist. Yet even this praise fails to convey the music that is there in Miller's language: for that we have to turn for analogy to the greatest of the jazz soloists—Parker, say, or Art Tatum or Clifford Brown—where one astonishing chorus treads upon the notes of the next.

Miller could, of course, write more conventionally and indeed did so in his later years, as if the lessons of Paris had begun to fade for him and something of the younger New York Miller with all his intellectual and literary baggage hanging about him had returned to chide him for a career of excesses. Once, in his down-and-out Paris days, he had described himself as slouching emptily through the great city like a ghost at a banquet. Now that situation seemed oddly reprised, the ghost of the younger Miller haunting the voluptuous banquet the mature writer had prepared in the thirties, forties, and fifties. A photograph of him in the 1960s in the *impasse* of the Villa Seurat (where some of his best Paris work was done) shows an aging man, his hand raised to his lips in bemusement, as if asking, *"I* did this?" So it had been with the late Whitman, who wondered whether, after all the passion, the daring adventure in self-revelation, *Leaves of Grass* was "only a language experiment."

Miller, however, stuck by his Paris vision of how a man must write. When he was eighty with more than fifty books behind him, he told an interviewer that the only writers he had respect for "are those who have put themselves completely into their work. Not those who use their skillful hands to do something. This isn't writing, in my opinion." He preferred, he went on, the man who is "unskillful, who is an awkward writer, but who has something to say, who is dealing himself one time on every page." He had never, so he claimed, been drawn to the classics (though it is evident he had read a good many of them) because there the writing was "too skillful, and following old patterns . . . , improving on them—but the breakthroughs have occurred with rare men who spoke with their own voices."

One is never in doubt as to who speaks in Henry Miller's work. His is one of the most distinctive voices in American letters, sustained through a remarkable range of novels, short stories, sketches, travel literature, cultural and literary criticism, letters, biography, and, of course, autobiography. Anarchical, irreverent, crude, at times downright cruel and bigoted, it is the voice of a singer who has reinvented himself out of nothingness and failure, expressing something deep in the native grain.

NOTE ON THE SELECTIONS

Despite the vast amount of material available, it is no easy matter to anthologize Henry Miller. This is because early on he flouted literary conventions like chapter and paragraph divisions; transitions; narrative chronology, and continuity of subject matter: he might, for instance, begin writing about a visit to Knossos, then suddenly veer off into a jazz fugue critique on modern civilization. Often the divagations are more captivating than the original line of thought. These early revolutionary intentions remained as habits of composition as Miller grew older, and if, as he once said, he intended to cause trouble for his biographers and for the literary critics, so has he also for anthologists. In making the following selections, I have been concerned to represent Miller's distinctive literary characteristics; to suggest the impressive range of his achievement, including passages from as many works as practicable, without at the same time giving mere snippets in the service of comprehensiveness; and to display a kind of chronology of the writer's life from his Brooklyn boyhood to his Big Sur years. I did not make selections from some of Miller's best known works—*Black Spring* and *The Rosy Crucifixion* —which might be reason enough for the making of another anthology. In Miller's case this would be all to the good, and it is certain that the author himself wouldn't have had it any other way.

—Frederick Turner

TROPIC OF CAPRICORN

From Tropic of Capricorn. *Begun in Paris in the summer of 1932 and published there seven years later,* Capricorn *was unavailable in America until the Grove Press edition of 1961.* Miller *began it in the afterglow of* Tropic of Cancer, *but had to set it aside numerous times because he couldn't find a way to tell the profoundly troubling story of his relationship to June Smith. He had already failed at this in the novel he called "Crazy Cock" (and some would argue, as Norman Mailer does, that he failed yet again in* The Rosy Crucifixion). *But* Tropic of Capricorn *succeeds, and wildly so, because Miller was temporarily able to evade his obsession with that relationship and focus instead on the larger, more resonant story of his hero's boyhood and young manhood in the boiling world of New York at the turn of the century.*

I'm thinking now about the rock fight one summer's afternoon long long ago when I was staying with my Aunt Caroline up near Hell Gate. My cousin Gene and I had been corralled by a gang of boys while we were playing in the park. We didn't know which side we were fighting for but we were fighting in dead earnest amidst the rock pile by the river bank. We had to show even more courage than the other boys because we were suspected of being sissies. That's how it happened that we killed one of the rival gang. Just as they were charging us my cousin Gene let go at the ringleader and caught him in the guts with a handsome-sized rock. I let go almost at the same instant and my rock caught him in the temple and when he went down he lay there for good and not a peep out of him. A few minutes later the cops came and the boy was found dead. He was eight or nine years old, about the same age as us. What they would have done to us if they had caught us I don't know. Anyway, so as not to arouse any suspicion we hurried home; we had cleaned up a bit on the way and had combed our hair. We walked in looking almost as immaculate as when we had left the house. Aunt Caroline gave us our usual two big slices of sour rye with fresh butter and a little sugar over it and we sat there at the kitchen table listening to her with an angelic smile. It was an extremely hot day and she thought we had better stay in the house, in the big front room where the blinds had been pulled down, and play marbles with our little friend Joey Kasselbaum. Joey had the reputation of being a little backward and ordinarily we would have trimmed him, but that afternoon, by a sort of mute understanding, Gene and I allowed him to win everything we had. Joey was so happy that he took us down to his cellar later and made his sister pull up her dress and show us what was underneath. Weesie, they called her, and I remember that she was stuck on me instantly. I came from another part of the city, so far away it seemed to them, that it was almost like coming from another country. They even seemed to think that I talked differently from them. Whereas the other urchins used to pay to make Weesie lift her dress up, for us it was done with love. After a while we persuaded her not to do it any more for the other boys—we were in love with her and we wanted her to go straight.

When I left my cousin the end of the summer I didn't see him again for twenty years or more. When we did meet what deeply impressed me was the look of innocence he wore—the same expression as the day of the rock fight. When I spoke to him about the fight I was still more amazed to discover that he had forgotten that it was we who had killed the boy; he remembered the boy's death but he spoke of it as though neither he nor I had any part in it. When I mentioned Weesie's name he had difficulty in placing her. Don't you remember the cellar next door . . . *Joey Kesselbaum?* At this a faint smile passed over his face. He thought it extraordinary that I should remember such things. He was already married, a father, and working in a factory making fancy pipe cases. He considered it extraordinary to remember events that had happened so far back in the past.

On leaving him that evening I felt terribly despondent. It was as though he had attempted to eradicate a precious part of my life, and himself with it. He seemed more attached to the tropical fish which he was collecting than to the wonderful past. As for me I recollect everything, everything that happened that summer, and particularly the day of the rock fight. There are times, in fact, when the taste of that big slice of sour rye which his mother handed me that afternoon is stronger in my mouth than the food I am actually tasting. And the sight of Weesie's little bud almost stronger than the actual feel of what is in my hand. The way the boy lay there after we downed him, far far more impressive than the history of the World War. The whole long summer, in fact, seems like an idyll out of the Arthurian legends. I often wonder what it was about this particular summer which makes it so vivid in my memory. I have only to close my eyes a moment in order to relive each day. The death of the boy certainly caused me no anguish—it was forgotten before a week had elapsed. The sight of Weesie standing in the gloom of the cellar with her dress lifted up, that too passed easily away. Strangely enough, the thick slice of rye bread which his mother handed me each day seems to possess more potency than any other image of that period. I wonder about it . . . wonder deeply. Perhaps it is that whenever she handed me the slice of bread it was with a tenderness and a sympathy that I had never known before. She was a very homely woman, my Aunt Caroline. Her face was marked by the pox, but it was a kind, winsome face which no disfigurement could mar. She was enormously stout and she had a very soft, a very caressing voice. When she addressed me she seemed to give me even more attention, more consideration, than her own son. I would like to have stayed with her always: I would have chosen her for my own mother had I been permitted. I remember distinctly how when my mother arrived on a visit she seemed peeved that I was so contented with my new life. She even remarked that I was ungrateful, a remark I never forgot, because then I realized for the first time that to be ungrateful was perhaps necessary and good for one. If I close my eyes now and I think about it, about the slice of bread, I think almost at once that in this house I never knew what it was to be scolded. I think if I had told my Aunt Caroline that I had killed a boy in the lot, told her just how it happened, she would have put her arms around me and forgiven me—instantly. That's why perhaps that summer is so precious to me. It was a summer of tacit and complete absolution. That's why I can't forget Weesie either. She was full of a natural goodness, a child who was in love with me and who made no reproaches. She was the first of the other sex to admire me for being *different*. After Weesie it was the other way round. I was loved, but I was hated too for being what I was. Weesie made an effort to understand. The very fact that I came from a strange country, that I spoke another language, drew her closer to me. The way her eyes shone when she presented me to her little friends is something I will never forget. Her eyes seemed to be bursting with love and admiration. Sometimes the three of us would walk to the riverside in the evening and sitting on the bank we would talk as children talk when they are out of sight of their elders. We talked then, I know it now so well, more sanely and more profoundly than our parents. To give us that thick slice of bread each day the parents had to pay a heavy penalty. The worst penalty was that they became estranged from us. For, with each slice they fed us we became not only more indifferent to them, but we became more and more superior to them. In our ungratefulness was our strength and our beauty. Not being devoted we were innocent of all crime. The boy whom I saw drop dead, who lay there motionless, without making the slightest sound or whimper, the killing of that boy seems almost like a clean, healthy performance. The struggle for food, on the other hand, seems foul and degrading and when we stood in the presence of our parents we sensed that they had come to us unclean and for that we could never forgive them. The thick slice of bread in the afternoons, precisely because it was not earned, tasted delicious to us. Never again will bread taste this way. Never again will it be given this way. The day of the murder it was even tastier than ever. It had a slight taste of terror in it which has been lacking ever since. And it was received with Aunt Caroline's tacit but complete absolution.

There is something about the rye bread which I am trying to fathom—something vaguely delicious, terrifying and liberating, something associated with first discoveries. I am thinking of another slice of sour rye which was connected with a still earlier period, when my little friend Stanley and I used to rifle the icebox. That was *stolen* bread and consequently even more marvelous to the palate than the bread which was given with love. But it was in the act of eating the rye bread, the walking around with it and talking at the same time, that something in the nature of revelation occurred. It was like a state of grace, a state of complete ignorance, of self-abnegation. Whatever was imparted to me in these moments I seem to have retained intact and there is no fear that I shall ever lose the knowledge that was gained. It was just the fact perhaps that it was not knowledge as we ordinarily think of it. It was almost like receiving a truth, though truth is almost too precise a word for it. The important thing about the sour rye discussions is that they always took place away from home, away from the eyes of our parents whom we feared but never respected. Left to ourselves there were no limits to what we might imagine. Facts had little importance for us; what we demanded of a subject was that it allow us opportunity to expand. What amazes me, when I look back on it, is how well we understood one another, how well we penetrated to the essential character of each and every one, young or old. At seven years of age we knew with dead certainty, for example, that such a fellow would end up in prison, that another would be a drudge, and another a good for nothing, and so on. We were absolutely correct in our diagnoses, much more correct, for example, than our parents, or our teachers, more correct, indeed, than the so-called psychologists. Alfie Betcha turned out to be an absolute bum; Johnny Gerhardt went to the penitentiary; Bob Kunst became a work horse. Infallible predictions. The learning we received only tended to obscure our vision. From the day we went to school we learned nothing; on the contrary, we were made obtuse, we were wrapped in a fog of words and abstractions.

With the sour rye the world was what it is essentially, a primitive world ruled by magic, a world in which fear plays the most important role. The boy who could inspire the most fear was the leader and he was respected as long as he could maintain his power. There were other boys who were rebels, and they were admired, but they never became the leader. The majority were clay in the hands of the fearless ones; a few could be depended on, but the most not. The air was full of tension—nothing could be predicted for the morrow. This loose, primitive nucleus of a society created sharp appetites, sharp emotions, sharp curiosity. Nothing was taken for granted; each day demanded a new test of power, a new sense of strength or of failure. And so, up until the age of nine or ten, we had a real taste of life—we were on our own. That is, those of us who were fortunate enough not to have been spoiled by our parents, those of us who were free to roam the streets at night and to discover things with our own eyes.

What I am thinking of, with a certain amount of regret and longing, is that this thoroughly restricted life of early boyhood seems like a limitless universe and the life which followed upon it, the life of the adult, a constantly diminishing realm. From the moment when one is put in school one is lost; one has the feeling of having a halter put around his neck. The taste goes out of the bread as it goes out of life. Getting the bread becomes more important than the eating of it. Everything is calculated and everything has a price upon it.

My cousin Gene became an absolute nonentity; Stanley became a first-rate failure. Besides these two boys, for whom I had the greatest affection, there was another, Joey, who has since become a letter carrier. I could weep when I think of what life has made them. As boys they were perfect, Stanley least of all because Stanley was more temperamental. Stanley went into violent rages now and then and there was no telling how you stood with him from day to day. But Joey and Gene were the essence of goodness; they were friends in the old meaning of the word. I think of Joey often when I go out into the country because he was what is called a country boy. That meant, for one thing, that he was more loyal, more sincere, more tender, than the boys we knew. I can see Joey now coming to meet me; he was always running with arms wide open and ready to embrace me, always breathless with adventures that he was planning for my partici-pation, always loaded with gifts which he had saved for my coming. Joey received me like the monarchs of old received their guests. Everything I looked at was mine. We had innumerable things to tell each other and nothing was dull or boring. The difference between our respective worlds was enormous.

Though I was of the city too, still, when I visited my cousin Gene, I became aware of an even greater city, a city of New York proper in which my sophistication was negligible. Stanley knew no excursions from his own neighborhood, but Stanley had come from a strange land over the sea, Poland, and there was always between us the mark of the voyage. The fact that he spoke another tongue also increased our admiration for him. Each one was surrounded by a distinguishing aura, by a well-defined identity which was preserved inviolate. With the entrance into life these traits of difference fell away and we all became more or less alike and, of course, most unlike our own selves. And it is this loss of the peculiar self, of the perhaps unimportant individuality, which saddens me and makes the rye bread stand out glowingly. The wonderful sour rye went into the making of our individual selves; it was like the communion loaf in which all participate but from which each one receives only according to his peculiar state of grace. Now we are eating of the same bread, but without benefit of communion, without grace. We are eating to fill our bellies and our hearts are cold and empty. We are separate but not individual.

There was another thing about the sour rye and that was that we often ate a raw onion with it. I remember standing with Stanley in the late afternoons, a sandwich in hand, in front of the veterinary's which was just opposite my home. It always seemed to be late afternoon when Dr. McKinney elected to castrate a stallion, an operation which was done in public and which always gathered a small crowd. I remember the smell of the hot iron and the quivering of the horse's legs, Dr. McKinney's goatee, the taste of the raw onion and the smell of the sewer gas just behind us where they were laying in a new gas main. It was an olfactory performance through and through and, as Abélard so well describes it, practically painless. Not knowing the reason for the operation we used to hold long discussions afterwards which usually ended in a brawl. Nobody liked Dr. McKinney either; there was a smell of iodoform about him and of stale horse piss. Sometimes the gutter in front of his office was filled with blood and in the wintertime the blood froze into the ice and gave a strange look to his sidewalk. Now and then the big two-wheeled cart came, an open cart which smelled like the devil, and they whisked a dead horse into it. Rather it was hoisted in, the carcass, by a long chain which made a creaking noise like the dropping of an anchor. The smell of a bloated dead horse is a foul smell and our street was full of foul smells. On the corner was Paul Sauer's place where raw hides and trimmed hides were stacked up in the street; they stank frightfully too. And then the acrid odor coming from the tin factory behind the house—like the smell of modern progress. The smell of a dead horse, which is almost unbearable, is still a thousand times better than the smell of burning chemicals. And the sight of a dead horse with a bullet hole in the temple, his head lying in a pool of blood and his asshole bursting with the last spasmic evacuation, is still a better sight than that of a group of men in blue aprons coming out of the arched doorway of the tin factory with a hand truck loaded with bales of fresh-made tin. Fortunately for us there was a bakery opposite the tin factory and from the back door of the bakery, which was only a grill, we could watch the bakers at work and get the sweet, irresistible odor of bread and cake. And if, as I say, the gas mains were being laid there was another strange medley of smells—the smell of earth just turned up, of rotted iron pipes, of sewer gas, and of the onion sandwiches which the Italian laborers ate whilst reclining against the mounds of upturned earth. There were other smells too, of course, but less striking; such, for instance, as the smell of Silverstein's tailor shop where there was always a great deal of pressing going on. This was a hot, fetid stench which can be best apprehended by imagining that Silverstein, who was a lean, smelly Jew himself, was cleaning out the farts which his customers had left behind in their pants. Next door was the candy and stationery shop owned by two daffy old maids who were religious; here there was the almost sickeningly sweet smell of taffy, of Spanish peanuts, of jujubes and Sen-Sen and of Sweet Caporal cigarettes. The stationery store was like a beautiful cave, always cool, always full of intriguing objects; where the soda fountain was, which gave off another distinct odor, ran a thick marble slab which turned sour in the summertime and yet mingled pleasantly, the sourness, with the slightly ticklish, dry smell of the carbonated water when it was fizzed into the glass of ice cream.

With the refinements that come with maturity the smells faded out, to be replaced by only one other distinctly memorable, distinctly pleasurable smell—the odor of the cunt. More particularly the odor that lingers on the fingers after playing with a woman, for, if it has not been noticed before, this smell is even more enjoyable, perhaps because it already carries with it the perfume of the past tense, than the odor of the cunt itself. But this odor, which belongs to maturity, is but a faint odor compared with the odors attaching to childhood. It is an odor which evaporates, almost as quickly in the mind's imagination, as in reality. One can remember many things about the woman one has loved but it is hard to remember the smell of her cunt—with anything like certitude. The smell of wet hair, on the other hand, a woman's wet hair, is much more powerful and lasting—why, I don't know. I can remember even now, after almost forty years, the smell of my Aunt Tillie's hair after she had taken a shampoo. This shampoo was performed in the kitchen which was always overheated. Usually it was a late Saturday afternoon, in preparation for a ball, which meant again another singular thing—that there would appear a cavalry sergeant with very beautiful yellow stripes, a singularly handsome sergeant who even to my eyes was far too gracious, manly and intelligent for an imbecile such as my Aunt Tillie. But anyway, there she sat on a little stool by the kitchen table drying her hair with a towel. Beside her was a little lamp with a smoked chimney and beside the lamp two curling irons the very sight of which filled me with an inexplicable loathing. Generally she had a little mirror propped up on the table; I can see her now making wry faces at herself as she squeezed the blackheads out of her nose. She was a stringy, ugly, imbecilic creature with two enormous buck teeth which gave her a horsey look whenever her lips drew back in a smile. She smelled sweaty, too, even after a bath. But the smell of her hair—that smell I can never forget, because somehow the smell is associated with my hatred and contempt for her. This smell, when the hair was just drying, was like the smell that comes up from the bottom of a marsh. There were two smells—one of the wet hair and another of the same hair when she threw it into the stove and it burst into flame. There were always curled knots of hair which came from her comb, and they were mixed with dandruff and the sweat of her scalp which was greasy and dirty. I used to stand by her side and watch her, wondering what the ball would be like and wondering how she would behave at the ball. When she was all primped up she would ask me if she didn't look beautiful and if I didn't love her, and of course I would tell her yes. But in the water closet later, which was in the hall just next to the kitchen, I would sit in the flickering light of the burning taper which was placed on the window ledge, and I would say to myself that she looked crazy. After she was gone I would pick up the curling irons and smell them and squeeze them. They were revolting and fascinating—like spiders. Everything about this kitchen was fascinating to me. Familiar as I was with it I never conquered it. It was at once so public and so intimate. Here I was given my bath, in the big tin tub, on Saturdays. Here the three sisters washed themselves and primped themselves. Here my grandfather stood at the sink and washed himself to the waist and later handed me his shoes to be shined. Here I stood at the window in the winter time and watched the snow fall, watched it dully, vacantly, as if I were in the womb and listening to the water running while my mother sat on the toilet. It was in the kitchen where the secret confabulations were held, frightening, odious sessions from which they always reappeared with long, grave faces or eyes red with weeping. Why they ran to the kitchen I don't know. But it was often while they stood thus in secret conference, haggling about a will or deciding how to dispense with some poor relative, that the door suddenly opened and a visitor would arrive, whereupon the atmosphere immediately changed. Changed violently, I mean, as though they were relieved that some outside force had intervened to spare them the horrors of a protracted secret session. I remember now that, seeing that door open and the face of an unexpected visitor peering in, my heart would leap with joy. Soon I would be given a big glass pitcher and asked to run to the corner saloon where I would hand the pitcher in, through the little window at the family entrance, and wait until it was returned brimming with foamy suds. This little run to the corner for a pitcher of beer was an expedition of absolutely incalculable proportions. First of all there was the barber shop just below us, where Stanley's father practiced his profession. Time and again, just as I was dashing out for something, I would see the father giving Stanley a drubbing with the razor strop, a sight that made my blood boil. Stanley was my best friend and his father was nothing but a drunken Polack. One evening, however, as I was dashing out with the pitcher, I had the intense pleasure of seeing another Polack go for Stanley's old man with a razor. I saw his old man coming through the door backwards, the blood running down his neck, his face white as a sheet. He fell on the sidewalk in front of the shop, twitching and moaning, and I remember looking at him for a minute or two and walking on feeling absolutely contented and happy about it. Stanley had sneaked out during the scrimmage and was accompanying me to the saloon door. He was glad too, though he was a bit frightened. When we got back the ambulance was there in front of the door and they were lifting him in on the stretcher, his face and neck covered with a sheet. Sometimes it happened that Father Carroll's pet choirboy strolled by the house just as I was hitting the air. This was an event of primary importance. The boy was older than any of us and he was a sissy, a fairy in the making. His very walk used to enrage us. As soon as he was spotted the news went out in every direction and before he had reached the corner he was surrounded by a gang of boys all much smaller than himself who taunted him and mimicked him until he burst into tears. Then we would pounce on him, like a pack of wolves, pull him to the ground and tear the clothes off his back. It was a disgraceful performance but it made us feel good. Nobody knew yet what a fairy was, but whatever it was we were against it. In the same way we were against the Chinamen. There was one Chinaman, from the laundry up the street, who used to pass frequently and, like the sissy from Father Carroll's church, he too had to run the gantlet. He looked exactly like the picture of a coolie which one sees in the schoolbooks. He wore a sort of black alpaca coat with braided button holes, slippers without heels, and a pigtail. Usually he walked with his hands in his sleeves. It was his walk which I remember best, a sort of sly, mincing, feminine walk which was utterly foreign and menacing to us. We were in mortal dread of him and we hated him because he was absolutely indifferent to our gibes. We thought he was too ignorant to notice our insults. Then one day when we entered the laundry he gave us a little surprise. First he handed us the package of laundry; then he reached down below the counter and gathered a handful of lichee nuts from the big bag. He was smiling as he came from behind the counter to open the door. He was still smiling as he caught hold of Alfie Betcha and pulled his ears; he caught hold of each of us in turn and pulled our ears, still smiling. Then he made a ferocious grimace and, swift as a cat, he ran behind the counter and picked up a long, ugly-looking knife which he brandished at us. We fell over ourselves getting out of the place. When we got to the corner and looked around we saw him standing in the doorway with an iron in his hand looking very calm and peaceful. After this incident nobody would go to the laundry any more; we had to pay little Louis Pirossa a nickel each week to collect the laundry for us. Louis's father owned the fruit stand on the corner. He used to hand us the rotten bananas as a token of his affection. Stanley was especially fond of the rotten bananas as his aunt used to fry them for him. The fried bananas were considered a delicacy in Stanley's home. Once, on his birthday, there was a party given for Stanley and the whole neighborhood was invited. Everything went beautifully until it came to the fried bananas. Somehow nobody wanted to touch the bananas, as this was a dish known only to Polacks like Stanley's parents. It was considered disgusting to eat fried bananas. In the midst of the embarrassment some bright youngster suggested that crazy Willie Maine should be given the fried bananas. Willie Maine was older than any of us but unable to talk. He said nothing but *Bjork! Bjork!* He said this to everything. So when the bananas were passed to him he said *Bjork!* and he reached for them with two hands. But his brother George was there and George felt insulted that they should have palmed off the rotten bananas on his crazy brother. So George started a fight and Willie, seeing his brother attacked, began to fight also, screaming *Bjork! Bjork!* Not only did he strike out at the other boys but at the girls too, which created a pandemonium.

Finally Stanley's old man, hearing the noise, came up from the barber shop with a strop in his hand. He took crazy Willie Maine by the scruff of the neck and began to lambast him. Meanwhile his brother George had sneaked off to call Mr. Maine senior. The latter, who was also a bit of a drunkard, arrived in his shirt sleeves and seeing poor Willie being beaten by the drunken barber, he went for him with two stout fists and beat him up unmercifully. Willie, who had gotten free meanwhile, was on his hands and knees, gobbling up the fried bananas which had fallen on the floor. He was stuffing them away like a billy goat, fast as he could find them. When the old man saw him there chewing away like a goat he became furious and picking up the strop he went after Willie with a vengeance. Now Willie began to howl—*Bjork! Bjork!*—and suddenly everybody began to laugh. That took the steam out of Mr. Maine and he relented. Finally he sat down and Stanley's aunt brought him a glass of wine. Hearing the racket some of the other neighbors came in and there was more wine and then beer and then schnapps and soon everybody was happy and singing and whistling and even the kids got drunk and then crazy Willie got drunk and again he got down on the floor like a billy goat and he yelled *Bjork! Bjork!* and Alfie Betcha, who was very drunk though only eight years old, bit crazy Willie Maine in the backside and then Willie bit him and then we all started biting each other and the parents stood by laughing and screaming with glee and it was very very merry and there were more fried bananas and everybody ate them this time and then there were speeches and more bumpers downed and crazy Willie Maine tried to sing for us but could only sing *Bjork! Bjork!* It was a stupendous success, the birthday party, and for a week or more no one talked of anything but the party and what good Polacks Stanley's people were. The fried bananas, too, were a success and for a time it was hard to get any rotten bananas from Louis Pirossa's old man because they were so much in demand. And then an event occurred which cast a pall over the entire neighborhood—the defeat of Joe Gerhardt at the hands of Joey Silverstein. The latter was the tailor's son; he was a lad of fifteen or sixteen, rather quiet and studious looking, who was shunned by the other older boys because he was a Jew. One day as he was delivering a pair of pants to Fillmore Place he was accosted by Joey Gerhardt who was about the same age and who considered himself a rather superior being. There was an exchange of words and then Joe Gerhardt pulled the pants away from the Silverstein boy and threw them in the gutter. Nobody had ever imagined that young Silverstein would reply to such an insult by recourse to his fists and so when he struck out at Joe Gerhardt and cracked him square in the jaw everybody was taken aback, most of all Joe Gerhardt himself. There was a fight which lasted about twenty minutes and at the end Joe Gerhardt lay on the sidewalk unable to get up. Whereupon the Silverstein boy gathered up the pair of pants and walked quietly and proudly back to his father's shop. Nobody said a word to him. The affair was regarded as a calamity. Who had ever heard of a Jew beating up a Gentile? It was something inconceivable, and yet it had happened, right before everyone's eyes. Night after night, sitting on the curb as we used to, the situation was discussed from every angle, but without any solution until . . . well until Joe Gerhardt's younger brother, Johnny, became so wrought up about it that he decided to settle the matter himself. Johnny, though younger and smaller than his brother, was as tough and invincible as a young puma. He was typical of the shanty Irish who made up the neighborhood. His idea of getting even with young Silverstein was to lie in wait for him one evening as the latter was stepping out of the store and trip him up. When he tripped him up that evening he had provided himself in advance with two little rocks which he concealed in his fists and when poor Silverstein went down he pounced on him and then with the two handsome little rocks he pounded poor Silverstein's temples. To his amazement Silverstein offered no resistance; even when he got up and gave him a chance to get to his feet Silverstein never so much as budged. Then Johnny got frightened and ran away. He must have been thoroughly frightened because he never came back again; the next that was heard of him was that he had been picked up out West somewhere and sent to a reformatory. His mother, who was a slatternly, jolly Irish bitch, said that it served him right and she hoped to God she'd never lay eyes on him again. When the boy Silverstein recovered he was not the same any more;

people said the beating had affected his brain, that he was a little daffy. Joe Gerhardt, on the other hand, rose to prominence again. It seems that he had gone to see the Silverstein boy while he lay in bed and had made a deep apology to him. This again was something that had never been heard of before. It was something so strange, so unusual, that Joe Gerhardt was looked upon almost as a knight errant. Nobody had approved of the way Johnny behaved, and yet nobody would have thought of going to young Silverstein and apologizing to him. That was an act of such delicacy, such elegance, that Joe Gerhardt was looked upon as a real gentleman—the first and only gentleman in the neighborhood. It was a word that had never been used among us and now it was on everybody's lips and it was considered a distinction to be a gentleman. This sudden transformation of the defeated Joe Gerhardt into a gentleman I remember made a deep impression upon me. A few years later, when I moved into another neighborhood and encountered Claude de Lorraine, a French boy, I was prepared to understand and accept "a gentlemen." This Claude was a boy such as I had never laid eyes on before. In the old neighborhood he would have been regarded as a sissy; for one thing he spoke too well, too correctly, too politely, and for another thing he was too considerate, too gentle, too gallant. And then, while playing with him, to hear him suddenly break into French as his mother or father came along, provided us with something like a shock. German we had heard and German was a permissible transgression, but French! why to talk French, or even to understand it, was to be thoroughly alien, thoroughly aristocratic, rotten, distingué. And yet Claude was one of us, as good as us in every way, even a little bit better, we had to admit secretly. But there was a blemish—his French! It antagonized us. He had no right to be living in our neighborhood, no right to be as capable and manly as he was. Often, when his mother called him in and we had said good-by to him, we got together in the lot and we discussed the Lorraine family backwards and forwards. We wondered what they ate, for example, because being French they must have different customs than ours. No one had ever set foot in Claude de Lorraine's home either—that was another suspicious and repugnant fact. Why? What were they concealing?

Yet when they passed us in the street they were always very cordial, always smiled, always spoke in English and a most excellent English it was. They used to make us feel rather ashamed of ourselves—they were superior, that's what it was. And there was still another baffling thing—with the other boys a direct question brought a direct answer, but with Claude de Lorraine there was never any direct answer. He always smiled very charmingly before replying and he was very cool, collected, employing an irony and a mockery which was beyond us. He was a thorn in our side, Claude de Lorraine, and when finally he moved out of the neighborhood we all breathed a sigh of relief. As for myself, it was only maybe ten or fifteen years later that I thought about this boy and his strange, elegant behavior. And it was then that I felt I had made a bad blunder. For suddenly one day it occurred to me that Claude de Lorraine had come up to me on a certain occasion obviously to win my friendship and I had treated him rather cavalierly. At the time I thought of this incident it suddenly dawned on me that Claude de Lorraine must have seen something different in me and that he had meant to honor me by extending the hand of friendship. But back in those days I had a code of honor, such as it was, and that was to run with the herd. Had I become a bosom friend of Claude de Lorraine I would have been betraying the other boys. No matter what advantages lay in the wake of such a friendship they were not for me; I was one of the gang and it was my duty to remain aloof from such as Claude de Lorraine. I remembered this incident once again, I must say, after a still greater interval—after I had been in France a few months and the word *raisonnable* had come to acquire a wholly new significance for me. Suddenly one day, overhearing it, I thought of Claude de Lorraine's overtures on the street in front of his house. I recalled vividly that he had used the word *reasonable*. He had probably asked me to be *reasonable,* a word which then would never have crossed my lips as there was no need for it in my vocabulary. It was a word, like gentleman, which was rarely brought out and then only with great discretion and circumspection. It was a word which might cause others to laugh at you. There were lots of words like that— *really,* for example. No one I knew had ever used the word *really*—until Jack Lawson came along. He used it because his parents were English and, though we made fun of him, we forgave him for it. *Really* was a word which reminded me immediately of little Carl Ragner from the old neighborhood. Carl Ragner was the only son of a politician who lived on the rather distinguished little street called Fillmore Place. He lived near the end of the street in a little red brick house which was always beautifully kept. I remember the house because passing it on my way to school I used to remark how beautifully the brass knobs on the door were polished. In fact, nobody else had brass knobs on their doors. Anyway, little Carl Ragner was one of those boys who was not allowed to associate with other boys. He was rarely seen, as a matter of fact. Usually it was a Sunday that we caught a glimpse of him walking with his father. Had his father not been a powerful figure in the neighborhood Carl would have been stoned to death. He was really impossible, in his Sunday garb. Not only did he wear long pants and patent leather shoes, but he sported a derby and a cane. At six years of age a boy who would allow himself to be dressed up in this fashion must be a ninny— that was the consensus of opinion. Some said he was sickly, as though that were an excuse for his eccentric dress. The strange thing is that I never once heard him speak. He was so elegant, so refined, that perhaps he had imagined it was bad manners to speak in public. At any rate, I used to lie in wait for him Sunday mornings just to see him pass with his old man. I watched him with the same avid curiosity that I would watch the firemen cleaning the engines in the firehouse. Sometimes on the way home he would be carrying a little box of ice cream, the smallest size they had, probably just enough for him, for his dessert. Dessert was another word which had somehow become familiar to us and which we used derogatorily when referring to the likes of little Carl Ragner and his family. We could spend hours wondering what these people ate for *dessert*, our pleasure consisting principally in bandying about this new-found word, *dessert*, which had probably been smuggled out of the Ragner household. It must also have been about this time that Santos Dumont came into fame. For us there was something grotesque about the name Santos Dumont. About his exploits we were not much concerned—just the name. For most of us it smelled of sugar, of Cuban plantations, of the strange Cuban flag which had a star in the corner and which was always highly regarded by those who saved the little cards which were given away with Sweet Caporal cigarettes and on which there were represented either the flags of the different nations or the leading soubrettes of the stage or the famous pugilists. Santos Dumont, then, was something delightfully foreign, in contradistinction to the usual foreign person or object, such as the Chinese laundry, or Claude de Lorraine's haughty French family. Santos Dumont was a magical word which suggested a beautiful flowing mustache, a sombrero, spurs, something airy, delicate, humorous, quixotic. Sometimes it brought up the aroma of coffee beans and of straw mats, or, because it was so thoroughly outlandish and quixotic, it would entail a digression concerning the life of the Hottentots. For there were among us, older boys who were beginning to read and who would entertain us by the hour with fantastic tales which they had gleaned from books such as *Ayesha* or Ouida's *Under Two Flags*. The real flavor of knowledge is most definitely associated in my mind with the vacant lot at the corner of the new neighborhood where I was transplanted at about the age of ten. Here, when the fall days came on and we stood about the bonfire roasting chippies and raw potatoes in the little cans which we carried, there ensued a new type of discussion which differed from the old discussions I had known in that the origins were always bookish. Some one had just read a book of adventure, or a book of science, and forthwith the whole street became animated by the introduction of a hitherto unknown subject. It might be that one of these boys had just discovered that there was such a thing as the Japanese current and he would try to explain to us how the Japanese current came into existence and what the purpose of it was. This was the only way we learned things— against the fence, as it were, while roasting chippies and raw potatoes. These bits of knowledge sunk deep—so deep, in fact, that later, confronted with a more accurate knowledge it was often difficult to dislodge the older knowledge. In this way it was explained to us one day by an older boy that the Egyptians had known about the circulation of the blood, something which seemed so natural to us that it was hard later to swallow the story of the discovery of the circulation of the blood by an Englishman named Harvey. Nor does it seem strange to me now that in those days most of our conversation was about remote places, such as China, Peru, Egypt, Africa, Iceland, Greenland. We talked about ghosts, about God, about the transmigration of souls, about Hell, about astronomy, about strange birds and fish, about the formation of precious stones, about rubber plantations, about methods of torture, about the Aztecs and the Incas, about marine life, about volcanoes and earthquakes, about burial rites and wedding ceremonies in various parts of the earth, about languages, about the origin of the American Indian, about the buffaloes dying out, about strange diseases, about cannibalism, about wizardry, about trips to the moon and what it was like there, about murderers and highwaymen, about the miracles in the Bible, about the manufacture of pottery, about a thousand and one subjects which were never mentioned at home or in school and which were vital to us because we were starved and the world was full of wonder and mystery and it was only when we stood shivering in the vacant lot that we got to talking seriously and felt a need for communication which was at once pleasurable and terrifying.

The wonder and the mystery of life—which is throttled in us as we become responsible members of society! Until we were pushed out to work the world was very small and we were living on the fringe of it, on the frontier, as it were, of the unknown. A small Greek world which was nevertheless deep enough to provide all manner of variation, all manner of adventure and speculation. Not so very small either, since it held in reserve the most boundless potentialities. I have gained nothing by the enlargement of my world; on the contrary, I have lost. I want to become more and more childish and to pass beyond childhood in the opposite direction. I want to go exactly contrary to the normal line of development, pass into a superinfantile realm of being which will be absolutely crazy and chaotic but not crazy and chaotic as the world about me. I have been an adult and a father and a responsible member of society. I have earned my daily bread. I have adapted myself to a world which never was mine. I want to break through this enlarged world and stand again on the frontier of an unknown world which will throw this pale, unilateral world into shadow. I want to pass beyond the responsibility of fatherhood to the irresponsibility of the anarchic man who cannot be coerced nor wheedled nor cajoled nor bribed nor traduced. I want to take as my guide Oberon the nightrider who, under the spread of his black wings, eliminates both the beauty and the horror of the past; I want to flee toward a perpetual dawn with a swiftness and relentlessness that leaves no room for remorse, regret, or repentance. I want to outstrip the inventive man who is a curse to the earth in order to stand once again before an impassable deep which not even the strongest wings will enable me to traverse. Even if I must become a wild and natural park inhabited only by idle dreamers I must not stop to rest here in the ordered fatuity of responsible, adult life. I must do this in remembrance of a life beyond all comparison with the life which was promised me, in remembrance of the life of a child who was strangled and stifled by the mutual consent of those who had surrendered. Everything which the fathers and the mothers created I disown. I am going back to a world even smaller than the old Hellenic world, going back to a world which I can always touch with outstretched arms, the world of what I know and see and recognize from moment to moment. Any other world is meaningless to me, and alien and hostile. In retraversing the first bright world which I knew as a child I wish not to rest there but to muscle back to a still brighter world from which I must have escaped. What this world is like I do not know, nor am I even sure that I will find it, but it is my world and nothing else intrigues me.

QUIET DAYS IN CLICHY

From Quiet Days in Clichy. *In February, 1940, Miller reluctantly returned to America, France having fallen to Germany. He still had no literary reputation, except perhaps as a writer of dirty books. Exiled from the city where he had forged a new identity, it would not be surprising if he began to apply to his Paris days and nights a nostalgic patina.* Quiet Days in Clichy *partakes of something of that. It is at the same time as high-spirited, raucous, and bawdy as either of the* Tropics. *Miller evidently wrote it in the spring of 1940, mislaid the manuscript for fifteen years, then rewrote it in 1956. Grove issued an American edition in 1965. In the section excerpted here, the narrator and his friend Carl have been vacationing in Luxembourg—a trip Miller himself made with Alfred Perlès in 1933—but they have become bored with the country's smug sanity and so return to Paris.*

To be truthful, it was a beautiful, orderly, prosperous, easy-going sort of world, everyone full of good humor, charitable, kindly, tolerant. Yet, for some reason, there was a rotten odor about the place. The odor of stagnation. The goodness of the inhabitants, which was negative, had deteriorated their moral fiber.

All they were concerned about was to know on which side their bread was buttered. They couldn't make bread, but they could butter it.

I felt thoroughly disgusted. Better to die like a louse in Paris than live here on the fat of the land, thought I to myself.

"Let's go back and get a good dose of clap," I said, rousing Carl from a state of near torpor.

"*What?* What are you talking about?" he mumbled thickly.

"Yes," I said, "let's get out of here, it stinks. Luxembourg is like Brooklyn, only more charming and more poisonous. Let's go back to Clichy and go on a spree. I want to wipe the taste of this out of my mouth."

It was about midnight when we arrived in Paris. We hurried to the newspaper office, where our good friend, King, ran the racing column. We borrowed more francs of him and rushed off.

I was in a mood to take the first whore that came along. "I'll take her, clap and all," thought I. "Shit, a dose of clap is something, after all. Those Luxembourg cunts are full of buttermilk."

Carl wasn't quite so keen about contracting another dose of clap. His cock already felt itchy, he confided. He was trying to think who could have given it to him, if it was the clap, as he suspected.

"If you've got it, there's no great harm in getting it again," I remarked cheerily. "Get a double dose and spread it abroad. Infect the whole continent! Better a good venereal disease than a moribund peace and quiet. Now I know what makes the world civilized: it's vice, disease, thievery, mendacity, lechery. Shit, the French are a great people, even if they're syphilitic. Don't ever ask me to go to a neutral country again. Don't let me look at any more cows, human or otherwise."

I was that peppery I could have raped a nun.

It was in this mood that we entered the little dance hall where our friend, the hat check girl, hung out. It was only a little after midnight, and we had plenty for a little fling. There were three or four whores at the bar and one or two drunks, English, of course. Pansies, most likely. We had a few dances and then the whores began to pester us.

It's amazing what one can do publicly in a French bar. To a *putain* anyone who speaks English, male or female, is a degenerate. A French girl doesn't degrade herself in putting on a show for the foreigner, any more than a sea-lion becomes civilized by being trained to do tricks.

Adrienne, the hat check girl, had come to the bar for a drink. She sat on a high stool with her legs spread apart. I stood beside her with an arm around one of her little friends. Presently I had my hand up her dress. I played with her a little while and then she slid down off her perch and, putting her arms around my neck, stealthily opened my fly and closed her hand over my balls. The musicians were playing a slow waltz, the lights dimmed. Adrienne led me to the floor, my fly wide open, and, holding me tight, she shifted me to the middle of the floor where we were soon packed like sardines. We could hardly move from the spot, the jam was so thick. Again she reached into my fly, took my pecker out, and placed it against her cunt. It was excruciating. To make it more excruciating, one of her little friends who was wedged next to us, brazenly caught hold of my prick. At this point I could hold back no longer—I squirted it into her hand.

When we drifted back to the bar, Carl was standing in a corner, crouched over a girl who seemed to be sagging to the ground. The barman looked annoyed. "This is a drinking place, not a boudoir," he said. Carl looked up in a daze, his face covered with lip rouge, his tie askew, his vest unbuttoned, his hair down over his eyes. "These aren't whores," he muttered, "they're nymphomaniacs."

He sat down on the stool with his shirt tail sticking out of his fly. The girl began buttoning his fly for him. Suddenly she changed her mind, ripped it open again and, pulling his pecker out, bent over and kissed it. This was going a little too far, apparently. The manager now sidled up to inform us that we would have to behave differently or beat it. He didn't appear to be angry with the girls; he simply scolded them, as if they were naughty children.

We were for leaving then and there, but Adrienne insisted that we wait until closing time. She said she wanted to go home with us.

When we finally called a cab and piled in, we discovered that there were five of us. Carl was for shoving one of the girls out, but couldn't make up his mind which one. On the way we stopped to buy some sandwiches, some cheese and olives, and a few bottles of wine.

"They're going to be disappointed when they see how much money we have left," said Carl.

"Good," said I, "maybe they'll all desert us then. I'm tired. I'd like to take a bath and tumble into bed."

As soon as we arrived I undressed and turned on the bath

water. The girls were in the kitchen spreading the table. I had just gotten into the tub, and begun soaping myself, when Adrienne and one of the other girls walked into the bathroom. They had decided that they would take a bath too. Adrienne quickly slipped out of her things and slid into the tub with me. The other girl also undressed, then came and stood beside the tub. Adrienne and I were facing each other, our legs entwined. The other girl leaned over the tub and started playing with me. I lay back in the luxuriously hot water and allowed her to twirl her soapy fingers around my cock. Adrienne was playing with her cunt, as if to say—"All right, let her play with that thing a little while, but when the time comes I'll snatch it out of her hand."

Presently the three of us were in the tub, a sandwich in one hand and a glass of wine in the other. Carl had decided to shave. His girl sat on the edge of the *bidet*, chatting and munching her sandwich. She disappeared for a moment to return with a full bottle of red wine which she poured down our necks. The soapy water quickly took on the hue of permanganate.

By this time I was in a mood for anything. Feeling a desire to urinate, I calmly proceeded to pee. The girls were horrified. Apparently I had done something unethical. Suddenly they became suspicious of us. Were we going to pay them? If so, how much? When Carl blithely informed them that he had about nine francs to distribute, there was an uproar. Then they decided that we were only joking—another bad little joke, like peeing in the bathtub. But no, we insisted that we were in earnest. They swore they had never heard the likes of it; it was simply incredible, monstrous, inhuman.

"They're a couple of dirty Huns," said one of the girls.

"No, *English*. Degenerate English," said the other.

Adrienne tried to mollify them. She said she had known us for a long time and that we had always acted like gentlemen with her, an announcement which sounded rather strange to my ears considering the nature of our relations with her. However, the word gentlemen connoted nothing more than that we had always paid cash for her little services.

She was trying desperately to retrieve the situation. I could almost hear her think.

"Couldn't you give them a check?" she begged.

At this Carl burst out laughing. He was about to say we had no check book when I interrupted him, saying: "Sure, that's an idea . . . we'll give each of you a check, how's that?" I went into Carl's room without another word and got out an old check book of his. I brought him his beautiful Parker pen and handed it to him.

At this point Carl displayed his astuteness. Pretending to be angry with me for having uncovered his check book and for meddling in his affairs, he said:

"It's always like this." (In French, of course, for their benefit.) "I'm the one who always pays for these follies. Why don't you hand out your own checks?"

To this I replied as shamefacedly as I could that my account was dry. Still he demurred, or pretended to.

"Why can't they wait until tomorrow?" he asked, turning to Adrienne. "Won't they trust us?"

"Why should we trust you?" said one of the girls. "A moment ago you pretended you had nothing. Now you want us to wait until tomorrow. Ah, no, that doesn't go with us."

"Well, then, you can all clear out," said Carl, throwing the check book on the floor.

"Don't be so mean," cried Adrienne. "Give us each a hundred francs and we won't speak about it any more. *Please!*"

"A hundred francs *each?*"

"Of course," she said. "That's not very much."

"Go ahead," I said, "don't be such a piker. Besides, I'll pay you back my half in a day or two."

"That's what you always say," Carl replied.

"Cut the comedy," I said, in English. "Write out the checks and let's get rid of them."

"Get rid of them? What, after giving them checks you want me to throw them out? No sir, I'm going to get full value for my money, even if the checks are no good. *They* don't know that. If we let them off too easy they'll smell a rat.

"Hey, *you!*" he shouted, waving a check at one of the girls. "What do I get for this? I want something unique, not just a lay."

He proceeded to distribute the checks. It looked comical,

handing checks around in the raw. Even had they been good, the checks, they looked phony. Possibly because we were all naked. The girls seemed to feel the same way, that it was a phony transaction. Except for Adrienne, who believed in us.

I was praying they'd put on an act rather than force us to go through with the "fucking" routine. I was all in. Dog tired. It would have to be a tall performance, on their part, to make me work up even the semblance of a hard-on. Carl, on the other hand, was behaving like a man who had genuinely doled out three hundred francs. He wanted something for his money, and he wanted something exotic.

While they were talking it over among themselves I climbed into bed. I was so far removed, mentally, from the situation, that I fell into a reverie about the story I had begun days ago and which I intended to resume writing on waking. It was about an axe murder. I wondered if I should attempt to compress the narrative and concentrate on the drunken murderer whom I had left sitting beside the headless body of the wife he had never loved. Perhaps I would take the newspaper account of the crime, telescope it, and begin my own rendition of the murder at the point, or moment, when the head rolled off the table. That would fit in nicely, I thought, with the bit about the armless, legless man who wheeled himself through the streets at night on a little platform, his head on a level with the knees of the passers-by. I wanted a bit of horror because I had a wonderful burlesque up my sleeve which I intended to use as a wind up.

In the brief interval of reverie allotted me I had regained the mood which had been broken days ago by the advent of our somnambulistic Pocahontas.

A nudge from Adrienne, who had made a place for herself beside me, roused me. She was whispering something in my ear. Something about money again. I asked her to repeat it, and, in order not to lose the thought which had just come to me, I kept repeating to myself—"Head rolls off table—head rolls off . . . little man on wheels . . . wheels . . . legs . . . millions of legs . . ."

"They would like to know if you wouldn't please try to dig up some change for a taxi. They live far away."

"Far away?" I repeated, looking at her vacantly. "How far away?" (*Remember*—wheels, legs, head rolls off . . . begin in the middle of a sentence.)

"Ménilmontant," said Adrienne.

"Get me a pencil and paper—there, on the desk," I begged.

"Ménilmontant . . . Ménilmontant . . ." I repeated hypnotically, scrawling a few key words, such as rubber wheels, wooden heads, corkscrew legs, and so on.

"What are you doing?" hissed Adrienne, tugging at me violently. "What's the matter with you?

"Il est fou," she exclaimed, rising from the bed and throwing up her hands in despair.

"Où est l'autre?" she demanded, looking for Carl.

"Mon Dieu!" I heard her say, as though from afar, *"il dort."* Then after a heavy pause: "Well, that beats everything. Come, let's get out of here! One is drunk and the other is inspired. We're wasting time. That's how foreigners are—always thinking of other things. They don't want to make love, they want to be titillated . . ."

Titillated. I wrote that down, too, I don't remember what she had said in French, but whatever it was, it had resuscitated a forgotten friend. *Titillated.* It was a word I hadn't used for ages. Immediately I thought of another word I only rarely used: *misling.* I was no longer sure what it meant. What matter? I'd drag it in anyway. There were lots of words which had fallen out of my vocabulary, living abroad so long.

I lay back and observed them making ready to leave. It was like watching a stage performance from a box seat. Being a paralytic, I was enjoying the spectacle from my wheelchair. If one of them should take it into her head to throw a pitcher of water over me, I wouldn't stir from the spot. I'd merely shake myself and smile— the way one smiles at frolicsome angels. (Were there such?) All I wanted was for them to go and leave me to my reverie. Had I had any coins on me I would have flung them at them.

After an aeon or so they made for the door. Adrienne was wafting a long distance kiss, a gesture so unreal that I became fascinated by the poise of her arm; I saw it receding down a long corridor where it was finally sucked through the narrow mouth of a funnel, the arm still bent at the wrist, but so diminished, so attenuated, that it finally resembled a wisp of straw.

"*Salaud!*" shouted one of the girls, and as the door banged shut I caught myself answering; "*Oui, c'est juste. Un salaud. Et vous, des salopes. Il n'y a que ça. N'y a que ça. Salaud, salope. La saloperie, quoi. C'est assoupissant.*"

I snapped out of it with a "Shit, what the hell am I talking about?"

Wheels, legs, head rolling off . . . Fine. Tomorrow will be like any other day, only better, juicier, rosier. The man on the platform will roll himself off the end of a pier. At Canarsie. He will come up with a herring in his mouth. A Maatjes herring, no less.

Hungry again. I got up and looked for the remnants of a sandwich. There wasn't a crumb on the table. I went to the bathroom absent-mindedly, thinking to take a leak. There were a couple of slices of bread, a few pieces of cheese, and some bruised olives scattered about. Thrown away in disgust, evidently.

I picked up a piece of bread to see if it were eatable. Someone had stamped on it with an angry foot. There was a little mustard on it. Or was it mustard? Better try another piece. I salvaged a fairly clean piece, a trifle soggy from lying on the wet floor, and slapped a piece of cheese on it. In a glass beside the *bidet* I found a drop of wine. I downed it, then gingerly bit into the bread. Not bad at all. On the contrary, it tasted good. Germs don't molest hungry people, or inspired people. All rot, this worrying about cellophane and whose hand touched it last. To prove it, I wiped my ass with it. Swiftly, to be sure. Then I gulped it down. *There!* What's to be sorry about? I looked for a cigarette. There were only butts left. I selected the longest one and lit it. Delicious aroma. Not that toasted sawdust from America! Real tobacco. One of Carl's *Gauloises Bleues*, no doubt.

Now what was it I was thinking about?

I sat down at the kitchen table and swung my feet up. Let's see now . . . What was it again?

I couldn't see or think a thing. I felt too absolutely wonderful. Why think anyway?

Yes, a big day. *Several*, indeed. Yes, it was only a few days ago that we were sitting here, wondering where to go. Might have been yesterday. Or a year ago. What difference? One gets stretched and then one collapses. Time collapses too. Whores collapse. Everything collapses. Collapses into a clap.

On the window-sill an early bird was tweeting. Pleasantly, drowsily, I remembered sitting thus on Brooklyn Heights years ago. In some other life. Would probably never see Brooklyn again. Nor Canarsie, nor Shelter Island, nor Montauk Point, nor Secaucus, nor Lake Pocotopaug, nor the Neversink River, nor scallops and bacon, nor finnan haddie, nor mountain oysters. Strange, how one can stew in the dregs and think it's home. Until someone says Minnehaha—or Walla Walla. *Home.* Home is if home lasts. Where you hang your hat, in other words. Far away, she said, meaning Ménilmontant. That's not far. China now, that's really far. Or Mozambique. Ducky, to drift everlastingly. It's unhealthy, Paris. Maybe she had something there. Try Luxembourg, little one. What the hell, there are thousands of places, Bali, for instance. Or the Carolines. Crazy, this asking for money all the time. Money, money. No money. Lots of money. Yeah, somewhere far, far away. And no books, no typewriter, no nothing. Say nothing, do nothing. Float with the tide. That bitch, Nys. Nothing but a cunt. *What a life!* Don't forget—*titillated!*

I got off my ass, yawned, stretched, staggered to the bed.

Off like a streak. Down, down, to the cosmocentric cesspool. Leviathans swimming around in strangely sunlit depths. Life going on as usual everywhere. Breakfast at ten sharp. An armless, legless man tending bar with his teeth. Dynamite falling through from the stratosphere. Garters descending in long graceful spirals. A woman with a gashed torso struggling desperately to screw her severed head on. Wants money for it. For what? She doesn't know *for what.* Just money. Atop an umbrella fern lies a fresh corpse full of bullet holes. An iron cross is suspended from its neck. Somebody's asking for a sandwich. The water is too agitated for sandwiches. Look under S in the dictionary!

A rich, fecundating dream, shot through with a mystic blue light, I had sunk to that dangerous level where, out of sheer bliss and wonder, one lapses back to the button mold. In some vague dreamy way I was aware that I must make a herculean effort. The struggle to reach the surface was agonizing, exquisitely agonizing. Now and then I succeeded in opening my eyes: I saw the room, as through a mist, but my body was down below in the shimmering marine depths. To swoon back was voluptuous. I fell clear through to the bottomless bottom, where I waited like a shark. Then slowly, very slowly, I rose. It was tantalizing. All cork and no fins. Nearing the surface I was sucked under again, pulled down, down, in delicious helplessness, sucked into the empty vortex, there to wait through endless passages of time for the will to gather and raise me like a sunken buoy.

I awoke with the sound of birds chirping in my ear. The room was no longer veiled in a watery mist but clear and recognizable. On my desk were two sparrows fighting over a crumb. I rested on an elbow and watched them flutter to the window, which was closed. Into the hallway they flew, then back again, frantically seeking an exit.

I got up and opened the window. They continued to fly about the room, as if stunned. I made myself very still. Suddenly they darted through the open window. *"Bonjour, Madame Oursel,"* they cheeped.

It was high noon, about the third or fourth day of spring . . .

TROPIC OF CANCER

From Tropic of Cancer. *There can be no book more important in all of Miller's work than* Cancer, *both for its effect on him and for its inherent qualities. In the writing of it Miller satisfied himself for the first time that he was a sure-enough writer instead of a pretend one or a failure. As he writes in the novel's opening passage, "A year ago, six months ago, I thought I was an artist. I no longer think about it, I am."*

In America I had a number of Hindu friends, some good, some bad, some indifferent. Circumstances had placed me in a position where fortunately I could be of aid to them; I secured jobs for them, I harbored them, and I fed them when necessary. They were very grateful, I must say; so much so, in fact that they made my life miserable with their attentions. Two of them were saints, if I know what a saint is; particularly Gupte who was found one morning with his throat cut from ear to ear. In a little boarding house in Greenwich Village he was found one morning stretched out stark naked on the bed, his flute beside him, and his throat gashed, as I say, from ear to ear. It was never discovered whether he had been murdered or whether he had committed suicide. But that's neither here nor there. . . .

I'm thinking back to the chain of circumstances which has brought me finally to Nanantatee's place. Thinking how strange it is that I should have forgotten all about Nanantatee until the other day when lying in a shabby hotel room on the Rue Cels. I'm lying there on the iron bed thinking what a zero I have become, what a cipher, what a nullity, when bango! out pops the word: NONENTITY! That's what we called him in New York—Nonentity. *Mister* Nonentity.

I'm lying on the floor now in that gorgeous suite of rooms he boasted of when he was in New York. Nanantatee is playing the good Samaritan; he has given me a pair of itchy blankets, horse blankets they are, in which I curl up on the dusty floor. There are little jobs to do every hour of the day—that is, if I am foolish enough to remain indoors. In the morning he wakes me rudely in order to have me prepare the vegetables for his lunch: onions, garlic, beans, etc. His friend, Kepi, warns me not to eat the food— he says it's bad. Bad or good what difference? *Food!* That's all that matters. For a little food I am quite willing to sweep his carpets with a broken broom, to wash his clothes and to scrape the crumbs off the floor as soon as he has finished eating. He's become absolutely immaculate since my arrival: everything has to be dusted now, the chairs must be arranged a certain way, the clock must ring, the toilet must flush properly. . . . A crazy Hindu if ever there was one! And parsimonious as a string bean. I'll have a great laugh over it when I get out of his clutches, but just now I'm a prisoner, a man without caste, an untouchable. . . .

If I fail to come back at night and roll up in the horse blankets he says to me on arriving: "Oh, so you didn't die then? I thought you had died." And though he knows I'm absolutely penniless he tells me every day about some cheap room he has just discovered in the neighborhood. "But I can't take a room yet, you know that," I say. And then, blinking his eyes like a Chink, he answers smoothly: "Oh, yes, I forgot that you had no money. I am always forgetting, Endree. . . . But when the cable comes . . . when Miss Mona sends you the money, then you will come with me to look for a room, eh?" And in the next breath he urges me to stay as long as I wish—"six months . . . seven months, Endree . . . you are very good for me here."

Nanantatee is one of the Hindus I never did anything for in America. He represented himself to me as a wealthy merchant, a pearl merchant, with a luxurious suite of rooms on the Rue Lafayette, Paris, a villa in Bombay, a bungalow in Darjeeling. I could see from first glance that he was a half-wit, but then half-wits sometimes have the genius to amass a fortune. I didn't know that he paid his hotel bill in New York by leaving a couple of fat pearls in the proprietor's hands. It seems amusing to me now that this little duck once swaggered about the lobby of that hotel in New York with an ebony cane, bossing the bellhops around, ordering luncheons for his guests, calling up the porter for theater tickets, renting a taxi by the day, etc., etc., all without a sou in his pocket. Just a string of fat pearls around his neck which he cashed one by one as time wore on. And the fatuous way he used to pat me on the back, thank me for being so good to the Hindu boys—"they are all very intelligent boys, Endree . . . very intelligent!" Telling me that the good lord so-and-so would repay me for my kindness. That explains now why they used to giggle so, these intelligent Hindu boys, when I suggested that they touch Nanantatee for a five-spot.

Curious now how the good lord so-and-so is requiting me for my benevolence. I'm nothing but a slave to this fat little duck. I'm at his beck and call continually. He needs me here—he tells me so to my face. When he goes to the crap-can he shouts: "Endree, bring me a pitcher of water, please. I must wipe myself." He wouldn't think of using toilet paper, Nanantatee. Must be against his religion. No, he calls for a pitcher of water and a rag. He's *delicate*, the fat little duck. Sometimes when I'm drinking a cup of pale tea in which he has dropped a rose leaf he comes alongside of me and lets a loud fart, right in my face. He never says "Excuse me!" The word must be missing from his Gujarati dictionary.

The day I arrived at Nanantatee's apartment he was in the act of performing his ablutions, that is to say, he was standing over a dirty bowl trying to work his crooked arm around toward the back of his neck. Beside the bowl was a brass goblet which he used to change the water. He requested me to be silent during the ceremony. I sat there silently, as I was bidden, and watched him as he sang and prayed and spat now and then into the washbowl. So this is the wonderful suite of rooms he talked about in New York! The Rue Lafayette! It sounded like an important street to me back there in New York. I thought only millionaires and pearl merchants inhabited the street. It sounds wonderful, the Rue Lafayette, when you're on the other side of the water. So does Fifth Avenue, when you're over here. One can't imagine what dumps there are on these swell streets. Anyway, here I am at last, sitting in the gorgeous suite of rooms on the Rue Lafayette. And this crazy duck with his crooked arm is going through the ritual of washing himself. The chair on which I'm sitting is broken, the bedstead is falling apart, the wallpaper is in tatters, there is an open valise under the bed crammed with dirty wash. From where I sit I can glance at the miserable courtyard down below where the aristocracy of the Rue Lafayette sit and smoke their clay pipes. I wonder now, as he chants the doxology, what that bungalow in Darjeeling looks like. It's interminable his chanting and praying.

He explains to me that he is obliged to wash in a certain prescribed way—his religion demands it. But on Sundays he takes a bath in the tin tub—the Great I AM will wink at that, he says. When he's dressed he goes to the cupboard, kneels before a little idol on the third shelf, and repeats the mumbo jumbo. If you pray like that every day, he says, nothing will happen to you. The good lord what's his name never forgets an obedient servant. And then he shows me the crooked arm which he got in a taxi accident on a day doubtless when he had neglected to rehearse the complete song and dance. His arm looks like a broken compass; it's not an arm any more, but a knucklebone with a shank attached. Since the arm has been repaired he has developed a pair of swollen glands in the armpit—fat little glands, exactly like a dog's testicles. While bemoaning his plight he remembers suddenly that the doctor had recommended a more liberal diet. He begs me at once to sit down and make up a menu with plenty of fish and meat. "And what about oysters, Endree— for *le petit frère?*" But all this is only to make an impression on me. He hasn't the slightest intention of buying himself oysters, or meat, or fish. Not as long as I am there, at least. For the time being we are going to nourish ourselves on lentils and rice and all the dry foods he has stored away in the attic. And the butter he bought last week that won't go to waste either. When he commences to cure the butter the smell is unbearable. I used to run out at first, when he started frying the butter, but now I stick it out. He'd be only too delighted if he could make me vomit up my meal—that would be something else to put away in the cupboard along with the dry bread and the moldy cheese and the little grease cakes that he makes himself out of the stale milk and the rancid butter.

For the last five years, so it seems, he hasn't done a stroke of work, hasn't turned over a penny. Business has gone to smash. He talks to me about pearls in the Indian ocean—big fat ones on which you can live for a lifetime. The Arabs are ruining the business, he says. But meanwhile he prays to the lord so-and-so every day, and that sustains him. He's on a marvelous footing with the deity: knows just how to cajole him, how to wheedle a few sous out of him. It's a pure commercial relationship. In exchange for the flummery before the cabinet every day he gets his ration of beans and garlic, to say nothing of the swollen testicles under his arm. He is confident that everything will turn out well in the end. The pearls will sell again some day, maybe five years hence, maybe twenty—when the Lord Boomaroom wishes it. "And when the business goes, Endree, you wil get ten per cent—for writing the letters. But first Endree, you must write the letter to find out if we can get credit from India. It will take about six months for an answer, maybe seven months . . . the boats are not fast in India." He has no conception of time at all, the little duck. When I ask him if he has slept well he will say: "Ah, yes, Endree, I sleep very well . . . I sleep sometimes ninety-two hours in three days."

Mornings he is usually too weak to do any work. His arm! That poor broken crutch of an arm! I wonder sometimes when I see him twisting it around the back of his neck how he will ever get it into place again. If it weren't for that little paunch he carries he'd remind me of one of those contortionists at the Cirque Médrano. All he needs is to break a leg. When he sees me sweeping the carpet, when he sees what a cloud of dust I raise, he begins to cluck like a pygmy. "Good! Very good, Endree. And now I will pick up the knots." That means that there are a few crumbs of dust which I have overlooked; it is a polite way he has of being sarcastic.

Afternoons there are always a few cronies from the pearl market dropping in to pay him a visit. They're all very suave, butter-tongued bastards with soft, doelike eyes; they sit around the table drinking the perfumed tea with a loud hissing noise while Nanantatee jumps up and down like a jack-in-the-box or points to a crumb on the floor and says in his smooth slippery voice—"Will you please to pick that up, Endree." When the guests arrive he goes unctuously to the cupboard and gets out the dry crusts of bread which he toasted maybe a week ago and which taste strongly now of the moldy wood. Not a crumb is thrown away. If the bread gets too sour he takes it downstairs to the concierge who, so he says, has been very kind to him. According to him, the concierge is delighted to get the stale bread—she makes bread pudding with it.

One day my friend Anatole came to see me. Nanantatee was delighted. Insisted that Anatole stay for tea. Insisted that he try little grease cakes and the stale bread. "You must come every day," he says, "and teach me Russian. Fine language, Russian . . . I want to speak it. How do you say that again, Endree—*borsht?* You will write that down for me, please, Endree. . . ." And I must write it on the typewriter, no less, so that he can observe my technique. He bought the typewriter, after he had collected on the bad arm, because the doctor recommended it as a good exercise. But he got tired of the typewriter shortly—it was an *English* typewriter.

When he learned that Anatole played the mandolin he said: "Very good! You must come every day and teach me the music. I will buy a mandolin as soon as business is better. It is good for my arm." The next day he borrows a phonograph from the concierge. "You will please teach me to dance, Endree. My stomach is too big." I am hoping that he will buy a porterhouse steak some day so that I can say to him: "You will please bite it for me, *Mister* Nonentity. My teeth are not strong!"

As I said a moment ago, ever since my arrival he has become extraordinarily meticulous. "Yesterday," he says, "you made three mistakes, Endree. First, you forgot to close the toilet door and so all night it makes boom-boom; second, you left the kitchen window open and so the window is cracked this morning. And you forgot to put out the milk bottle! Always you will put out the milk bottle please, before you go to bed, and in the morning you will please bring in the bread."

Every day his friend Kepi drops in to see if any visitors have arrived from India. He waits for Nanantatee to go out and then he scurries to the cupboard and devours the sticks of bread that are hidden away in a glass jar. The food is no good, he insists, but he puts it away like a rat. Kepi is a scrounger, a sort of human tick who fastens himself to the hide of even the poorest compatriot. From Kepi's standpoint they are all nabobs. For a Manila cheroot and the price of a drink he will suck any Hindu's ass. A Hindu's, mind you, but not an Englishman's. He has the address of every whorehouse in Paris, and the rates. Even from the ten franc joints he gets his little commission. And he knows the shortest way to any place you want to go. He will ask you first if you want to go by taxi; if you say no, he will suggest the bus, and if that is too high then the streetcar or the metro. Or he will offer to walk you there and save a franc or two, knowing very well that it will be necessary to pass a *tabac* on the way and that you will please be so good as to buy me a little cheroot.

Kepi is interesting, in a way, because he has absolutely no ambition except to get a fuck every night. Every penny he makes, and they are damned few, he squanders in the dance halls. He has a wife and eight children in Bombay, but that does not prevent him from proposing marriage to any little *femme de chambre* who is stupid and credulous enough to be taken in by him. He has a little room on the Rue Condorcet for which he pays sixty francs a month. He papered it all himself. Very proud of it, too. He uses violet-colored ink in his fountain pen because it lasts longer. He shines his own shoes, presses his own pants, does his own laundry. For a little cigar, a cheroot, if you please, he will escort you all over Paris. If you stop to look at a shirt or a collar button his eyes flash. "Don't buy it here," he will say. "They ask too much. I will show you a cheaper place." And before you have time to think about it he will whisk you away and deposit you before another show window where there are the same ties and shirts and collar buttons—maybe it's the very same store! but you don't know the difference. When Kepi hears that you want to buy something his soul becomes animated. He will ask you so many questions and drag you to so many places that you are bound to get thirsty and ask him to have a drink, whereupon you will discover to your amazement that you are again standing in a *tabac*—maybe the same *tabac!*—and Kepi is saying again in that small unctuous voice: "Will you please be so good as to buy me a little cheroot?" No matter what you propose doing, even if it's only to walk around the corner, Kepi will economize for you. Kepi will show you the shortest way, the cheapest place, the biggest dish, because whatever you have to do you *must* pass a *tabac*, and whether there is a revolution or a lockout or a quarantine Kepi must be at the Moulin Rouge or the Olympia or the Ange Rouge when the music strikes up.

The other day he brought a book for me to read. It was about a famous suit between a holy man and the editor of an Indian paper. The editor, it seems had openly accused the holy man of leading a scandalous life; he went further, and accused the holy man of being diseased. Kepi says it must have been the great French pox, but Nanantatee avers that it was the Japanese clap. For Nanantatee everything has to be a little exaggerated. At any rate, says Nanantatee cheerily: "You will please tell me what it says, Endree. I can't read the book—it hurts my arm." Then, by way of encouraging me—"it is a fine book about the fucking, Endree. Kepi has brought it for you. He thinks about nothing but the girls. So many girls he fucks—just like Krishna. We don't believe in that business, Endree. . . ."

A little later he takes me upstairs to the attic which is loaded down with tin cans and crap from India wrapped in burlap and firecracker paper. "Here is where I bring the girls," he says. And then rather wistfully: "I am not a very good fucker, Endree. I don't screw the girls any more. I hold them in my arms and I say the words. I like only to say the words now." It isn't necessary to listen any further: I know that he is going to tell me about his arm. I can see him lying there with that broken hinge dangling from the side of the bed. But to my surprise he adds: "I am no good for the fucking, Endree. I never was a very good fucker. My brother, he is good! Three times a day, every day! And Kepi, he is good—just like Krishna."

His mind is fixed now on the "fucking business." Downstairs, in the little room where he kneels before the open cabinet, he explains to me how it was when he was rich and his wife and the children were here. On holidays he would take his wife to the House of All Nations and hire a room for the night. Every room was appointed in a different style. His wife liked it there very much. "A wonderful place for the fucking, Endree. I know all the rooms. . . ."

The walls of the little room in which we are sitting are crammed with photographs. Every branch of the family is represented, it is like a cross section of the Indian empire. For the most part the members of this genealogical tree look like withered leaves: the women are frail and they have a startled, frightened look in their eyes: the men have a keen, intelligent look, like educated chimpanzees. They are all there, about ninety of them, with their white bullocks, their dung cakes, their skinny legs, their old-fashioned spectacles; in the background, now and then, one catches a glimpse of the parched soil, of a crumbling pediment, of an idol with crooked arms, a sort of human centipede. There is something so fantastic, so incongruous about this gallery that one is reminded inevitably of the great spawn of temples which stretch from the Himalayas to the tip of Ceylon, a vast jumble of architecture, staggering in beauty and at the same time monstrous, hideously monstrous because the fecundity which seethes and ferments in the myriad ramfications of design seems to have exhausted the very soil of India itself. Looking at the seething hive of figures which swarm the façades of the temples one is overwhelmed by the potency of these dark, handsome peoples who mingled their mysterious streams in a sexual embrace that has lasted thirty centuries or more. These frail men and women with piercing eyes who stare out of the photographs seem like the emaciated shadows of those virile, massive figures who incarnated themselves in stone and fresco from one end of India to the other in order that the heroic myths of the races who here intermingled should remain forever entwined in the hearts of their countrymen. When I look at only a fragment of these spacious dreams of stone, these toppling, sluggish edifices studded with gems, coagulated with human sperm, I am overwhelmed by the dazzling splendor of those imaginative flights which enabled half a billion people of diverse origins to thus incarnate the most fugitive expressions of their longing.

Is is a strange, inexplicable medley of feelings which assails me now as Nanantatee prattles on about the sister who died in childbirth. There she is on the wall, a frail, timid thing of twelve or thirteen clinging to the arm of a dotard. At ten years of age she was given in wedlock to this old roué who had already buried five wives. She had seven children, only one of whom survived her. She was given to the aged gorilla in order to keep the pearls in the family. As she was passing away, so Nanantatee puts it, she whispered to the doctor: "I am tired of this fucking. . . . I don't want to fuck any more, doctor." As he relates this to me he scratches his head solemnly with his withered arm. "The fucking business is bad, Endree," he says. "But I will give you a word that will always make you lucky; you must say it every day, over and over, a million times you must say it. It is the best word there is, Endree . . . say it now . . . OOMAHARUMOOMA!"

"OOMARABOO. . . ."

"No, Endree . . . like this . . . OOMAHARUMOOMA!"

"OOMAMABOOMBA. . . ."

"No, Endree . . . like this. . . ."

. . . But what with the murky light, the botchy print, the tattered cover, the jigjagged page, the fumbling fingers, the fox-trotting fleas, the lie-a-bed lice, the scum on his tongue, the drop in his eye, the lump in his throat, the drink in his pottle, the itch in his palm, the wail of his wind, the grief from his breath, the fog of his brainfag, the tic of his conscience, the height of his rage, the gush of his fundament, the fire in his gorge, the tickle of his tail, the rats in his garret, the hullabaloo and the dust in his ears, since it took him a month to steal a march, he was hard-set to memorize more than a word a week.

I suppose I would never have gotten out of Nanantatee's clutches if fate hadn't intervened. One night, as luck would have it, Kepi asked me if I wouldn't take one of his clients to a whorehouse nearby. The young man had just come from India and he had not very much money to spend. He was one of Gandhi's men, one of that little band who made the historic march to the sea during the salt trouble. A very gay disciple of Gandhi's I must say, despite the vows of abstinence he had taken. Evidently he hadn't looked at a woman for ages. It was all I could do to get him as far as the Rue Laferrière; he was like a dog with his tongue hanging out. And a pompous, vain little devil to boot! He had decked himself out in a corduroy suit, a beret, a cane, a Windsor tie; he had bought himself two fountain pens, a kodak, and some fancy underwear. The money he was spending was a gift from the merchants of Bombay; they were sending him to England to spread the gospel of Gandhi.

Once inside Miss Hamilton's joint he began to lose his *sang-froid*. When suddenly he found himself surrounded by a bevy of naked women he looked at me in consternation. "Pick one out," I said. "You can have your choice." He had become so rattled that he could scarcely look at them. "You do it for me," he murmured, blushing violently. I looked them over coolly and picked out a plump young wench who seemed full of feathers. We sat down in the reception room and waited for the drinks. The madam wanted to know why I didn't take a girl also. "Yes, you take one too," said the young Hindu. "I don't want to be alone with her." So the girls were brought in again and I chose one for myself, a rather tall, thin one with melancholy eyes. We were left alone, the four of us, in the reception room. After a few moments my young Gandhi leans over and whispers something in my ear. "Sure, if you like her better, take her," I said, and so, rather awkwardly and considerably embarrassed, I explained to the girls that we would like to switch. I saw at once that we had made a *faux pas*, but by now my young friend had become gay and lecherous and nothing would do but to get upstairs quickly and have it over with.

We took adjoining rooms with a connecting door between. I think my companion had in mind to make another switch once he had satisfied his sharp, gnawing hunger. At any rate, no sooner had the girls left the room to prepare themselves than I hear him knocking on the door. "Where is the toilet, please?" he asks. Not thinking that it was anything serious I urge him to do it in the *bidet*. The girls return with towels in their hands. I hear him giggling in the next room.

As I'm putting on my pants suddenly I hear a commotion in the next room. The girl is bawling him out, calling him a pig, a dirty little pig. I can't imagine what he has done to warrant such an outburst. I'm standing there with one foot in my trousers listening attentively. He's trying to explain to her in English, raising his voice louder and louder until it becomes a shriek.

I hear a door slam and in another moment the madam bursts into my room, her face as red as a beet, her arms gesticulating wildly. "You ought to be ashamed of yourself," she screams, "bringing a man like that to my place! He's a barbarian . . . he's a pig . . . he's a . . . !" My companion is standing behind her, in the doorway, a look of utmost discomfiture on his face. "What did you do?" I ask.

"What did he do?" yells the madam. "I'll show you. . . . Come here!" And grabbing me by the arm she drags me into the next room. "There! There!" she screams, pointing to the *bidet*.

"Come on, let's get out," says the Hindu boy.

"Wait a minute, you can't get out as easily as all that."

The madam is standing by the *bidet*, fuming and spitting. The girls are standing there too, with towels in their hands. The five of us are standing there looking at the *bidet*. There are two enormous turds floating in the water. The madam bends down and puts a towel over it. "Frightful! Frightful!" she wails. "Never have I seen anything like this! A pig! A dirty little pig!"

The Hindu boy looks at me reproachfully. "You should have told me!" he says. "I didn't know it wouldn't go down. I asked you where to go and you told me to use that." He is almost in tears.

Finally the madam takes me to one side. She has become a little more reasonable now. After all, it was a mistake. Perhaps the gentlemen would like to come downstairs and order another drink—for the girls. It was a great shock to the girls. They are not used to such things. And if the good gentlemen will be so kind as to remember the *femme de chambre*. . . . It is not so pretty for the *femme de chambre*—that mess, that ugly mess. She shrugs her shoulders and winks her eye. A lamentable incident. But an accident. If the gentlemen will wait here a few moments the maid will bring the drinks. Would the gentlemen like to have some champagne? Yes?

"I'd like to get out of here," says the Hindu boy weakly.

"Don't feel so badly about it," says the madam. "It is all over now. Mistakes will happen sometimes. Next time you will ask for the toilet." She goes on about the toilet—one on every floor, it seems. And a bathroom too. "I have lots of English clients," she says. "They are all gentlemen. The gentleman is a Hindu? Charming people, the Hindus. So intelligent. So handsome."

When we get into the street the charming young gentleman is almost weeping. He is sorry now that he bought a corduroy suit and the cane and the fountain pens. He talks about the eight vows that he took, the control of the palate, etc. On the march to Dandi even a plate of ice cream it was forbidden to take. He tells me about the spinning wheel—how the little band of Satyagrahists imitated the devotion of their master. He relates with pride how he walked beside the master and conversed with him. I have the illusion of being in the presence of one of the twelve disciples.

During the next few days we see a good deal of each other; there are interviews to be arranged with the newspaper men and lectures to be given to the Hindus of Paris. It is amazing to see how these spineless devils order one another about; amazing also to see how ineffectual they are in all that concerns practical affairs. And the jealousy and the intrigues, the petty, sordid rivalries. Wherever there are ten Hindus together there is India with her sects and schisms, her racial, lingual, religious, political antagonisms. In the person of Gandhi they are experiencing for a brief moment the miracle of unity, but when he goes there will be a crash, an utter relapse into that strife and chaos so characteristic of the Indian people.

The young Hindu, of course, is optimistic. He has been to America and he has been contaminated by the cheap idealism of the Americans, contaminated by the ubiquitous bathtub, the five-and-ten-cent store bric-a-brac, the bustle, the efficiency, the machinery, the high wages, the free libraries, etc., etc. His ideal would be to Americanize India. He is not at all pleased with Gandhi's retrogressive mania. *Forward*, he says, just like a YMCA man. As I listen to his tales of America I see how absurd it is to expect of Gandhi that miracle which will deroute the trend of destiny. India's enemy is not England, but America. India's enemy is the time spirit, the hand which cannot be turned back. Nothing will avail to offset this virus which is poisoning the whole world. America is the very incarnation of doom. She will drag the whole world down to the bottomless pit.

He thinks the Americans are a very gullible people. He tells me about the credulous souls who succored him there—the Quakers, the Unitarians, the Theosophists, the New Thoughters, the Seventh-day Adventists, etc. He knew where to sail his boat, this bright young man. He knew how to make the tears come to his eyes at the right moment; he knew how to take up a collection, how to appeal to the minister's wife, how to make love to the mother and daughter at the same time. To look at him you would think him a saint. And he is a saint, in the modern fashion; a contaminated saint who talks in one breath of love, brotherhood, bathtubs, sanitation, efficiency, etc.

The last night of his sojourn in Paris is given up to "the fucking business." He has had a full program all day—conferences, cablegrams, interviews, photographs for the newspapers, affectionate farewells, advice to the faithful, etc., etc. At dinner time he decides to lay aside his troubles. He orders champagne with the meal, he snaps his fingers at the *garçon* and behaves in general like the boorish little peasant that he is. And since he has had a bellyful of all the good places he suggests now that I show him something more primitive. He would like to go to a very cheap place, order two or three girls at once. I steer him along the Boulevard de la Chapelle, warning him all the while to be careful of his pocketbook. Around Aubervilliers we duck into a cheap dive and immediately we've got a flock of them on our hands. In a few minutes he's dancing with a naked wench, a huge blonde with creases in her jowls. I can see her ass reflected a dozen times in the mirrors that line the room—and those dark, bony fingers of his clutching her tenaciously. The table is full of beer glasses, the mechanical piano is wheezing and gasping. The girls who are unoccupied are sitting placidly on the leather benches, scratching themselves peacefully just like a family of chimpanzees. There is a sort of subdued pandemonium in the air, a note of repressed violence, as if the awaited explosion required the advent of some utterly minute detail, something microscopic but thoroughly unpremeditated, completely unexpected. In that sort of half-reverie which permits one to participate in an event and yet remain quite aloof, the little detail which was lacking began obscurely but insistently to coagulate, to assume a freakish, crystalline form, like the frost which gathers on the windowpane. And like those frost patterns which seem so bizarre, so utterly free and fantastic in design, but which are nevertheless determined by the most rigid laws, so this sensation which commenced to take form inside me seemed also to be giving obedience to ineluctable laws. My whole being was responding to the dictates of an ambiance which it had never before experienced; that which I could call myself seemed to be contracting, condensing, shrinking from the stale, customary boundaries of the flesh whose perimeter knew only the modulations of the nerve ends.

And the more substantial, the more solid the core of me became, the more delicate and extravagant appeared the close, palpable reality out of which I was being squeezed. In the measure that I became more and more metallic, in the same measure the scene before my eyes became inflated. The state of tension was so finely drawn now that the introduction of a single foreign particle, even a microscopic particle, as I say, would have shattered everything. For the fraction of a second perhaps I experienced that utter clarity which the epileptic, it is said, is given to know. In that moment I lost completely the illusion of time and space: the world unfurled its drama simultaneously along a meridian which had no axis. In this sort of hair-trigger eternity I felt that everything was justified, supremely justified; I felt the wars inside me that had left behind this pulp and wrack; I felt the crimes that were seething here to emerge tomorrow in blatant screamers; I felt the misery that was grinding itself out with pestle and mortar, the long dull misery that dribbles away in dirty handkerchiefs. On the meridian of time there is no injustice: there is only the poetry of motion creating the illusion of truth and drama. If at any moment anywhere one comes face to face with the absolute, that great sympathy which makes men like Gautama and Jesus seem divine freezes away; the monstrous thing is not that men have created roses out of this dung heap, but that, for some reason or other, they should *want* roses. For some reason or other man looks for the miracle, and to accomplish it he will wade through blood. He will debauch himself with ideas, he will reduce himself to a shadow if for only one second of his life he can close his eyes to the hideousness of reality. Everything is endured—disgrace, humiliation, poverty, war, crime, *ennui*—in the belief that overnight something will occur, a miracle, which will render life tolerable. And all the while a meter is running inside and there is no hand that can reach in there and shut it off. All the while someone is eating the bread of life and drinking the wine, some dirty fat cockroach of a priest who hides away in the cellar guzzling it, while up above in the light of the street a phantom host touches the lips and the blood is pale as water. And out of the endless torment and misery no miracle comes forth, no microscopic vestige even of relief. Only ideas, pale, attenuated ideas which have to be fattened by slaughter; ideas which come forth like bile, like the guts of a pig when the carcass is ripped open.

And so I think what a miracle it would be if this miracle which man attends eternally should turn out to be nothing more than these two enormous turds which the faithful disciple dropped in the *bidet*. What if at the last moment, when the banquet table is set and the cymbals clash, there should appear suddenly, and wholly without warning, a silver platter on which even the blind could see that there is nothing more, and nothing less, than two enormous lumps of shit. That, I believe would be more miraculous than anything which man has looked forward to. It would be miraculous because it would be undreamed of. It would be more miraculous than even the wildest dream because *anybody* could imagine the possibility but nobody ever has, and probably nobody ever again will.

Somehow the realization that nothing was to be hoped for had a salutary effect upon me. For weeks and months, for years, in fact, all my life I had been looking forward to something happening, some extrinsic event that would alter my life, and now suddenly, inspired by the absolute hopelessness of everything, I felt relieved, felt as though a great burden had been lifted from my shoulders. At dawn I parted company with the young Hindu, after touching him for a few francs, enough for a room. Walking toward Montparnasse I decided to let myself drift with the tide, to make not the least resistance to fate, no matter in what form it presented itself. Nothing that had happened to me thus far had been sufficient to destroy me; nothing had been destroyed except my illusions. I myself was intact. The world was intact. Tomorrow there might be a revolution, a plague, an earthquake; tomorrow there might not be left a single soul to whom one could turn for sympathy, for aid, for faith. It seemed to me that the great calamity had already manifested itself, that I could be no more truly alone than at this very moment. I made up my mind that I would hold on to nothing, that I would expect nothing, that henceforth I would live as an animal, a beast of prey, a rover, a plunderer. Even if war were declared, and it were my lot to go, I would grab the bayonet and plunge it, plunge it up to the hilt. And if rape were the order of the day then rape I would, and with a vengeance. At this very moment, in the quiet dawn of a new day, was not the earth giddy with crime and distress? Had one single element of man's nature been altered, vitally, fundamentally altered, by the incessant march of history? By what he calls the better part of his nature, man has been betrayed, that is all. At the extreme limits of his spiritual being man finds himself again naked as a savage. When he finds God, as it were, he has been picked clean: he is a skeleton. One must burrow into life again in order to put on flesh. The word must become flesh; the soul thirsts. On whatever crumb my eye fastens, I will pounce and devour. If to live is the paramount thing, then I will live, even if I must become a cannibal. Heretofore I have been trying to save my precious hide, trying to preserve the few pieces of meat that hid my bones. I am done with that. I have reached the limits of endurance. My back is to the wall; I can retreat no further. As far as history goes I am dead. If there is something beyond I shall have to bounce back. I have found God, but he is insufficient. I am only spiritually dead. Physically I am alive. Morally I am free. The world which I have departed is a menagerie. The dawn is breaking on a new world, a jungle world in which the lean spirits roam with sharp claws. If I am a hyena I am a lean and hungry one: I go forth to fatten myself.

THE WISDOM OF THE HEART

From The Wisdom of the Heart, *"The Eye of Paris." Miller's second American publication,* Wisdom *is a collection of sketches, essays, and portraits New Directions published in 1940. Although censorship laws prevented publisher James Laughlin from exhibiting the full range of Miller's talent,* Wisdom *does give a good sample of Miller's interests and prejudices. Miller was a skilled and often brilliant portraitist, as shown here in his depiction of Brassai (Gyula Halész), the Hungarian-born photographer whom Miller met in 1930 and whose work in nighttime Paris was akin to what Miller was trying to capture in words.*

THE EYE OF PARIS

Brassai has that rare gift which so many artists despise—*normal vision.* He has no need to distort or deform, no need to lie or to preach. He would not alter the living arrangement of the world by one iota; he sees the world precisely as it is and as few men in the world see it because seldom do we encounter a human being endowed with normal vision. Everything to which his eye attaches itself acquires value and significance, a value and significance, I might say, heretofore avoided or ignored. The fragment, the defect, the commonplace—he detects in them what there is of novelty or perfection. He explores with equal patience, equal interest, a crack in the wall or the panorama of a city. Seeing becomes an end in itself. For Brassai is an eye, a living eye.

When you meet the man you see at once that he is equipped with no ordinary eyes. His eyes have that perfect, limpid sphericity, that all-embracing voracity which makes the falcon or the shark a shuddering sentinel of reality. He has the eyeball of the insect which, hypnotized by its myopic scrutiny of the world, raises its two huge orbs from their sockets in order to acquire a still greater flexibility. Eye to eye with this man you have the sensation of a razor operating on your own eyeball, a razor which moves with such delicacy and precision that you are suddenly in a ball room in which the act of undressing follows upon the wish. His gaze pierces the retina like those marvelous probes which penetrate the labyrinth of the ear in order to sound for dead bone, which tap at the base of the skull like the dull tick of a watch in moments of complete silence. I have felt the penetration of his gaze like the gleam of a searchlight invading the hidden recesses of the eye, pushing open the sliding doors of the brain. Under that keen, steady gaze I have felt the seat of my skull glowing like an asbestos grill, glowing with short, violet waves which no living matter can resist. I have felt the cool, dull tremors in every vertebra, each socket, each nodule, cushion and fiber vibrating at such a speed that the whole backbone together with my rudimentary tail is thrown into incandescent relief. My spine becomes a barometer of light registering the pressure and deflection of all the waves which escape the heavy, fluid substance of matter. I feel the feathery, jubilant weight of his eye rising from its matrix to brush the prisms of light. Not the eye of a shark, nor a horse, nor a fly, not any known flexible eye, but the eye of a coccus newborn, a coccus traveling on the wave of an epidemic, always a millimeter in advance of the crest. The eye that gloats and ravages. The eye that precedes doom. The waiting, lurking eye of the ghoul, the torpid, monstrously indifferent eye of the leper, the still, all-inclusive eye of the Buddha which never closes. *The insatiable eye.*

It is with this eye that I see him walking through the wings of the Folies-Bergère, walking across the ceiling with sticky, clinging feet, crawling on all fours over candelabras, warm breasts, crinolines, training that huge, cold searchlight on the inner organs of a Venus, on the foam of a wave of lace, on the cicatrices that are dyed with ink in the satin throat of a puppet, on the pulleys that will hoist a Babylon in paint and papier-mâché, on the empty seats which rise tier upon tier like layers of sharks' teeth. I see him walking across the proscenium with his beautiful suede gloves, see him peeling them off and tossing them to the

inky squib which has swallowed the seats and the glass chandeliers, the fake marble, the brass posts, the thick velvet cords and
the chipped plaster. I see the world of behind the scenes upside
down, each fragment a new universe, each human body or
puppet or pulley framed in its own inconceivable niche. I see the
lovely Venus prone and full athwart her strange axis, her hair
dipped in laudanum, her mouth bright with asphodels; she lies in
the neap of the tide, taut with starry sap, her toes tinctured with
light, her eyes transfixed. He does not wait for the curtain to rise;
he waits for it to fall. He waits for that moment when all the
conglomerations artificially produced resolve back into their natural component entities, when the nymphs and the dryads
strewing themselves like flowers over the floor of the stage gaze
vacantly into the mirror of the tank where a moment ago,
tesselated with spotlights, they swam like goldfish.

Deprived of the miracle of color, registering everything in
degrees of black and white, Brassai nevertheless seems to convey
by the purity and quality of his tones all the effects of sunlight,
and even more impressively the effects of night light. A man of
the city, he limits himself to that spectacular feast which only
such a city as Paris can offer. No phase of cosmopolitan life has
escaped his eye. His albums of black and white comprise a vast
encyclopaedia of the city's architecture, its growth, its history, its
origins. Whatever aspect of the city his eye seizes upon the result
is a vast metaphor whose brilliant arc, studded with incalculable
vistas backward and forward, glistens now like a drop of dew
suspended in the morning light. The Cemetery Montmartre, for
example, shot from the bridge at night is a phantasmagoric
creation of death flowering in electricity; the intense patches of
night lie upon the tombs and crosses in a crazy patchwork of steel
girders which fade with the sunlight into bright green lawns and
flower beds and graveled walks.

Brassai strikes at the accidental modulations, the illogical syn-
tax, the mythical juxtaposition of things, at that anomalous,
sporadic form of growth which a walk through the streets or a
glance at a map or a scene in a film conveys to the sleeping portion
of the brain. What is most familiar to the eye, what has become
stale and commonplace, acquires through the flick of his magic

lens the properties of the unique. Just as a thousand diverse types may write automatically and yet only one of them will bear the signature of André Breton, so a thousand men may photograph the Cemetery Montmartre but one of them will stand out triumphantly as Brassai's. No matter how perfect the machine, no matter how little of human guidance is involved, the mark of personality is always there. The photograph seems to carry with it the same degree of personality as any other form or expression of art. Brassai is Brassai and Man Ray is Man Ray. One man may try to interfere as little as possible with the apparatus, or the results obtained from the apparatus; the other may endeavor to subjugate it to his will, to dominate it, control it, use it like an artist. But no matter what the approach or the technique involved the thing that registers is the stamp of individuality.

Perhaps the difference which I observe between the work of Brassai and that of other photographers lies in this—that Brassai seems overwhelmed by the fullness of life. How else are we to explain that a chicken bone, under the optical alchemy of Brassai, acquires the attributes of the marvelous, whereas the most fantastic inventions of other men often leave us with a sense of unfulfillment? The man who looked at the chicken bone transferred his whole personality to it in looking at it; he transmitted to an insignificant phenomenon the fullness of his knowledge of life, the experience acquired from looking at millions of other objects and participating in the wisdom which their relationships one to another inspired. The desire which Brassai so strongly evinces, a desire not to tamper with the object but regard it as it is, was this not provoked by a profound humility, a respect and reverence for the object itself? The more the man detached from his view of life, from the objects and identities that make life, all intrusion of individual will and ego, the more readily and easily he entered into the multitudinous identities which ordinarily remain alien and closed to us. By depersonalizing himself, as it were, he was enabled to discover his personality everywhere in everything.

Perhaps this is not the method of art. Perhaps art demands the wholly personal, the catalytic power of will. *Perhaps.* All I know is that when I look at these photographs which seem to have been taken at random by a man loath to assert any values except what were inherent in the phenomena, I am impressed by their authority. I realize in looking at his photos that by looking at things aesthetically, just as much as by looking at things moralistically or pragmatically, we are destroying their value, their significance. Objects do not fade away with time: *they are destroyed!* From the moment that we cease to regard them awesomely they die. They may carry on an existence for thousands of years, but as dead matter, as fossil, as archaeologic data. What once inspired an artist or a people can, after a certain moment, fail to elicit even the interest of a scientist. Objects die in proportion as the vision of things dies. The object and the vision are one. Nothing flourishes after the vital flow is broken, neither the thing seen, nor the one who sees.

It happens that the man who introduced me to Brassaï is a man who has no understanding of him at all, a sort of human cockroach living out his dream of the 18th century. He knows all the Metro stations by heart, can recite them backwards for you, line by line; he can give you the history of each *arrondissement*, can tell you precisely where and how one street intersects another, can give you the genesis of every statue and monument in Paris. But he has absolutely no feeling for the streets, no wanderlust, no curiosity, no reverence. He secretes himself in his room and lives out in imagination the hermeneutic life of the 18th century.

I mention this only as an example of the strange fatality by which two men of kindred spirit are sometimes brought together. I mention it by way of showing that even the despised cockroach serves a purpose in life. I see that the cockroach living out its dream of the 18th century can serve as a link to bind the living. It was this same cockroach, I must also confess, who revealed to me the glamor of the 13th *arrondissement*. In the very heart of it, like a spider luring me to its lair, there lived all the while this man Brassaï whom I was destined to meet. I remember vividly how, when I first came to Paris, I wandered one day to his hotel looking for a painter. The man who received me was not the man I had expected to see. He was a petty, niggardly, querulous soul who had once painted a knife and fork and rested there. I had to return to America, come back to France once again, starve, roam the streets, listen to silly, idiotic theories of life and art, take up with this failure and that, and finally surrender to the cockroach before it was possible to know the man who like myself had taken in Paris without effort of will, the man who, without my knowing it, was silently slaving away at the illustrations for my books. And when one day the door was finally thrust open I beheld to my astonishment a thousand replicas of all the scenes, all the streets, all the walls, all the fragments of that Paris wherein I died and was born again. There on his bed, in myriad pieces and arrangements, lay the cross to which I had been nailed and crucified, the cross on which I was resurrected to live again and forever in the spirit.

How then am I to describe these morsels of black and white, how refer to them as photographs or specimens of art? Here on this man's bed, drained of all blood and suffering, radiant now with only the life of the sun, I saw my own sacred body exposed, the body that I have written into every stone, every tree, every monument, park, fountain, statue, bridge, and dwelling of Paris. I see now that I am leaving behind me a record of Paris which I have written in blood—but also in peace and good will. The whole city—every *arrondissement*, every *carrefour*, every impasse, every enchanted street. Through me Paris will live again, a little more, a little brighter.

Tenderly, reverently, as if I were gathering to my breast the most sentient morsels of myself, I pick up these fragments which lie on the bed. Once again I traverse the road that led me to the present, to this high, cool plateau whence I can look about me in serenity. What a procession passes before my eyes! What a throng of men and women! What strange cities—and situations stranger still! The mendicant sitting on the public bench, thirsting for a glimmer of sun, the butcher standing in a pool of blood with knife upraised, the scows and barges dreaming in the shadows of the bridges, the pimp standing against a wall with cigarette in hand, the street cleaner with her broom of reddish twigs, her thick, gnarled fingers, her high stomach draped in black, a shroud over her womb, rinsing away the vomit of the night before so that when I pass over the cobblestones my feet will gleam with the light of morning stars. I see the old hats, the sombreros and fedoras, the velours and Panamas that I painted with a clutching fury; I see the corners of walls eroded by time and weather which I passed in the night and in passing felt the erosion going on in myself, corners of my own walls crumbling away, blown down, dispersed, reintegrated elsewhere in mysterious shape and essence. I see the old tin urinals where, standing in the dead silence of the night, I dreamed so violently that the past sprang up like a white horse and carried me out of the body.

Looking for an instant into the eyes of this man I see therein the image of myself. Two enormous eyes I see, two glowing discs which look up at the sun from the bottom of a pool; two round, wondrous orbs that have pushed back the heavy, opaque lids in order to swim up to the surface of the light and drink with unslakeable thirst. Heavy tortoise eyes that have drunk from every stratum; soft, viscous eyes that have burrowed into the mud sinks, tracked the worm and shell; hard, sclerotic gems, bead and nugget, over which the heel of man has passed and left no imprint. Eye that lurks in the primal ooze, lord and master of all it surveys; not waiting on history, not waiting on time. The cosmologic eye, persisting through wrack and doom, impervious, inchoate, *seeing only what is.*

Now and then, in wandering through the streets, suddenly one comes awake, perceives with a strange exultation that he is moving through an absolutely fresh slice of reality. Everything has the quality of the marvelous—the murky windows, the rain-sodden vegetables, the contours of the houses, the bill-posters, the slumping figures of men and women, the tin soldiers in the stationery shops, the colors of the walls—everything written down in an unfamiliar script. After the moment of ecstasy has passed what is one's amazement but to discover that the street through which he is walking with eyes popping is the street on which he lives. He has simply come upon it unaware, from the wrong end perhaps. Or, moving out of the confines of an unknown region, the sense of wonder and mystery prolonged itself in defiance of reality. It is as if the eye itself had been freshened, as if it had forgotten all that it had been taught. In this condition it happens that one really does see things he had never seen before—not the fantastic, harrowing, hallucinating objects of dream or drug, but the most banal, the most commonplace things, seen as it were for the first time.

Walking one night along a dark, abandoned street of Levallois-Perret suddenly across the way I notice a window lit up. As I approach the reddish glow of the room awakens something in me, some obscure memory which stirs sleepily, only to be drowned again in deeper memories. The hideous pattern of the wallpaper, which I can only vaguely decipher, seems as familiar to me as if I had lived with it all my life. The weird, infernal glow of the room throws the pattern of the wallpaper into violent relief; it leaps out from the wall like the frantic gesture of a madman. My heart is in my throat. My step quickens. I have the sensation of being about to look into the privacy of a room such as no man has seen before.

As I come abreast of the window I notice the glass bells suspended from the chandelier—three glass bells such as are manufactured by the million and which are the pride of every poverty-stricken home wherever there are progress and invention. Under this modern, universal whatnot are gathered three of the most ordinary people that could possibly be grouped together—a tintype of honest toil snapped on the threshold of Utopia. Everything in the room is familiar to me, nauseatingly familiar: the cupboard, the chairs, the table, the tablecloth, the rubber plant, the bird cage, the alarm clock, the calendar on the wall, the Sunday it registers and the saint who rules it. And yet never have I seen such a tintype as this. This is so ordinary, so familiar, so stale, so commonplace, that I have never really noticed it before.

The group is composed of two men and a woman. They are standing around the cheap, polished walnut table—the table that is not yet paid for. One man is in his shirt sleeves and wears a cap; the other man is wearing a pair of striped flannel pajamas and has a black derby tilted on the back of his head. The woman is in a dressing sack and one of her titties is falling out. A large juicy teat with a dark, mulberry nipple swimming in a deep coffee stain full of fine wrinkles. On the table is a large dishpan filled with boiling water. The man with cap and shirt sleeves has just doused something in the pan; the other man stands with his hands in his pockets and quietly puffs a cigarette, allowing the ash to fall on his pajama coat and from there to the table.

Suddenly the woman grabs the queer-looking object from the man with the cap and, holding it somewhat above her head, she commences plucking at it with lean, tenacious fingers. It is a dead chicken with black and red feathers and a bright red-toothed comb. While she holds the legs of the chicken with one hand the man with the cap holds the neck; at intervals they lower the dead chicken into the pan of boiling water. The feathers come out easily, leaving the slightly yellowish skin full of black splinters. They stand there facing each other without uttering a word. The woman's fingers move nimbly from one area of the chicken to another—until she comes to the little triangular flap over the vent when with one gleeful clutch she rips out all the tail feathers at once and flinging them on the floor drops the chicken on the table.

Strike me pink if I have ever seen anything more grotesque! Taken in combination, under that light, at that hour of the night, the three tintypes, the peculiar deadness of the chicken, the scene remains unique in my memory. Every other chicken, dressed or undressed, is scalded from my memory. Henceforth whenever I say chicken there will always come to mind two kinds—*this* chicken, whose name I do not know, and all other chickens. Chicken *prime*, let us say, so as to distinguish it from all other chicken integers that were and will be tomorrow, henceforth and forevermore.

And so it is, when I look at the photographs of Brassai, that I say to myself—chicken *prime*, table *prime*, chair *prime*, Venus *prime*, etc. That which constitutes the uniqueness of an object, the first, the original, the imperishable vision of things. When Shakespeare painted a horse, said a friend of mine once, it was a horse for all time. I must confess that I am largely unfamiliar with the horses of Shakespeare, but knowing as I do certain of his human characters, and knowing also that they have endured throughout several centuries, I am quite willing to concede that his horses too, whoever and wherever they are, will have a long and abiding life. I know that there are men and women who belong just as distinctly and inexpugnably to Rembrandt's world, or Giotto's, or Renoir's. I know that there are sleeping giants who belong to the Grimm family or to Michelangelo, and dwarfs who belong to Velasquez or Hieronymus Bosch, or to Toulouse-Lautrec. I know that there are physiognomic maps and relics of the human body which is all that we possess of buried epochs, all that is personal and understandable to us, and that these maps and relics bear the distinguished imprimatur of Dante, da Vinci, Petronius and such like. I know too that even when the human body has been disintegrated and made an inhuman part of a fragmented world—such as the one we now inhabit—I mean that when the human body, having lost its distinction and kingship, serves the painter with no more inspiration, no more reverence than a table or chair or discarded newspaper, still it is possible to recognize one sort of hocus-pocus from another, to say this is Braque, that is Picasso, the other Chirico.

We have reached the point where we do not want to know any longer whose work it is, whose seal is affixed, whose stamp is upon it; what we want, and what at last we are about to get, are individual masterpieces which triumph in such a way as to completely subordinate the accidental artists who are responsible for them. Every man today who is really an artist is trying to kill the artist in himself—and he must, if there is to be any art in the future. We are suffering from a plethora of art. We are art-ridden. Which is to say that instead of a truly personal, truly creative vision of things, we have merely an *aesthetic* view. Empty as we are, it is impossible for us to look at an object without annexing it to our collection. We have not a single chair, for example, in the sweep and memory of our retina, that does not bear a label; if, for the space of a week, a man working in absolute secrecy were to turn out chairs unique and unrecognizable, the world would go mad. And yet every chair that is brought into existence is howling for recognition *as chair*, as chair in its own right, unique and perdurable.

I think of chair because among all the objects which Brassai has photographed his chair with the wire legs stands out with a majesty that is singular and disquieting. It is a chair of the lowest denomination, a chair which has been sat on by beggars and by royalty, by little trot-about whores and by queenly opera divas. It is a chair which the municipality rents daily to any and every one who wishes to pay fifty centimes for sitting down in the open air. A chair with little holes in the seat and wire legs which come to a loop at the bottom. The most unostentatious, the most inexpensive, the most ridiculous chair, if a chair can be ridiculous, which could be devised. Brassai chose precisely this insignificant chair and, snapping it where he found it, unearthed what there was in it of dignity and veracity. THIS IS A CHAIR. Nothing more. No sentimentalism about the lovely backsides which once graced it, no romanticism about the lunatics who fabricated it, no statistics about the hours of sweat and anguish that went into the creation of it, no sarcasm about the era which produced it, no odious comparisons with chairs of other days, no humbug about the dreams of the idlers who monopolize it, no scorn for the nakedness of it, no gratitude either. Walking along a path of the Jardin des Tuileries one day he saw this chair standing on the edge of a grating. He saw at once chair, grating, tree, clouds, sun, people. He saw that the chair was as much a part of that fine spring day as the tree, the clouds, the sun, the people. He took it as it was, with its honest little holes, its slender wire legs. Perhaps the Prince of Wales once sat on it, perhaps a holy man, perhaps a leper, perhaps a murderer or an idiot. *Who* sat on it did not interest Brassai in the least. It was a spring day and the foliage was greening; the earth was in a ferment, the roots convulsed with sap. On such a day, if one is alive, one can well believe that out of the dead body of the earth there will spring forth a race of men immortal in their splendor. On such a day there is visible in the stalest object a promise, a hope, a possibility. Nothing is dead, except in the imagination. Animate or inanimate, all bodies under the sun give expression to their vitality. Especially on a fine day in spring!

And so on that day, in that glorious hour, the homely, inexpensive chair belonging to the municipality of Paris became the empty throne which is always beseeching the restless spirit of man to end his fear and longing and proclaim the kingdom of man.

THE COLOSSUS OF MAROUSSI

From The Colossus of Maroussi. *During the years when Miller's novels were unavailable, this spirited account of his trip to Greece in the summer of 1939 was said to be his best work. That judgment, of course, could be but a partial one, subject to revision when the novels became available in the 1960s. But* Colossus *is in fact a gem of a book, one of the best things Miller wrote. Like his hero, D. H. Lawrence, Miller is one of those very rare writers who manages to make himself as interesting as the terrain he covers. And though he is often accused of writing only about himself, in his Greek book he establishes a delightful balance between himself as picaresque narrator and the ancient landscape through which he moves.*

For twenty years it had been my dream to visit Knossus. I never realized how simple it would be to make the journey. In Greece you have only to announce to some one that you intend to visit a certain place and presto! in a few moments there is a carriage waiting for you at the door. This time it turned out to be an aeroplane. Seferiades had decided that I should ride in pomp. It was a poetic gesture and I accepted it like a poet.

I had never been in a plane before and I probably will never go up again. I felt foolish sitting in the sky with hands folded; the man beside me was reading a newspaper, apparently oblivious of the clouds that brushed the window-panes. We were probably making a hundred miles an hour, but since we passed nothing but clouds I had the impression of not moving. In short, it was unrelievedly dull and pointless. I was sorry that I had not booked passage on the good ship Acropolis which was to touch at Crete shortly. Man is made to walk the earth and sail the seas; the conquest of the air is reserved for a later stage of his evolution, when he will have sprouted real wings and assumed the form of the angel which he is in essence. Mechanical devices have nothing to do with man's real nature—they are merely traps which Death has baited for him.

We came down at the seaport of Herakleion, one of the principal towns of Crete. The main street is almost a ringer for a movie still in a third-rate Western picture. I found a room quickly in one of the two hotels and set out to look for a restaurant. A gendarme, whom I accosted, took me by the arm and graciously escorted me to a modest place near the public fountain. The meal was bad but I was now within reach of Knossus and too excited to be disturbed about such a trifle. After lunch I went across the street to a café and had a Turkish coffee. Two Germans who had arrived by the same plane were discussing the lecture on Wagner which they were to give that evening; they seemed to be fatuously unaware that they had come with their musical poison to the birthplace of Venizelos. I left to take a quick stroll through the town. A few doors away, in a converted mosque, a cinema announced the coming of Laurel and Hardy. The children who were clustered about the billboards were evidently as enthusiastic about these clowns as the children of Dubuque or Kenosha might be. I believe the cinema was called "The Minoan." I wondered vaguely if there would be a cinema at Knossus too, announcing perhaps the coming of the Marx Brothers.

Herakleion is a shabby town bearing all the ear-marks of Turkish domination. The principal streets are filled with open shops in which everything for men's needs are made by hand as in medieval times. From the countryside the Cretans come in garbed in handsome black raiment set off by elegant high boots, of red or white leather ofttimes. Next to Hindus and Berbers they are the most handsome, noble, dignified males I have ever seen. They are far more striking than the women: they are a race apart.

I walked to the edge of the town where as always in the Balkans everything comes to an end abruptly, as though the monarch who had designed the weird creation had suddenly become demented, leaving the great gate swinging on one hinge. Here the buses collect like broken-down caterpillars waiting for the dust of the plains to smother them in oblivion. I turned back and dove into the labyrinth of narrow, twisting streets which forms the residential quarter and which, though thoroughly Greek, has the atmospheric flavor of some English outpost in the West Indies. I had long tried to imagine what the approach to Crete would be like. In my ignorance I had supposed that the island was sparsely inhabited, that there was no water to be had except what was brought in from the mainland; I thought that one would see a deserted-looking coast dotted with a few scintillating ruins which would be Knossus, and beyond Knossus there would be a wasteland resembling those vast areas of Australia where the dodo bird, shunned by other feathered species of the bush, forlornly buries his head in the sand and whistles out the other end. I remembered that a friend of mine, a French writer, had been stricken with dysentery here and transported on the back of a donkey to a small boat whence by some miracle he was transported to a passing freighter and returned to the mainland in a state of delirium. I wandered about in a daze, stopping now and then to listen to a cracked record from a horned phonograph standing on a chair in the middle of the street. The butchers were draped in blood-red aprons; they stood before primitive chopping blocks in little booths such as one may still see at Pompeii. Every so often the streets opened up into a public square flanked by insane buildings devoted to law, administration, church, education, sickness and insanity; the architecture was of that startling reality which characterizes the work of the popular primitives such as Bombois, Peyronnet, Kane, Sullivan and Vivin. In the dazzling sunlight a detail such as a grilled gate of a defenseless bastion stands out with hair-raising exactitude such as one sees only in the paintings of the very great or the insane. Every inch of Herakleion is paintable; it is a confused, nightmarish town, thoroughly anomalous, thoroughly heterogeneous, a place-dream suspended in a void between Europe and Africa, smelling strongly of raw hides, caraway seeds, tar and sub-tropical fruits. It has been brutalized by the Turk and infected with the harmless rose water vaporings of the back pages of Charles Dickens. It has no relation whatever to Knossus or Phaestos; it is Minoan in the way that Walt Disney's creations are American; it is a carbuncle on the face of time, a sore spot which one rubs like a horse while asleep on four legs.

I had in my pocket a card of introduction to the leading literary figure of Crete, a friend of Katsimbalis. Towards evening I found him in the café where the Germans had been hatching their Wagnerian machinations. I shall call him Mr. Tsoutsou as I have unfortunately forgotten his name. Mr. Tsoutsou spoke French, English, German, Spanish, Italian, Russian, Portuguese, Turkish, Arabic, demotic Greek, newspaper Greek and ancient Greek. He was a composer, poet, scholar and lover of food and drink. He began by asking me about James Joyce, T. S. Eliot, Walt Whitman, André Gide, Breton, Rimbaud, Lautréamont, Lewis Carroll, Monk Lewis, Heinrich Georg and Rainer Maria Rilke. I say he asked me about them, much as you would ask about a relative or a mutual friend. He spoke of them as if they were all alive, which they are, thank God. I rubbed my head. He started off on Aragon—had I read *Le Paysan de Paris?* Did I remember the Passage Jouffroy in Paris? What did I think of St. Jean Perse? Or *Nadja* of Breton? Had I been to Knossus yet? I ought to stay a few weeks at least—he would take me over the island from one end to another. He was a very hale and hearty fellow and when he understood that I liked to eat and drink he beamed most approvingly. He regretted sincerely that he was not free for the evening, but hoped to see me the following day; he wanted to introduce me to the little circle of literati in Herakleion. He was excited by the fact that I came from America and begged me to tell him something about New York which I found it almost impossible to do because I had long ceased to identify myself with that odious city.

I went back to the hotel for a nap. There were three beds in the room, all of them very comfortable. I read carefully the sign warning the clients to refrain from tipping the employees. The room cost only about seventeen cents a night and I became involved willy-nilly in a fruitless speculation as to how many drachmas one would give as a tip if one could tip. There were only three or four clients in the hotel. Walking through the wide corridors looking for the W. C. I met the maid, an angelic sort of spinster with straw hair and watery blue eyes who reminded me vividly of the Swedenborgian caretaker of the Maison Balzac in Passy. She was bringing me a glass of water on a tray made of lead, zinc and tin. I undressed and as I was pulling in the blinds I observed two men and a stenographer gazing at me from the window of some outlandish commercial house across the way. It seemed unreal, this transaction of abstract business in a place like Herakleion. The typewriter looked surrealistic and the men with sleeves rolled up as in commercial houses everywhere appeared fantastically like the freaks of the Western world who move grain and corn and wheat around in carload lots by means of the telephone, the ticker, the telegraph. Imagine what it would be like to find two business men and a stenographer on Easter Island! Imagine how a typewriter would sound in that Oceanic silence! I fell back on the bed and into a deep, drugged sleep. No tipping allowed—that was the last thought and a very beautiful one to a weary traveler.

When I awoke it was dark. I opened the blinds and looked down the forlorn main street which was now deserted. I heard a telegraph instrument clicking. I got into my things and hurried to the restaurant near the fountain. The waiter seemed to expect me and stood ready to translate for me into that Iroquois English which the itinerant Greek has acquired in the course of his wanderings. I ordered some cold fish with the skin on it and a bottle of dark-red Cretan wine. While waiting to be served I noticed a man peering through the large plate-glass window; he walked away and came back again in a few minutes. Finally he made up his mind to walk in. He walked directly up to my table and addressed me—in English. Was I not Mr. Miller who had arrived by plane a few hours ago? I was. He begged leave to introduce himself. He was Mr. So-and-So, the British Vice Consul at Herakleion. He had noticed that I was an American, a writer. He was always happy to make the acquaintance of an American. He paused a moment, as if embarrassed, and then went on to say that his sole motive for introducing himself was to let me know that as long as I remained in Crete I was to consider his humble services entirely at my disposal. He said that he was originally from Smyrna and that every Greek from Smyrna was eternally indebted to the American people. He said that there was no favor too great for me to ask of him.

The natural reply was to ask him to sit down and share a meal with me, which I did. He explained that he would be unable to accept the honor as he was obliged to dine in the bosom of his family, *but*—would I do him the honor of taking a coffee with him and his wife at their home after dinner? As the representative of the great American people (not at all sure of the heroic role we had played in the great disaster of Smyrna) I most graciously accepted, rose, bowed, shook his hand and escorted him to the door where once again we exchanged polite thanks and mutual felicitations. I went back to the table, unskinned the cold fish and proceeded to wet my whistle. The meal was even lousier than at noon, but the service was extraordinary. The whole restaurant was aware that a distinguished visitor had arrived and was partaking with them of their humble food. Mr. Tsoutsou and his wife appeared for just a moment to see how I was faring, commented bravely on the delicious, appetizing appearance of the skinned fish and disappeared with bows and salaams which sent an electric thrill through the assembled patrons of Herakleion's most distinguished restaurant. I began to feel as though something of vast import were about to happen. I ordered the waiter to send the *chasseur* out for a coffee and cognac. Never before had a vice consul or any form of public servant other than a constable or gendarme sought me out in a public place. The plane was responsible for it. It was like a letter of credit.

The home of the vice consul was rather imposing for Herakleion. In truth, it was more like a museum than a home. I felt somewhat hysterical, somewhat disoriented. The vice consul was a good, kind-hearted man but vain as a peacock. He drummed nervously on the arm of the chair, waiting impatiently for his wife to leave off about Paris, Berlin, Prague, Budapest et cetera in order to confide that he was the author of a book on Crete. He kept telling his wife that I was a journalist, an insult which normally I find hard to swallow, but in this case I found it easy not to take offense since the vice consul considered all writers to be journalists. He pressed a button and very sententiously commanded the maid to go to the library and find him a copy of the book he had written on Crete. He confessed that he had never written a book before but, owing to the general state of ignorance and confusion regarding Crete in the mind of the average tourist, he had deemed it incumbent upon him to put down what he knew about his adopted land in more or less eternal fashion. He admitted that Sir Arthur Evans had expressed it all in unimpeachable style but then there were little things, trifles by comparison of course, which a work of that scope and grandeur could not hope to encompass. He spoke in this pompous, ornate, highly fatuous way about his masterpiece. He said that a journalist like myself would be one of the few to really appreciate what he had done for the cause of Crete et cetera. He handed me the book to glance at. He handed it over as if it were the Gutenberg Bible. I took one glance and realized immediately that I was dealing with one of the "popular masters of reality," a blood-brother to the man who had painted "A Rendezvous with the Soul." He inquired in a pseudo-modest way if the English were all right, because English was not his native tongue. The implication was that if he had done it in Greek it would be beyond criticism. I asked him politely where I might hope to obtain a copy of this obviously extraordinary work whereupon he informed me that if I came to his office in the morning he would bestow one upon me as a gift, as a memento of this illustrious occasion which had culminated in the meeting of two minds thoroughly attuned to the splendors of the past. This was only the beginning of a cataract of flowery horse shit which I had to swallow before going through the motions of saying good-night. Then came the Smyrna disaster with a harrowing, detailed recital of the horrors which the Turks perpetrated on the helpless Greeks and the merciful intervention of the American people which no Greek would ever forget until his dying day. I tried desperately, while he spun out the horrors and atrocities, to recall what I had been doing at this black moment in the history of Greece. Evidently the disaster had occurred during one of those long intervals when I had ceased to read the newspapers. I hadn't the faintest remembrance of any such catastrophe. To the best of my recollection the event must have taken place during the year when I was looking for a job without the slightest intention of taking one. It reminded me that, desperate as I thought myself then to be, I had not even bothered to look through the columns of the want ads.

Next morning I took the bus in the direction of Knossus. I had to walk a mile or so after leaving the bus to reach the ruins. I was so elated that it seemed as if I were walking on air. At last my dream was about to be realized. The sky was overcast and it sprinkled a bit as I hopped along. Again, as at Mycenae, I felt that I was being drawn to the spot. Finally, as I rounded a bend, I stopped dead in my tracks; I had the feeling that I was there. I looked about for traces of the ruins but there were none in sight. I stood for several minutes gazing intently at the contours of the smooth hills which barely grazed the electric blue sky. This must be the spot, I said to myself, I can't be wrong. I retraced my steps and cut through the fields to the bottom of a gulch. Suddenly, to my left, I discovered a bald pavilion with columns painted in raw, bold colors—the palace of King Minos. I was at the back entrance of the ruins amidst a clump of buildings that looked as if they had been gutted by fire. I went round the hill to the main entrance and followed a little group of Greeks in the wake of a guide who spoke a boustrophedonous language which was sheer Pelasgian to me.

There has been much controversy about the aesthetics of Sir Arthur Evans' work of restoration. I found myself unable to come to any conclusion about it; I accepted it as a fact. However Knossus may have looked in the past, however it may look in the future, this one which Evans has created is the only one I shall ever know. I am grateful to him for what he did, grateful that he had made it possible for me to descend the grand staircase, to sit on that marvellous throne chair the replica of which at the Hague Peace Tribunal is now almost as much of a relic of the past as the original.

Knossus in all its manifestations suggests the splendor and sanity and opulence of a powerful and peaceful people. It is gay— gay, healthful, sanitary, salubrious. The common people played a great role, that is evident. It has been said that throughout its long history every form of government known to man was tested out; in many ways it is far closer in spirit to modern times, to the twentieth century, I might say, than other later epochs of the Hellenic world. One feels the influence of Egypt, the homely human immediacy of the Etruscan world, the wise, communal organizing spirit of Inca days. I do not pretend to know, but I felt, as I have seldom felt before the ruins of the past, that here throughout long centuries there reigned an era of peace. There is something down to earth about Knossus, the sort of atmosphere which is evoked when one says Chinese or French. The religious note seems to be graciously diminished; women played an important, equal role in the affairs of this people; a spirit of play is markedly noticeable. In short, the prevailing note is one of joy. One feels that man lived to live, that he was not plagued by thoughts of a life beyond, that he was not smothered and restricted by undue reverence for the ancestral spirits, that he was religious in the only way which is becoming to man, by making the most of everything that comes to hand, by extracting the utmost of life from every passing minute. Knossus was worldly in the best sense of the word. The civilization which it epitomized went to pieces fifteen hundred years before the coming of the Saviour, having bequeathed to the Western world the greatest single contribution yet known to man—the alphabet. In another part of the Island, at Gortyna, this discovery is immortalized in huge blocks of stone which run over the countryside like a miniature Chinese wall. Today the magic has gone out of the alphabet; it is a dead form to express dead thoughts.

Walking back to meet the bus I stopped at a little village to get a drink. The contrast between past and present was tremendous, as though the secret of life had been lost. The men who gathered around me took on the appearance of uncouth savages. They were friendly and hospitable, extraordinarily so, but by comparison with the Minoans they were like neglected domesticated animals. I am not thinking of the comforts which they lacked, for in point of comfort I make no great distinction between the life of a Greek peasant, a Chinese coolie and a migratory American jack-of-all-trades. I am thinking now of the lack of those essential elements of life which make possible a real society of human beings. The great fundamental lack, which is apparent everywhere in our civilized world, is the total absence of anything approaching a communal existence. We have become spiritual nomads; whatever pertains to the soul is derelict, tossed about by the winds like flotsam and jetsam. The village of Hagia Triada, looked at from any point in time, stands out like a jewel of consistency, integrity, significance. When a miserable Greek village, such as the one I am speaking of, and the counterpart of which we have by the thousand in America, embellishes its meagre, stultified life by the adoption of telephone, radio, automobile, tractor, et cetera, the meaning of the word communal becomes so fantastically distorted that one begins to wonder what is meant by the phrase "human society." There is nothing human about these sporadic agglomerations of beings; they are beneath any known level of life which this globe has known. They are less in every way than the pygmies who are truly nomadic and who move in filthy freedom with delicious security.

As I sipped my glass of water, which had a strange taste, I listened to one of these glorified baboons reminisce about the glorious days he had spent in Herkimer, New York. He had run a candy store there and seemed grateful to America for having permitted him to save the few thousand dollars which he required to return to his native land and resume the degrading life of toil which he was accustomed to. He ran back to the house to fetch an American book which he had kept as a souvenir of the wonderful money-making days. It was a farmer's almanac, badly thumb-marked, fly-bitten, louse-ridden. Here in the very cradle of our civilization a dirty baboon hands me a precious monstrosity of letters—the almanac.

The owner of the almanac and myself were seated at a table off the road in the center of a group of louts who were visibly impressed. I ordered cognac for the crowd and surrendered myself to the interlocutor. A man came over and put his big hairy finger on the photograph of a farm implement. The interlocutor said: "good machine, he like this." Another one took the book in his hands and went through it with a wet thumb, grunting now and then to signify his pleasure. Interlocutor said: "Very interesting book. He like American book." Suddenly he espied a friend in the background. "Come here," he called. He presented him to me. "Nick! He work in Michigan. Big farm. He like America too." I shook hands with Nick. Said Nick: "You New York? Me go New York once." He made a motion with his hands to indicate the skyscrapers. Nick spoke animatedly to the others. Suddenly there was a silence and the interlocutor spoke up. "They want to know how you like Greece." "It's marvellous," I answered. He laughed. "Greece very poor country, yes? No money. America rich. Everybody got money, yes?" I said yes to satisfy him. He turned to the others and explained that I had agreed—America was a very rich country, everybody rich, lots of money. "How long you stay in Greece?" he asked. "Maybe a year, maybe two years," I answered. He laughed again, as though I were an idiot. "What your business?" I told him I had no business. "You millionaire?" I told him I was very poor. He laughed, more than ever. The others were listening intently. He spoke a few words to them rapidly. "What you have to drink?" he asked. "Cretan people like Americans. Cretan people good people. You like cognac, yes?" I nodded.

Just then the bus came along. I made as if to go. "No hurry," said the interlocutor. "He no go yet. He make water here." The others were smiling at me. What were they thinking? That I was a queer bird to come to a place like Crete? Again I was asked what my business was. I made the motion of writing with a pen. "Ah!" exclaimed the interlocutor. "Newspaper!" He clapped his hands and spoke excitedly to the innkeeper. A Greek newspaper was produced. He shoved it into my hands. "You read that?" I shook my head. He snatched the paper out of my hand. He read the headline aloud in Greek, the others listening gravely. As he was reading I noticed the date—the paper was a month old. The interlocutor translated for me. "He say President Roosevelt no want fight. Hitler bad man." Then he got up and seizing a cane from one of the by-standers he put it to his shoulder and imitated a man firing point-blank. Bang-bang! he went, dancing around and aiming at one after the other. Bang-bang! Everybody laughed heartily. "Me," he said, jerking his thumb towards his breast, "me good soldier. Me kill Turks . . . many Turks. Me kill, kill, kill" and he made a ferocious, blood-thirsty grimace. "Cretan people good soldiers. Italians no good." He went up to one of the men and seized him by the collar. He made as if he were slitting the man's throat. "Italians, bah!" He spat on the ground. "Me kill Mussolini . . . like a that! Mussolini bad man. Greek no like Mussolini. We kill all Italians." He sat down grinning and chuckling. "President Roosevelt, he help Greeks, yes?" I nodded. "Greek good fighter. He kill everybody. He no 'fraid of nobody.

Look! Me, one man . . ." He pointed to the others. "Me one
Greek." He pointed to the others, snatching the cane again and
brandishing it like a club. "Me kill everybody—German, Italian,
Russian, Turk, French. Greek no 'fraid." The others laughed and
nodded their heads approvingly. It was convincing, to say the
least.

The bus was getting ready to move. The whole village seemed
to have gathered to see me off. I climbed aboard and waved good-
bye. A little girl stepped forward and handed me a bunch of
flowers. The interlocutor shouted Hooray! A gawky young lad
yelled *All right!* and they all laughed.

After dinner that evening I took a walk to the edge of the town.
It was like walking through the land of Ur. I was making for a
brilliantly lit café in the distance. About a mile away, it seemed, I
could hear the loud-speaker blasting out the war news—first in
Greek, then in French, then in English. It seemed to be proclaim-
ing the news throughout a wasteland. Europe speaking. Europe
seemed remote, on some other continent. The noise was deafen-
ing. Suddenly another one started up from the opposite direction. I turned back towards the little park facing a cinema where a
Western picture was being advertised. I passed what looked like
an immense fortress surrounded by a dry moat. The sky seemed
very low and filled with tattered clouds through which the moon
sailed unsteadily. I felt out of the world, cut off, a total stranger in
every sense of the word. The amplifiers increased this feeling of
isolation: they seemed to have tuned up to the wildest pitch in
order to carry far beyond me—to Abyssinia, Arabia, Persia,
Beluchistan, China, Tibet. The waves were passing over my
head; they were not intended for Crete, they had been picked up
accidentally. I dove into the narrow winding streets which led to
the open square. I walked right into a crowd which had gathered
outside a tent in which freaks were being exhibited. A man
squatting beside the tent was playing a weird melody on the
flute. He held the flute up towards the moon which had grown
larger and brighter in the interval. A belly-dancer came out of the
tent, dragging a cretin by the hand. The crowd giggled. Just then I
turned my head and to my astonishment I saw a woman with a

vase on her shoulder descending a little bluff in bare feet. She had
the poise and grace of a figure on an ancient frieze. Behind her
came a donkey laden with jars. The flute was getting more weird,
more insistent. Turbaned men with long white boots and black
frock coats were pushing towards the open tent. The man beside
me held two squawking chickens by the legs; he was rooted to the
spot, as if hypnotized. To the right of me was evidently a barracks
barred by a sentry box before which a soldier in white skirts
paraded back and forth.

There was nothing more to the scene than this, but for me it
held the enchantment of a world I was yet to glimpse. Even
before I had sailed for Crete I had been thinking of Persia and
Arabia and of more distant lands still. Crete is a jumping off
place. Once a still, vital, fecund center, a navel of the world, it
now resembles a dead crater. The aeroplane comes along, lifts
you up by the seat of the pants, and spits you down in Bagdad,
Samarkand, Beluchistan, Fez, Timbuctoo, as far as your money
will take you. All these once marvellous places whose very names
cast a spell over you are now floating islets in the stormy sea of
civilization. They mean homely commodities like rubber, tin,
pepper, coffee, carborundum and so forth. The natives are derelicts exploited by the octopus whose tentacles stretch from Lon-
don, Paris, Berlin, Tokyo, New York, Chicago to the icy tips of
Iceland and the wild reaches of Patagonia. The evidences of this
so-called civilization are strewn and dumped higgledy-piggledy
wherever the long, slimy tentacles reach out. Nobody is being
civilized, nothing is being altered in any real sense. Some are
using knives and forks who formerly ate with their fingers; some
have electric lights in their hovels instead of the kerosene lamp or
the wax taper; some have Sears-Roebuck catalogues and a Holy
Bible on the shelf where once a rifle or a musket lay; some have
gleaming automatic revolvers instead of clubs; some are using
money instead of shells and cowries; some have straw hats which
they don't need; some have Jesus Christ and don't know what to
do with Him. But all of them, from the top to the bottom, are
restless, dissatisfied, envious, and sick at heart. All of them suffer
from cancer and leprosy, in their souls. The most ignorant and
degenerate of them will be asked to shoulder a gun and fight for a

civilization which has brought them nothing but misery and degradation. In a language which they cannot understand the loud-speaker blares out the disastrous news of victory and defeat. It's a mad world and when you become slightly detached it seems even more mad than usual. The aeroplane brings death; the radio brings death; the machine gun brings death; the tinned goods bring death; the tractor brings death; the priest brings death; the schools bring death; the laws bring death; the electricity brings death; the plumbing brings death; the phonograph brings death; the knives and forks bring death; the books bring death; our very breath brings death, our very language, our very thought, our money, our love, our charity, our sanitation, our joy. No matter whether we are friends or enemies, no matter whether we call ourselves Jap, Turk, Russian, French, English, German or American, wherever we go, wherever we cast our shadow, wherever we breathe, we poison and destroy. Hooray! shouted the Greek. I too yell Hooray! Hooray for civilization! *Hooray! We will kill you all, everybody, everywhere. Hooray for Death! Hooray! Hooray!*

The next morning I paid a visit to the museum where to my astonishment I encountered Mr. Tsoutsou in the company of the Nibelungen racketeers. He seemed highly embarrassed to be discovered in their presence but, as he explained to me later, Greece was still a neutral country and they had come armed with letters of introduction from men whom he once considered friends. I pretended to be absorbed in the examination of a Minoan chessboard. He pressed me to meet him in the cafe later in the day. As I was leaving the museum I got the jitterbugs so bad that I made caca in my pants. I thought of my French friend immediately. Fortunately I had in my little notebook a remedy against such ailments; it had been given me by an English traveler whom I met in a bar one night in Nice. I went back to the hotel, changed my clothes, wrapped the old ones in a bundle with the idea of throwing them in a ravine and, armed with the prescription of the English globe-trotter, I made for the drug store.

I had to walk a considerable time before I could drop the bundle unobserved. By that time the jitterbugs had come on again. I made for the bottom of the moat near a dead horse swarming with bottle-flies.

The druggist spoke nothing but Greek. Diarrhoea is one of those words you never think to include in a rough and ready vocabulary—and good prescriptions are in Latin which every druggist should know but which Greek druggists are sometimes ignorant of. Fortunately a man came in who knew a little French. He asked me immediately if I were English and when I said yes he dashed out and in a few minutes returned with a jovial-looking Greek who turned out to be the proprietor of a cafe nearby. I explained the situation rapidly and, after a brief colloquy with the druggist, he informed me that the prescription couldn't be filled but that the druggist had a better remedy to suggest. It was to abstain from food and drink and go on a diet of soggy rice with a little lemon juice in it. The druggist was of the opinion that it was nothing—it would pass in a few days—everybody gets it at first.

I went back to the cafe with the big fellow—Jim he called himself—and listened to a long story about his life in Montreal where he had amassed a fortune, as a restaurateur, and then lost it all in the stock market. He was delighted to speak English again. "Don't touch the water here," he said. "My water comes from a spring twenty miles away. That's why I have such a big clientèle."

We sat there talking about the wonderful winters in Montreal. Jim had a special drink prepared for me which he said would do me good. I was wondering where to get a good bowl of thick soupy rice. Beside me was a man puffing away at a nargileh; he seemed to be in a stony trance. Suddenly I was back in Paris, listening to my occult friend Urbanski who had gone one winter's night to a bordel in Montreal and when he emerged it was spring. I have been to Montreal myself but somehow the image of it which I retain is not mine but Urbanski's. I see myself standing in his shoes, waiting for a street car on the edge of the town. A rather elegant woman comes along bundled in furs. She's also waiting for the street car. How did Krishnamurti's name come up? And then she's speaking of Topeka, Kansas, and it seems as if I had lived there all my life. The hot toddy also came in quite naturally. We're at the door of a big house that has the air of a deserted mansion. A colored woman opens the door. It's her place, just as she described it. A warm, cosy place too. Now and then the door-bell rings. There's the sound of muffled laughter, of glasses clinking, of slippered feet slapping through the hall. . . .

I had listened to this story so intently that it had become a part of my own life. I could feel the soft chains she had slipped around him, the too comfortable bed, the delicious, drowsy indolence of the pasha who had retired from the world during a season of snow and ice. In the spring he had made his escape but I, I had remained and sometimes, like now, when I forget myself, I'm there in a hotbed of roses trying to make clear to her the mystery of Arjuna's decision.

Towards evening I went round to the cafe to meet Mr. Tsoutsou. He insisted that I accompany him to his studio where he had planned to present me to the little circle of literati. I was wondering about the bowl of rice and how to get it.

The retreat was hidden away in the loft of a dilapidated building which reminded me forcibly of Giono's Biblical birthplace in Manosque. It was the sort of den which St. Jerome might have created for himself during his exile in a foreign land. Outside, in the volcanic hinterland of Herakleion, Augustine ruled; here, amidst the musty books, the paintings, the music, was Jerome's world. Beyond, in Europe proper, another world was going to ruin. Soon one would have to come to a place like Crete to recover the evidences of a civilization which had disappeared. In this little den of Tsoutsou's there was a cross-cut of everything which had gone to make the culture of Europe. This room would live on as the monks lived on during the Dark Ages.

One by one his friends came, poets most of them. French was the common language. Again there came up the names of Eliot, Breton, Rimbaud. They spoke of Joyce as a Surrealist. They thought America was experiencing a cultural renascence. We clashed. I can't stand this idea, which is rooted in the minds of little peoples, that America is the hope of the world. I brought up the names of their own writers, the contemporary poets and novelists of Greece. They were divided as to the merits of this one and that one. They were not sure of their own artists. I deplored that.

Food was served, and wine, and beautiful grapes, all of which I had to refuse. "I thought you liked to eat and drink," said Tsoutsou. I told him I was indisposed. "Oh, come you can eat a little cold fish," he insisted. "And this wine—you *must* taste it—I ordered it especially for you." The law of hospitality bade me to accept. I raised the glass and drank a toast to the future of Greece. Somebody insisted that I try the wonderful olives—and the famous goat cheese. Not a grain of rice in sight. I saw myself dashing for the bottom of the moat again beside the dead horse with the poisonous fat green flies.

"And what about Sinclair Lewis—surely he was one of America's great writers?"

When I said no they all seemed to be highly dubious of my critical faculties. Who *was* a great American writer, then, they demanded. I said: "Walt Whitman. He's the only great writer we ever had."

"And Mark Twain?"

"For adolescents," I answered.

They laughed, as the troglodytes had laughed at me the other morning.

"So you think Rimbaud is greater than all the American poets put together?" said one young man challengingly.

"Yes, I do. I think he's greater than all the *French* poets put together too."

This was like throwing a bomb in their midst. As always, the greatest defenders of French tradition are to be found outside France. Tsoutsou was of the opinion that they ought to listen to me at length; he thought my attitude was typical, representative of the American spirit. He applauded as one would applaud a trained seal after it has given a performance with the cymbals. I was somewhat depressed by this atmosphere of futile discussion. I made a long speech in bad French in which I admitted that I was no critic, that I was always passionate and prejudiced, that I had no reverence for anything except what I liked. I told them that I was an ignoramus, which they tried to deny vigorously. I said I would rather tell them stories. I began—about a bum who had tried to hit me up for a dime one evening as I was walking towards the Brooklyn Bridge. I explained how I had said No to the man automatically and then, after I had walked a few yards it suddenly came to me that a man had asked me for something and I ran back and spoke to him. But instead of giving him a dime or a quarter, which I could easily have done, I told him that I was broke, that I had wanted to let him know that, that was all. And the man had said to me—"do you mean that, buddy? Why, if that's the way it is, I'll be glad to give you a dime myself." And I let him give it to me, and I thanked him warmly, and walked off.

They thought it a very interesting story. So that's how it was in America? Strange country . . . anything could happen there.

"Yes," I said, "a very strange country," and I thought to myself that it was wonderful not to be there any more and God willing I'd never return to it.

"And what is it about Greece that makes you like it so much?" asked some one.

I smiled. "The light and the poverty," I said.

"You're a romantic," said the man.

"Yes," I said, "I'm crazy enough to believe that the happiest man on earth is the man with the fewest needs. And I also believe that if you have light, such as you have here, all ugliness is obliterated. Since I've come to your country I know that light is holy: Greece is a holy land to me."

"But have you seen how poor the people are, how wretchedly they live?"

"I've seen worse wretchedness in America," I said. "Poverty alone doesn't make people wretched."

"You can say that because you have sufficient . . ."

"I can say it because I've been poor all my life," I retorted. "I'm poor now," I added, "I have just enough to get back to Athens. When I get to Athens I'll have to think how to get more. It isn't money that sustains me—it's the faith I have in myself, in my own powers. In spirit I'm a millionaire—maybe that's the best thing about America, that you believe you'll rise again."

"Yes, yes," said Tsoutsou, clapping his hands, "that's the

wonderful thing about America: you don't know what defeat is."
He filled the glasses again and rose to make a toast. "To America!" he said, "long may it live!"

"To Henry Miller!" said another, "because he believes in
himself."

I got back to the hotel in the nick of time. Tomorrow I would
surely start the rice diet. I lay in bed watching the men in shirt
sleeves across the way. The scene reminded me of similar ones
in dingy lofts in the vicinity of the Broadway Central Hotel, New
York—Greene or Bleecker Street, for example. The intermediate
zone between high finance and grovelling in the bowels of the
earth. Paper box representatives . . . celluloid collars . . .
twine . . . mouse traps. The moon was scudding through the
clouds. Africa not far distant. At the other end of the island a
place called Phaestos. As I was dozing off Mlle. Swedenborg
knocked at the door to inform me that there had been a telephone
call from the prefect of police. "What does he want?" I asked. She
didn't know. I was disturbed. The word police fills me with
panic. I got up automatically to search my wallet for the *permis de
séjour*. I examined it to make sure that I was *en règle*. What could
that bastard want of me? Was he going to ask how much money I
had on me? In out of the way places they always think of petty
little things to harass you about. *"Vive la France!"* I muttered
absent-mindedly. Another thought came to me. I slipped on my
bathrobe and wandered from one floor to another to make sure
that I could find the W. C. in a hurry if necessary. I felt thirsty. I
rang and asked if they had any mineral water. The maid couldn't
understand what I meant. "Water, water," I repeated, looking
around in vain for a bottle to illustrate what I meant. She
disappeared to return with a pitcher of iced water. I thanked her
and turned out the lights. My tongue was parched. I got up and
wet my lips, fearful lest a stray drop slip down my burning throat.

Next morning I remembered that I had forgotten to call at the
vice consul's office for the book he had promised me. I went to his
office and waited for him to make his appearance. He arrived
beaming with pleasure. He had already written an inscription in
the book; he wanted me to be sure to let him know, immediately I

had read the book, what I thought of it. I brought up the rice problem as delicately as I could, after he had tried to sell me the idea of visiting the leper colony somewhere on the island. Boiled rice? Nothing could be easier. His wife would fix it for me every day—it would be a pleasure. Somehow I was touched by his alacrity in aiding me. I tried to imagine a French functionary speaking this way—it was just impossible. On the contrary, the image that came to mind was that of the Frenchwoman who ran the *tabac* in a certain neighborhood where I had lived for several years and how one day, when I was short two sous, she had snatched the cigarettes from my hand and shouted to me in a panicky voice that they couldn't possibly give credit to any one, it would ruin them, and so forth. I thought of a scene in another *bistrot*, where I was also a good customer, and how they had refused to lend me the two francs I needed to make the admission to a movie. I remembered how enraged I became when the woman pretended to me that she was not the proprietress but the cashier and how I had taken the change out of my pocket, just to prove to her that I had some money on me, and flinging it into the street I said—*"there*, that's what I think of your lousy francs!" And the waiter had immediately run out into the street and begun searching for the dirty little coins.

A little later, strolling about the town, I stopped into a shop near the museum where they sold souvenirs and post-cards. I looked over the cards leisurely; the ones I liked best were soiled and wrinkled. The man, who spoke French fluently, offered to make the cards presentable. He asked me to wait a few minutes while he ran over to the house and clean and ironed them. He said he would make them look like new. I was so dumbfounded that before I could say anything he had disappeared, leaving me in charge of the shop. After a few minutes his wife came in. I thought she looked strange for a Greek woman. After a few words had passed I realized that she was French and she, when she learned that I hailed from Paris, was overjoyed to speak with me. We got along beautifully until she began talking about Greece. She hated Crete, she said. It was too dry, too dusty, too hot, too bare. She missed the beautiful trees of Normandy, the gardens with the high walls, the orchards, and so on. Didn't I agree with her? I said NO, flatly. *"Monsieur!"* she said, rising up in her pride and dignity, as if I had slapped her in the face.

"I don't miss anything," I said, pressing the point home. "I think this is marvellous. I don't like your gardens with their high walls; I don't like your pretty little orchards and your well-cultivated fields. I like this. . . ." and I pointed outdoors to the dusty road on which a sorely-laden donkey was plodding along dejectedly. "But it's not civilized," she said, in a sharp, shrill voice which reminded me of the miserly tobacconiste in the Rue da la Tombe-Issoire.

"Je m'en fous de la civilisation européenne!" I blurted out.

"Monsieur!" she said again, her feathers ruffled and her nose turning blue with malice.

Fortunately her husband reappeared at this point with the post-cards which he had given a dry-cleaning. I thanked him warmly and bought another batch of cards which I selected at random. I stood a moment looking about, wondering what I might buy to show my appreciation. The woman had overlooked my remarks in her zeal to sell me some trifle. She was holding up a hand-woven scarf and patting it affectionately. "Thank you," I said, "I never wear them." "But it would make a beautiful gift," she said—"from Crete, which you are so enamored of." At this her husband pricked up his ears.

"You like it here?" he asked, looking at me approvingly.

"It's a wonderful place," I said. "It's the most beautiful land I've ever seen. I wish I could live here all my life."

The woman dropped the scarf in disgust. "Come back again," begged the man. "We will have a drink together, yes?" I shook hands with him and gave a cold nod to his wife.

That dried-up prune, I thought to myself. How could a full-blooded Greek live with a thing like that? She was probably berating him already for the trouble he had put himself to to please an ignorant foreigner. I could hear her saying in that squeaky, shoe-stringed voice: *"Les américains, ils sont tous les mêmes; ils ne savent pas ce que c'est la vie. Des barbares, quoi!"*

And out on the hot, dusty road, the flies biting like mad, the sun blistering the warts off my chin, the land of Ur reeling in its auto-intoxicated emptiness, I answer her blithely: *"Oui, tu as raison, salope que tu es. Mais moi je n'aime pas les jardins, les pots de fleurs, la petite vie adoucie. Je n'aime pas la Normandie. J'aime la soleil, la nudité, la lumière. . . ."*

With that off my chest I let a song go out of my heart, praising God that the great Negro race which alone keeps America from falling apart had never known the vice of husbandry. I let a song go out of my heart to Duke Ellington, that suave, super-civilized, double-jointed cobra with the steel-flanged wrists—and to Count Basie (*sent for you yesterday here you come today*), long lost brother of Isidore Ducasse and last direct lineal descendant of the great and only Rimbaud.

Madame, since you were speaking of gardens, let me tell you once and for all how the Dipsy Doodle works. Here's a passacaglia to embroider tonight when you're doing the drop stitch. As Joe Dudley of Des Moines says, the drums give a feeling of something present. I'll begin with a one o'clock jump, a maxixe à la Huysmanns.

Madame, it's like this. . . . Once there was a land. And there were no walls and there were no orchards. There was just a Boogie Woogie man whose name was Agamemnon. After a time he gave birth to two sons—Epaminondas and Louis the Armstrong. Epaminondas was for war and civilization and, in his treacherous way (which made even the angels weep), he fulfilled himself, thereby bringing on the white plague which ended in the basement of Clytemnestra's palace where the cesspool now stands. Louis was for peace and joy. *"Peace, it's wonderful!"* he shouted all day long.

Agamemnon, seeing that one of his sons had wisdom, bought him a golden torque, saying unto him: "Go forth now and trumpet peace and joy everywhere!" He said nothing about walls or gardens or orchards. He said nothing about building cathedrals. He said: "Go, my son, and riff it through the land!" And Louis went out into the world, which had already fallen into a state of sadness, and he took with him nothing save the golden torque.

Louis soon found that the world was divided into black and

white, very sharp and very bitterly. Louis wanted to make everything golden, not like coins or ikons but like ripe ears of corn, gold like the goldenrod, gold that everybody could look at and feel and roll around in.

When he had walked as far as Monemvasia, which is at the lower end of the Peloponnesus, Louis boarded the gin mill special for Memphis. The train was full of white people whom his brother Epaminondas had driven mad with misery. Louis had a great desire to leave the train and run his sore, aching feet through the river Jordan. He wanted to take a riff in the blue, blow his top.

Now it happened that the train came to a stop at Tuxedo Junction, not far from the corner of Munson Street. It was high time because Louis felt a break-down coming on. And then he remembered what his father, the illustrious Agamemnon, had told him once—to first get tight and quiet as a fiend, *and then blow!* Louis put his thick loving lips to the golden torque and blew. He blew one great big sour note like a rat bustin' open and the tears came to his eyes and the sweat rolled down his neck. Louis felt that he was bringing peace and joy to all the world. He filled his lungs again and blew a molten note that reached so far into the blue it froze and hung in the sky like a diamond-pointed star. Louis stood up and twisted the torque until it became a great shining bulge of ecstasy. The sweat was pouring down him like a river. Louis was so happy that his eyes began to sweat too and they made two golden pools of joy one of which he named the King of Thebes in honor of Oedipus, his nearest of kin, who had lived to meet the Sphinx.

On a certain day it became the Fourth of July, which is Dipsy-Doodle day in Walla Walla. Louis had by this time made a few friends as he went riffin' his way through the new land. One was a Count and another was a Duke. They carried little white rats on their finger-tips and when they couldn't stand it any longer, the sad, white gut bucket of a world, they bit with the ends of their fingers and where they bit it was like a laboratory of guinea pigs going crazy with experimentation. The Count was a two-fingered specialist, built small and round like a rotunda, with a little moustache. He always began—*bink-bink!* Bink for poison, bink for arson. He was quiet and steady like, a sort of introverted gorilla who, when he got bogged in the depths of the gerundive, would speak French like a marquis or babble in Polish or Lithuanian. He never started twice the same way. And when he came to the end, unlike other poison and arson men, he always stopped. He stopped sudden like, and the piano sank with him and the little white rats too. Until the next time. . . .

The Duke, on the other hand, always slid down from above in a silver-lined bathrobe. The Duke had been educated in Heaven where at an early age he had learned to play the pearly harp and other vibrafoid instruments of the celestial realm. He was always suave, always composed. When he smiled wreaths of ectoplasm formed around his mouth. His favorite mood was indigo which is that of the angels when all the world is sound asleep.

There were others too of course—Joe the chocolate cherub, Chick who was already sprouting wings, Big Sid, and Fats and Ella and sometimes Lionel the golden boy who carried everything in his hat. There was always Louis, of course, Louis just like he is, with that broad, million dollar smile like the Argive plain itself and smooth, polished nostrils that gleamed like the leaves of the magnolia tree.

On Dipsy-Doodle day they gathered together round the golden torque and they made jam—missionary jam. That is, Chick, who was like peppered lightning, always flashing his teeth, always spitting out dice and doodle balls, Chick would web it to the jungle and back again like a breeze. What for? you say. Why to fetch a big greasy missionary, to boil him in oil, that's what for. Joe, whose business it was to give that reassuring feeling of something present, Joe would keep to the background like a rubber pelvis.

Boil 'em alive, feathers and all—that's how the Dipsy-Doodle works. It's barbarious, Madame, but that's how it is. Ain't no more orchards, ain't no more walls. King Agamemnon say to his son: "Boy, bring that land!" And boy, he bring it back. He bring it back tootlin' and buglin'. He bring back goldenrods and yellow sassafras; he bring back golden cockerels and spaniels red as tigers. No more missionary culturization, no more Pammy Pamondas. Might be Hannibal, M. O., might be Carthage, Illy-Illy.

Might be the moon be low, might be a sort of funeralization. Might be nuthin' neither, 'cause I ain't thought to name it yet.

Madame, I'm gonna blow you down so low you're gonna quiver like a snake. I'm gonna take a fat rat bustin' note and blow you back to Kingdom Come. Hear that tappin' and rappin'? Hear that chicken liver moanin'? That's Boogie Woogie drawin' his breath. That's missionary man foamin' like a stew. Hear that screamin' high and shrill? That's Meemy the Meemer. She's little and low, sort of built up from the ground. Jam today, jam tomorrow. Nobody care, nobody worry. Nobody die sad no more. 'Cause the old glad land is full of torque. Blow wind! Blow dust in the eye! Blow hot and dry, blow brown and bare! Blow down them orchards, blow down them walls. Boogie Woogie's here again. Boogie Woogie go bink-bink. Bink for poison, bink for arson. He ain't got no feet, he ain't got no hands. Boogie Woogie done swish it up and down the land. Boogie Woogie scream. Boogie Woogie scream again. Boogie Woogie scream again, again, again, again. No walls, no trees, no nuthin'. Tish and pish and pish and tish. Rats movin.' Three rats, four rats, ten rats. One cockerel, one rat. Locomotive make choo-choo. Sun out and the road is hot and dusty. Trees jell, leaves shell. No knees, no hands, no toes between his fingers. Makin' hominy, that's all. He's comin' down the road with a banjo on his knees. He's a-tappin' and a-slappin'. Tappin' the Tappahanna, rappin' the Rappahanna. He's got blood on his fingers and blood in his hair. He's bogged down, kit and boodle, and the blood is on his knees.

Louis's back in the land with a horse shoe round his neck. He's makin' ready to blow a fat rat-bustin' note that'll knock the blue and the gray into a twisted torquemada. Why he wanna do that? To show he's satisfied. All them wars and civilizations ain't brought nobody no good. Just blood everywhere and people prayin' for peace.

In the tomb where they buried him alive lies his father Agamemnon. Agamemnon was a shining god-like man who was indeed a god. He gave birth to two sons who traveled far apart. One sowed misery throughout the world and the other sowed joy.

Madame, I am thinking of you now, of that sweet and fetid stench of the past which you throw off. You are Madame Nostalgia rotting in the cemetery of inverted dreams. You are the black satin ghost of everything which refuses to die a natural death. You are the cheap paper flower carnation of weak and useless womanhood. I repudiate you, your country, your walls, your orchards, your tempered, hand-laundered climate. I call up the malevolent spirits of the jungle to assassinate you in your sleep. I turn the golden torque on you to harass you in your last agonies. You are the white of a rotten egg. You stink.

Madame, there are always two paths to take: one back towards the comfort and security of death, the other forward to nowhere. You would like to fall back amongst your quaint tomb-stones and familiar cemetery walls. Fall back, then, fall deep and fathomless into the ocean of annihilation. Fall back into that bloody torpor which permits idiots to be crowned as kings. Fall back and writhe in torment with the evolutionary worms. I am going on, on past the last black and white squares. The game is played out, the figures have melted away, the lines are frazzled, the board is mildewed. Everything has become barbarious again.

What makes it so lovely and barbarious? The thought of annihilation. Boogie Woogie came back with blood on his knees. He made a one o'clock jump into the land of Jehoshaphat. They took him for a buggy ride. They poured kerosene on his kinky hair and fried him upside down. Sometimes, when the Count goes bink-bink, when he says to himself—what kind of sorrowful tune will I play now?—you can hear the flesh sizzlin' and stretchin'. When he was little and low they bashed him flat with a potato masher. When he was bigger and higher they caught him in the gut with a pitchfork.

Epaminondas sure did a swell job civilizationing everybody with murder and hatred. The whole world has become one great big organism dying of ptomaine poison. It got poisoned just when everything was beautifully organized. It became a gut bucket, the white and wormy gut of a rotten egg that died in the shell. It brought on rats and lice, it brought on trench feet and trench teeth, it brought on declarations and preambles and protocols, it brought on bandy-legged twins and bald-headed eunuchs, it brought on Christian Science and poison gases and plastic underwear and glass shoes and platinum teeth.

Madame, as I understand it, you want to preserve this *Ersatz* which is sadness and propinquity and status quo all rolled into a fat meat ball. You want to put it in the frying pan and fry it when you're hungry, is that it? It comforts you, even though there is no nourishment in it, to call it civilization, isn't that how it is? *Madame,* you are horribly, miserably, woefully, irrefragably mistaken. You were taught to spell a word which makes no sense. There ain't no such thing as civilization. There's one big barbarious world and the name of the rat-catcher is Boogie Woogie. He had two sons and one of them got caught in a wringer and died all mangled and twisted, his left hand thumpin' like a crazy fluke. The other is alive and procreating like a shad roe. He lives in joy barbariously with nothing but the golden torque. He took the gin mill special at Monemvasia one day and when he got to Memphis he rose up and blew a fat rat-bustin' note that knocked the meat ball out of the frying pan.

I'm going to leave you now, *Madame,* to wither in your own trimmed lard. I leave you to fade away to a grease spot. I leave you to let a song go out of my heart. I'm on my way to Phaestos, the last Paradise on earth. This is just a barbarious passacaglia to keep your fingers busy when you fall back on the drop stitch. Should you wish to buy a second-hand sewing machine get in touch with Murder, Death & Blight, Inc. of Oswego, Saskatchewan, as I am the sole, authorized, living agent this side of the ocean and have no permanent headquarters. As of this day forth, in witness whereof, heretofore solemnly sealed and affixed, I do faithfully demit, abdicate, abrogate, evaginate and fornicate all powers signatories, seals and offices in favor of peace and joy, dust and heat, sea and sky, God and angel, having to the best of my ability performed the duties of dealer, slayer, blighter, bludgeoner and betrayer of the Soiled & Civilized Sewing Machine manufactured by Murder, Death & Blight, Inc. of the Dominions of Canada, Australia, Newfoundland, Patagonia, Yucatan, Schleswig-Holstein, Pomerania and other allied, subjugated provinces registered under the Death and Destruction Act of the planet Earth during the whilomst hegemony of the Homo sapiens family this last twenty-five thousand years.

And now, *Madame*, since by the terms of this contract we have only a few thousand more years to run, I say *bink-bink* and bid you good-day. This is positively the end. *Bink-bink!*

Before the rice diet got properly under way it began to rain, not heavy rains, but moist, intermittent rains, a half hour's sprinkle, a thunder shower, a drizzle, a warm spray, a cold spray, an electric needle bath. It went on for days. The aeroplanes couldn't land because the flying field had become too soggy. The roads had become a slimy yellow mucus, the flies swarmed in dizzy, drunken constellations round one's head and bit like fiends. Indoors it was cold, damp, fungus-bitten; I slept in my clothes with my overcoat piled on top of the blankets and the windows closed tight. When the sun came out it was hot, an African heat which caked and blistered the mud, which made your head ache and gave you a restlessness which increased as soon as the rain began to fall. I was eager to go to Phaestos but I kept putting it off for a change of weather. I saw Tsoutsou again; he told me that the prefect had been inquiring about me. "He wants to see you," he said. I didn't dare to ask what for; I said I would pay him a visit shortly.

Between drizzles and downpours I explored the town more thoroughly. The outskirts of the city fascinated me. In the sun it was too hot, in the rain it was creepily cold. On all sides the town edged off abruptly, like an etching drowned in a plate of black zinc. Now and then I passed a turkey tied to a door knob by a string; the goat was ubiquitous and the donkey. There were wonderful cretins and dwarves too who wandered about with freedom and ease; they belonged to the scene, like the cactus, like the deserted park, like the dead horse in the moat, like the pet turkeys tied to the door knobs.

Along the waterfront there was a fang-like row of houses behind a hastily made clearing, strangely reminiscent of certain old quarters in Paris where the municipality has begun to create light and air for the children of the poor. In Paris one roams from quarter to quarter through imperceptible transitions, as if moving through invisible beaded curtains. In Greece the changes are sharp, almost painful. In some places you can pass through all the changes of fifty centuries in the space of five minutes. Everything is delineated, sculptured, etched. Even the waste lands have an eternal cast about them. You see everything in its uniqueness—*a* man sitting on *a* road under *a* tree: *a* donkey climbing *a* path near *a* mountain: *a* ship in *a* harbor in *a* sea of turquoise: *a* table on *a* terrace beneath *a* cloud. And so on. Whatever you look at you see as if for the first time; it won't run away, it won't be demolished overnight; it won't disintegrate or dissolve or revolutionize itself. Every individual thing that exists, whether made by God or man, whether fortuitous or planned, stands out like a nut in an aureole of light, of time and of space. The shrub is the equal of the donkey; a wall is as valid as a belfry; a melon is as good as a man. Nothing is continued or perpetuated beyond its natural time; there is no iron will wreaking its hideous path of power. After a half hour's walk you are refreshed and exhausted by the variety of the anomalous and sporadic. By comparison Park Avenue seems insane and no doubt is insane. The oldest building in Herakleion will outlive the newest building in America. Organisms die; the cell lives on. Life is at the roots, embedded in simplicity, asserting itself uniquely.

I called regularly at the vice consul's home for my bowl of rice. Sometimes he had visitors. One evening the head of the merchant tailors' association dropped in. He had lived in America and spoke a quaint, old-fashioned English. "Gentleman, will you have a cigar?" he would say. I told him I had been a tailor myself once upon a time. "But he's a journalist now," the vice consul hastily put in. "He's just read my book." I began to talk about alpaca sleeve linings, bastings, soft rolled lapels, beautiful vicunas, flap pockets, silk vests and braided cutaways. I talked about these things madly for fear the vice consul would divert the conversation to his pet obsession. I wasn't quite sure whether the boss tailor had come as a friend or as a favored menial. I didn't care, I decided to make a friend of him if only to keep the conversation off that infernal book which I had pretended to have read but which I couldn't stomach after page three.

"Where was your shop, gentleman?" asked the tailor.

"On Fifth Avenue," I said. "It was my father's shop."

"Fifth Avenue—that's a very rich street, isn't it?" he said, whereupon the vice consul pricked up his ears.

"Yes," I said, "we had only the best customers—nothing but bankers, brokers, lawyers, millionaires, steel and iron magnates, hotel keepers, and so on."

"And you learned how to cut and sew?" he said.

"I could only cut pants," I answered. "Coats were too complicated."

"How much did you charge for a suit, gentleman?"

"Oh, at that time we asked only a hundred or a hundred and twenty-five dollars. . . ."

He turned to the vice consul to ask him to calculate what that would be in drachmas. They figured it out. The vice consul was visibly impressed. It *was* a staggering sum in Greek money— enough to buy a small ship. I felt that they were somewhat sceptical. I began talking carload lots—about telephone books, skyscrapers, ticker tape, paper napkins and all the ignominious paraphernalia of the big city which makes the yokel roll his eyes as if he'd seen the Red Sea opening up. The ticker tape arrested the tailor's attention. He had been to Wall Street once, to visit the stock exchange. He wanted to speak about it. He asked me diffidently if there weren't men in the street who ran their own little markets. He began making deaf and dumb signs as they used to do in the curb market. The vice consul looked at him as if he were slightly touched. I came to his rescue. Of course there were such men, thousands of them, all trained in this special deaf and dumb language, I asserted vigorously. I stood up and made a few signs myself, to demonstrate how it was done. The vice consul smiled. I said I would take them inside the stock exchange, on the floor itself. I described that mad house in detail, ordering myself slices of Anaconda Copper, Amalgamated Tin, Tel & Tel, anything I could remember of that crazy Wall Street past whether volatile, combustible or analgesic. I ran from one corner of the room to the other, buying and selling like a maniac, standing at the vice consul's commode and telephoning my broker to flood the market, calling my banker to make a loan of fifty thousand immediately, calling the telegraph jakes to take a string of telegrams, calling the grain and wheat trusters in Chicago to dump a load in the Mississippi, calling the Secretary of the Interior to inquire if he had passed that bill about the Indians, calling my chauffeur to tell him to put a new spare tire on the back behind the rumble seat, calling my shirt-maker to curse him for making the neck too tight on the pink and white shirt and what about my initials. I ran across the seat and gobbled a sandwich at the Exchange Buffet. I said hello to a friend of mine who was going upstairs to his office to blow his brains out. I bought the racing edition and stuck a carnation in my button hole. I had my shoes shined, while answering telegrams and telephoning with the left hand. I bought a few thousand railroad stocks absent-mindedly and switched to Consolidated Gas on a hunch that the new pork barrel bill would improve the housewives' lot. I almost forgot to read the weather report; fortunately I had to run back to the cigar store to fill my breast pocket with a handful of Corona-Coronas and that reminded me to look up the weather report to see if it had rained in the Ozark region.

The tailor was listening to me goggle-eyed. "That's the truth," he said excitedly to the vice consul's wife who had just made another bowl of soggy rice for me. And then suddenly it occurred to me that Lindbergh was coming back from Europe. I ran for the elevator and took the express to the 109th floor of a building that hadn't been built yet. I ran to the window and opened it. The street was choked with frantically cheering men, women, boys, girls, horse cops, motorcycle cops, ordinary cops, thieves, bulls, plain clothes men, Democrats, Republicans, farmers, lawyers, acrobats, thugs, bank clerks, stenographers, floor-walkers, anything with pants or skirts on, anything that could cheer, holler, whistle, stamp, murder or evaginate. Pigeons were flying through the canyon. It was Broadway. It was the year something or other and our hero was returning from his great transcontinental flight. I stood at the window and cheered until I was hoarse. I don't believe in aeroplanes but I cheered anyway. I took a drink of rye to clear my throat. I grabbed a telephone book. I tore it to pieces like a crazed hyena. I grabbed some ticker tape. I threw that down on the flyspecks—Anaconda Copper, Amalgamated Zinc, U.S. Steel—$57\frac{1}{2}$, 34, 138, minus two, plus $6\frac{3}{4}$, 51, going up, going higher, Atlantic Coast Line, Seaboard Air Line, here he comes, he's coming, that's him, that's Lindbergh, Hooray, Hooray, some guy, the eagle of the skies, a hero, the greatest hero of all time. . . .

I took a mouthful of rice to quiet myself.

"How high is the tallest building?" asked the vice consul.

I looked at the tailor. "You answer it," I said.

He guessed about 57 stories.

I said—"A hundred and forty two, not counting the flag pole."

I stood up again to illustrate. Best way is to count the windows. The average skyscraper has roughly 92,546 windows back and front. I undid my belt and put it on again clumsily, as if I were a window-cleaner. I went to the window and sat on the sill outside. I cleaned the window thoroughly. I unhooked myself and went to the next window. I did that for four and a half hours, making roughly 953 windows cleaned, scraped and waterproofed.

"Doesn't it make you dizzy?" asked the tailor.

"No, I'm used to it," I said. "I was a steeple-jack once—after I quit the merchant tailoring business." I looked at the ceiling to see if I could do any demonstrating with the chandeliers.

"You'd better eat your rice," said the vice consul's wife.

I took another spoonful by way of politeness and absent-mindedly reached for the decanter in which there was the cognac. I was still excited about Lindbergh's homecoming. I forgot that actually, on that day when he landed at the Battery, I was digging a ditch for the Park Department in the County of Catawpa. The Commissioner was making a speech at a bowling club, a speech I had written for him the day before.

The vice consul was completely at home now in the New World. He had forgotten about his contribution to life and letters. He was pouring me another drink.

Had the gentleman tailor ever gone to a ball game, I inquired. He hadn't. Well, he surely must have heard of Christy Matthewson—or Walter Johnson? He hadn't. Had he ever heard of a spitball? He hadn't. Or a home run? He hadn't. I threw the sofa cushions around on the parlor floor—first, second, third base and home plate. I dusted the plate with the napkin. I put on my cage. I caught a fast one right over the plate. Strike! Two more and he's out, I explained. I threw off the mask and ran towards the infield. I looked up through the roof and I saw the ball dropping out of the planet Pluto. I caught it with one hand and threw it to the short stop. He's out, I said, it was a fly. Three more innings to go. How about a little pop corn? Have a bottle of pop, then? I took out a package of Spearmint and I stuck a rib in my throat. Always buy Wrigley's, I said, it lasts longer. Besides, they spend $5,000,000,963.00 a year for advertising. Gives people work. Keeps the subways clean. . . . How about the Carnegie Library? Would you like to pay a visit to the library? Five million, six hundred and ninety eight thousand circulating subscribers. Every book thoroughly bound, filed, annotated, fumigated and wrapped in cellophane. Andrew Carnegie gave it to the City of New York in memory of the Homestead Riots. He was a poor boy who worked his way to the top. He never knew a day of joy. He was a very great millionaire who proved that it pays to work hard and save your pennies. He was wrong, but that doesn't make any difference. He's dead now and he left us a chain of libraries which makes the working people more intelligent, more cultured, more informed, in short, more miserable and unhappy than they ever were, bless his heart. Let's go now to Grant's Tomb. . . .

The tailor looked at his watch. It was getting late, he thought. I poured myself a night cap, picked up the first, second and third bases and looked at the parrot which was still awake because they had forgotten to put the hood over the cage.

"It's been a wonderful evening," I said, shaking hands all around, shaking hands with the maid too by mistake. "You must come and see me when I get back to New York. I have a town house and a country house, you know. The weather is excellent in the fall, when the smoke has cleared away. They're building a new dynamo over near Spuyten Duyvil: it runs by ether waves. The rice was excellent tonight. And the cognac too. . . ."

THE AIR-CONDITIONED NIGHTMARE

From The Air-Conditioned Nightmare. *Back in the country he had, however reluctantly, to call his own, Miller set about rediscovering it for himself. In the summer of 1940, he purchased a '32 Buick; took some driving lessons from Kenneth Patchen; and in the company of Abraham Rattner, whom he had known in Paris, set out on a year-long exploration. He went south first, then west along the Gulf. Finally, he joined Route 66 and like so many others followed it to California where he set about writing his book of American impressions. New Directions issued it in 1945.*

I left Paris three months before the war broke out, to spend a Sabbatical year in Greece. Little did I dream then that I would encounter Abe Rattner in New York or plan with him this tour of America which I am now embarked upon. A singular coincidence, too, that he should have been able to accompany me on this trip only as far as New Iberia! Looking back upon it all, it almost seems as though everything had been planned and arranged by some unseen power.

We arrived at "The Shadows" towards dusk on a day in January. Our host was waiting for us at a gas station on the highway, in front of the house. He had been waiting to intercept us in order, as he explained, to have us enter the grounds from the rear. I saw at once that he was a character, a rich, amiable personality, such as my friend Rattner had so faithfully portrayed. Everything had to be done in a prescribed way, not because he was domineering or tyrannical, but because he wanted his guests to derive the utmost from every situation or event.

"The Shadows," as the house is called, is not at all in the traditional Louisiana style of architecture. Technically it would be defined as of the Roman Doric order, but to speak in architectural language of a house which is as organically alive, sensuous, and mellow as a great tree is to kill its charm. For me, perhaps because of the rich pinkish brick which gives to the whole atmosphere of the place a warm, radiant glow, "The Shadows" at once summoned to my mind the image of Corinth which I also had the good fortune to come upon towards the close of day. The wonderful masonry columns, so sturdy and yet so graceful, so full of dignity and simplicity, were also reminiscent of Corinth. Corinth has always been synonymous for me with opulence, a roseate, insidious opulence, fragrant with the heavy bloom of summer.

All through the South I had been made aware again and again of the magnificence of a recent past. The days of the great plantations bequeathed to the brief and bleak pattern of our American life a color and warmth suggestive, in certain ways, of that lurid, violent epoch in Europe known as the Renaissance. In America, as Weeks Hall puts it, the great houses followed the great crops: in Virginia tobacco, in South Carolina rice, in Mississippi cotton, in Louisiana sugar. Supporting it all, a living foundation, like a great column of blood, was the labor of the slaves. The very bricks of which the walls of the famous houses are made were shaped by the hands of the Negroes. Following the bayous the landscape is dotted with the cabined shacks of those who gave their sweat and blood to help create a world of extravagant splendor. The pretensions which were born of this munificence, and which still endure amidst the soulless ruins of the great pillared houses, are rotting away, but the cabins remain. The Negro is anchored to the soil; his way of life has changed hardly at all since the great débâcle. He is the real owner of the land, despite all titular changes of possession. No matter what the whites say, the South could not exist without the easy, casual servitude of the blacks. The blacks are the weak and flexible backbone of this decapitated region of America.

It had been a wonderful ride up from New Orleans, past towns and villages with strange French names, such as Paradis and Des Allemands, at first following the dangerous winding road that runs beside the levee, then later the meandering Bayou Black and finally the Bayou Teche. It was early in January and hot as blazes though a few days previously, coming into New Orleans, the cold was so mean and penetrating that our teeth were chattering. New Iberia is in the very heart of the Acadian country, just a few miles from St. Martinsville where the memories of Evangeline color the atmosphere.

January in Louisiana! Already the first signs of spring were manifesting themselves in the cabin door-yards: the paper-white narcissus and the German iris whose pale gray-green spikes are topped by a sort of disdainful white plume. In the transparent black waters of the bayous the indestructible cypress, symbol of silence and death, stands knee-deep. The sky is everywhere, dominating everything. How different the sky as one travels from region to region! What tremendous changes between Charleston, Asheville, Biloxi, Pensacola, Aiken, Vicksburg, St. Martinsville! Always the live oak, the cypress, the chinaball tree; always the swamp, the clearing, the jungle; cotton, rice, sugar cane; thickets of bamboo, banana trees, gum trees, magnolias, cucumber trees, swamp myrtle, sassafras. A wild profusion of flowers: camellias, azaleas, roses of all kinds, salvias, the giant spider lily, the aspidistra, jasmine, Michaelmas daisies; snakes, screech-owls, raccoons; moons of frightening dimensions, lurid, pregnant, heavy as mercury. And like a leit-motif to the immensity of sky are the tangled masses of Spanish moss, that peculiar spawn of the South which is allied to the pineapple family. An epiphyte, rather than a parasite, it lives an independent existence, sustaining itself on air and moisture; it flourishes just as triumphantly on a dead tree or a telegraph wire as on the live oak. "None but the Chinese," says Weeks Hall, "can ever hope to paint this moss. It has a baffling secret of line and mass which has never been remotely approached. It is as difficult to do as a veronica. The live oaks tolerate it—they do not seem to be at one with it. But to the Louisiana cypress it seems to want to act as a bodyguard. A strange phenomenon." It is also a profitable one, as the mattress and upholstery industry of Louisiana would indicate.

There are people from the North and the Mid-West who

actually shudder when they first come upon the giant be-whiskered live oaks; they sense something dismal and forbidding in them. But when one sees them in majestic, stately rows, as on the great estates around Beaufort, S.C., or at Biloxi—at Biloxi they come to apotheosis!—one must bow down before them in humble adoration for they are, if not monarchs of the tree world, certainly the sages or the magi.

It was in the shade of one of these great trees that the three of us stood admiring the back of the house. I say the three of us because our host—and that is one of the things I like about Weeks Hall—can stop and examine the place he lives in any hour of the day or night. He can talk for hours about any detail of the house or gardens; he speaks almost as if it were his own creation, though the house and the trees which surround it came into existence over a century ago. It is all that remains of estates which once comprised several thousand acres, including Weeks Island, a Spanish royal grant made to David Weeks by Baron Carondelet in 1792. The entrance to the property, now reduced to three acres, is on Main Street, which is a continuation of Highway 90. Driving past it in a car one would never in the world suspect what lies hidden behind the dense hedge of bamboo which encircles the grounds.

As we stood there talking, Theophile came up to inform our friend that some women were at the front gate demanding permission to visit the grounds. "Tell them I'm out," said our host. "The tourists!" he said wryly, turning to Rattner. "They pour through here like ants; they overrun the place. Thousands and thousands of them—it's like the plague." And then he began to relate one anecdote after another about the women who insist on inspecting the rooms, which is forbidden. "They would follow me into the bathroom," he said, "if I permitted them. It's almost impossible to have any privacy when you live in a place like this." Most of them were from the Middle West, I gathered. They were the type one sees in Paris, Rome, Florence, Egypt, Shanghai—harmless souls who have a mania for seeing the world and gathering information about anything and everything. A curious thing about these show places, and I have visited a number of them, is that the owners, despite the martyrdom inflicted upon them by the steady hordes of visitors, almost never feel at liberty to exclude the public. They all seem to possess a sense of guilt about living alone in such ancient splendor. Some of course can not afford to spurn the modest revenue which this traffic brings, but for the most part there exists a feeling of obligation towards the public, whether conscious or unconscious.

Later, in looking over the register, I came across many interesting names, that of Paul Claudel surprising me not a little. "Claudel, ah yes! He said a wonderful thing about the camellia— how in Japan, when the blossom falls, they speak of it as a beheading." He went on to talk about the camellia, of which he has some marvelous varieties, including the largest Lady Hume's Blush in America. Its rarity, I was informed, is almost legendary; a plant of this size, in fact, is comparable to a black pearl. He dwelt at length on the tones and colors, the Lady Hume's Blush, he insisted, being of the palest pink ivory, whereas the Madame Strekaloff was of a peach-blossom pink streaked with rose, a rose with reddish stripes. He spoke of the tight little blossoms which might have been born under the glass domes of wax flowers. "The new varieties are lush but never sensuous; they have a beauty which forbids. They are coldly unaffected by praise and admiration. Pink cabbages, that's what they are!" And so on and so forth. It seemed to me that the man had given his life to the study of camellias, to say nothing of his wealth. But the more I listened to him the more I realized that he had an almost encyclopaedic knowledge about a great diversity of things. A superabundant vitality also, which permits him, when he feels inclined to talk, to continue like a fount from morning till night. He had always been a great talker, I learned, even before the injury to his arm limited his painting. That first evening, after the dishes had been cleared away, I watched him in fascination as he paced up and down the room, lighting one cigarette after another—he smokes almost a hundred a day—and telling us of his travels, his dreams, his weaknesses and vices, his passions, his prejudices, his ambitions, his observations, his studies, his frustrations. At three in the morning, when we finally begged leave to retire, he was wide awake, making himself a fresh cup of black coffee which he shares with his dog, and preparing to take a stroll about the garden and meditate on things past and future. One of the weaknesses, shall I call it, which sometimes comes upon him in the wee hours of the morning is the desire to telephone some one in California or Oregon or Boston. The anecdotes about these early morning enthusiasms of his are related from one end of the country to the other. Telephoning is not the only one of his imperative impulses; the others are even more spectacular, more weird, such as impersonating a non-existent idiot twin brother . . .

When the guests retire he communes with his dog. There is an unholy sort of bond between them, something quite out of the ordinary. I have forgotten the dog's name—Spot or Queenie, some common name like that. She is an English setter, a bitch, and rather seedy now and smelly, though it would break her master's heart if he should hear me say a thing like that. Weeks Hall's contention about this Alice or Elsie is this—that she does not know that she is a dog. According to him, she does not like other dogs, doesn't even recognize them, so to speak. He contends that she has the most beautiful manners—the manners of a lady. Perhaps. I am no judge of dogs. But of one thing I am in agreement with him—she has absolutely human eyes. That her coat is like falling water, that her ears remind you of Mrs. Browning's portrait, that she makes things handsome with her casual languor—such subtleties are beyond me. But when you look into her eyes, no matter how much or how little you know about dogs, you must confess that this puzzling creature is no ordinary bitch. She looks at you with the soulful eyes of some departed human who has been condemned to crawl about on all fours in the body of this most companionable setter. Weeks Hall would have it that she is sad because of her inability to speak, but the feeling she gave me was that she was sad because nobody except her master had the intelligence to recognize her as a human being and not just a dog. I could never look her in the eyes for more than a moment at a time. The expression, which I have caught now and then on the face of a writer or painter suddenly interrupted in the midst of an inspiration, was that of a wanderer between two worlds. It was the sort of look which makes one desire to withdraw discreetly, lest the separation between body and soul become irreparable.

The next morning, after breakfast, as I was about to open a door which had blown shut, I saw to my astonishment the signatures in pencil on the back of the door of hundreds of celebrities, written in every scrawl imaginable. Of course we had to add our own to the collection. I signed mine under that of a Hungarian named Bloor Schleppey, a fascinating name which unleashed a story about the door that is worth recounting. The present names, it seems, are all of recent origin. Originally there was an even more scintillating array of names, but about the time of Bloor Schleppey, perhaps because the name had such an uncommon effect upon our host, the latter, after a debauch lasting several days, was so disgusted with the condition of the house that he ordered the servants to clean it from top to bottom. "I want it to be immaculate when I wake up," were his orders. They tried to tell him that it was impossible to put a house of such proportions in order in such a short space of time. There were only two of them. "Well, then, hire a gang," said our host. And they did. And when he awoke from his slumber the house was indeed spic and span, as he had commanded it to be. Certain things, to be sure, had disappeared, what with the zeal and frenzy of the house-cleaners. The real coup came when he observed, in the course of his inspection, that the door with the names had been washed down and the names obliterated. That was a blow. At first he stormed and cussed, but when he had quieted down suddenly an inspiration came to him. He would unhinge the door, crate it, and send it on a round robin to be re-signed by his distinguished visitors. What a journey! The idea was so fasincating that presently he began to think it was too good a treat to offer a mere door—he would go himself from place to place, carrying the door along, and begging like a monk for a fresh signature. Some of the visitors had come from China, some from Africa, some from India. Better to supervise it personally than entrust it to the post or express agencies. Nobody, as far as he knew, had ever travelled around the world with a door. It would be quite a feat, a sensation, in fact. To find Bloor Schleppey, that would be something. God only knew where he had disappeared. The others he thought of as relatively fixed, like certain stars. But Bloor Schleppey—he hadn't the faintest idea where Bloor Schleppey had departed to. And then, as he was planning his itinerary—a delight which lasted for weeks—who should arrive, unheralded, in the dead of night, accompanied by three great Danes on a leash, but Bloor Schleppey himself! Well, to make the story short, the door was put back on its hinges, Bloor Schleppey inscribed his signature again, and the idea of a world tour with a door on his back gradually faded away, like all whimsical ideas. A strange thing about the people identified with this door, which I feel compelled to add in conclusion, is this— that many of them, as if in answer to a silent summons, have returned to sign their names again. It may also be, of course, that some of them were summoned back by an early morning telephone call—who can say?

In the course of a century or more curious events must naturally have occurred in a remote and idyllic domain of this sort. At night, lying in the center of a huge four-poster bed staring at the brass ornament in the center of the tester, the stillness of the house seemed the stillness not of an empty house but of one in which a great family was sleeping the profound and peaceful sleep of the dead. Awakened from a light sleep by the buzz of a mosquito I would get to thinking about the statues in the garden, about that fluid, silent communion which went on like music between these guardians of the Four Seasons. Sometimes I would get up and go out on the broad balcony overlooking the garden, stand there half-naked puffing a cigarette, hypnotized by the warmth, the silence, the fragrance which enveloped me. So many strange, startling phrases were dropped in the course of a day— they would come back to me at night and plague me. Little remarks, such as the one he dropped about the pool, for instance. "A dozen square feet of pool mean more to them than all the soil: it is a transparent mystery." The pool! It brought back memories of the dead fountain which graces the entrance to the now abandoned Mississippi Lunatic Asylum. I know that water is soothing to the insane, just as music is. A little pool in an enclosed and enchanted garden, such as this one, is an inexhaustible source of wonder and magic. One evening, standing thus in a dream, I remembered that there was a typewritten description of the place framed and posted near the pool. I descended the outer staircase and with the aid of a match I read the thing through. I re-read the paragraph about the garden, as though it contained some magic incantation. Here it is:

> "A rectangular formal garden to the east of the house is enclosed by a clipped bamboo hedge and is bordered by walks of hand-shaped brick, at the four corners of which are marble statues of the Four Seasons which were once in the gardens of the old Hester plantation. The center of the grass rectangle has a clump of old Camellia trees planted when the house was built. The signed marble sundial is inscribed with the French adage—'Abundance is the Daughter of Economy and Work,' and is dated 1827."

A heavy mist had descended. I walked cautiously in my bare feet for the old bricks were slippery with moss. As I got to the far corner of the rectangle the light of the moon broke full and clear on the serene face of the goddess there enshrined. I leaned over impulsively and kissed the marble lips. It was a strange sensation. I went to each of them in turn and kissed their cold, chaste lips. Then I strolled back to the trellised garden house which lies on the banks of the Bayou Teche. The scene before my eyes was that of a Chinese painting. Sky and water had become one: the whole world was floating in a nebular mist. It was indescribably beautiful and bewitching. I could scarcely believe that I was in America. In a moment or so a river boat loomed up, her colored lights scattering the dense mist into a frayed kaleidoscope of ribboned light. The deep fog horn sounded and was echoed by the hooting of invisible owls. To the left the draw-bridge slowly raised its broken span, the soft edges illumined by fulgurant lights of red and green. Slowly, like a white bird, the river boat glided past my vision, and in her wake the mist closed in, bearing down the sky, a fistful of frightened stars, the heavy wet limbs of the moss-covered trees, the density of night, and watery, smothered sounds. I went back to bed and lay there not just wide awake but super-conscious, alive in every tip and pore of my being. The portrait of an ancestor stared at me from the wall—a Manchu portrait, with the dress folded and pressed in the frame. I could hear Weeks Hall's booming voice saying to me: "I should like to do a garden which would not be a seed-catalogue by daylight, but strange, sculptural blossoms by night, things hanging in trees and moving like metronomes, transparent plastics in geometrical shapes, silhouettes lit by lights and changing with the changing hours. A garden is a show—why not make one enormous garden, one big, changing show?" I lay there wondering about those several thousand letters and documents which he had exhumed from the garret and stored in the Archives at Baton Rouge. What a story they would make! And the garret itself—that enormous room on the third floor with the forty trunks! Forty trunks, with the hair still intact on the bear-skin hides. Containing enormous hat boxes for the tall hats of the fifties, a stereoscope of mahogany and pictures for it taken in the sixties, fencing foils, shotgun cases, an old telescope, early side-saddles, dog baskets, linen dancing cloths with rings to fit over the carpets in the drawing room, banjos, guitars, zithers. Doll trunks too, and a doll house replica of the great house itself. All smelling dry and lightly fragrant. The smell of age, not of dust.

A strange place, the attic, with twelve huge closets and the ceiling slanting throughout the length of the house. Strange house. To get to any room you had to walk through every other room of the house. Nine doors leading outside—more than one finds in most public buildings. The both staircases originally built on the outside—a somewhat mad idea. No central hall. A row of three identical double wooden doors placed in the dead center of the grave façade on the ground floor.

And the strange Mr. Persac, the itinerant painter who left a brace of microscopically done wash drawings in black enamel gilt frames on the walls of the reception room where we held our nightly pow-wows. Up and down the country, especially the Teche region, he wandered, just a few years before the War between the States. Making pictures of the great houses and living on the fat of the land. An honest painter who, when the task got beyond his powers, would cut out a figure from a magazine and paste it on the picture. Thus in one of his master-

pieces the child standing by the garden gate has disappeared—
but the balloon which she held in her hand is still visible. I adore
the work of these travelling artists. How infinitely more agreeable
and enriching than the life of the present day artist! How much
more genuine and congenial their work than the pretentious
efforts of our contemporaries! Think of the simple lunch that was
served them in the old plantation days. I cull a menu at random
from one of Lyle Saxon's books on old Louisiana: "a slice of bread
and butter spread with marmalade or guava jelly, accompanied
by a slab of jujube paste and washed down with lemonade or
orange-flower syrup or tamarind juice." Think of his joy if he had
the good fortune to be invited to a ball. I give a description of one
culled from the same book:

". . . Gorgeous costumes of real lace . . . jewels, plumes. The
staircase was garlanded in roses for full three flights. Vases on mantels
and brackets filled with fragrant flowers . . . and gentlemen sam-
pling Scotch or Irish whiskey . . . About midnight supper was announced and the hostess led the way to the dining room. On the
menu, the cold meats, salads, salamis, galantines quaking in jellied
seclusion, and an infinite variety of *à las,* were served from side tables,
leaving the huge expanse of carved oak besilvered, belinened and
belaced, for flowers trailing from the tall silver *épergne* in the center to
the corsage bouquet at each place; fruits, cakes in pyramids or layers or
only solid deliciousness, iced and ornamented; custards, pies, jellies,
creams, Charlotte Russes or home-concocted sponge cake spread with
raspberry jam encircling a veritable Mont Blanc of whipped cream
dotted with red cherry stars; towers of nougat or caramel, sherbets and
ice creams served in little baskets woven of candied orange peel and
topped with sugared rose leaves or violets . . . Various wines in cut
glass decanters, each with its name carved in the silver grapeleaf
suspended from its neck; iced champagne deftly poured by the waiters
into gold-traced or Bohemian glasses . . . Illuminating the whole
were wax candles in crystal chandeliers, and on the table, in silver
candelabra . . . More dancing followed supper and at dawn when
the guests were leaving a plate of hot gumbo, a cup of strong black
coffee and enchanting memories sustained them on the long drive to
their abodes."*

*Courtesy of Miss Louise Butler.

Well, Monsieur Persac or Persat, whichever it was, I felicitate you for having had the good fortune to be born in such times! I hope you are chewing the cud of these rich and pleasant memories in the Bardo beyond. When morning comes I shall go down to the reception room and look again at the balloon which is suspended above the gate. If I am in good fettle I will look around for a little child capable of holding such a beautiful balloon and I will paste her back in the picture as I know you would wish me to do. May you rest in peace!

I suppose there is no region in America like the old South for good conversation. Here men talk rather than argue and dispute. Here there are more eccentric, bizarre characters, I imagine, than in any other part of the United States. The South breeds character, not sterile intellectualism. With certain individuals the fact that they are shut off from the world tends to bring about a forced bloom; they radiate power and magnetism, their talk is scintillating and stimulating. They live a rich, quiet life of their own, in harmony with their environment and free of the petty ambitions and rivalries of the man of the world. Usually they did not settle down without a struggle, for most of them possess talents and energies unsuspected by the curious invader. The real Southerner, in my opinion, is more gifted by nature, more far-seeing, more dynamic, more inventive and without a doubt more filled with the zest for life than the man of the North or West. When he elects to retire from the world it is not because of defeatism but because, as with the French and the Chinese, his very love of life instills him with a wisdom which expresses itself in renunciation. The most difficult adjustment an expatriate has to make, on returning to his native land, is in this realm of conversation. The impression one has, at first, is that there *is* no conversation. We do not talk—we bludgeon one another with facts and theories gleaned from cursory readings of newspapers, magazines and digests. Talk is personal and if of any value must be creative. I had to come to the South before I heard such talk. I had to meet men whose names are unknown, men living in almost inaccessible spots, before I could enjoy what I call a real conversation.

I shall never forget one particular evening, after our friend Rattner had left, when I accompanied Weeks Hall to the home of an old friend of his. The man had given up his house and built himself a little wooden shack in the rear of what was once his home. Not a superfluous object in the place, but everything neat and tidy, as if it were occupied by a sailor. The man's life had been his education. He was a hunter who had temporarily decided to run a truck. I got the impression, after studying him quietly, that he had known great sorrow. He was very mellow, very sure of himself, and obviously reconciled with his lot. His hobby was books. He read widely, as his fancy dictated, seeking neither to improve his knowledge nor merely to kill time. Rather, so I gathered from his remarks, it was a vicarious way of dreaming, of lifting himself out of the world. The conversation originated, I remember, about the poisonous snakes of Louisiana, those with the cat's eye pupils. From that to sassafras and the habits of the Choctaw Indians, then to the various kinds of bamboo—edible and otherwise—and from that to the coral pink moss which is said to be very rare, very beautiful, and grows only on one side of the tree, always the same side too. And then, abruptly switching the conversation, suspecting too that I would receive an interesting response, I asked him point blank if he had read anything about Tibet. "Have I read about Tibet?" he said, pausing to exchange a smile of mutual understanding with his friend. "Why, I've read everything on that subject that I could lay hands on." At this point Weeks Hall got so excited that he had to excuse himself to relieve his bladder. In fact we all got excited and went out to the yard to relieve ourselves.

It's always amazing to me, even though I am prepared for it, to learn that some one is interested in Tibet. I can also say that I have never met any one who *is* deeply interested in the wonders and mysteries of this land with whom I have not established a strong link. Tibet seems to be the countersign for a world-wide community who have this much in common at least—they know that there is something more to life than is summed up in the empirical knowledge of the high priests of logic and science. On the island of Hydra in the Aegean Sea I remember having had a similar experience. Curious, too, how when this subject comes up—it is the same if you should happen to mention Rudolf Steiner's name or Blavatsky's or the Count Saint Germain—a schism immediately takes place and soon there are left in the room only those who are marked, as it were, by the passion for the secret and the obscure. Were a stranger suddenly to enter into the presence of such a gathering he would likely as not find the language employed quite unintelligible. I have had the experience more than once of being understood by some one who scarcely knew English and of not being understood at all by my English-speaking friends. And I have seen a man like Briffault, the author of *Europa,* in whose presence I happened to raise the subject one evening, go into a tantrum at the very mention of the word mysticism.

The conversation left us in an exalted mood. On our way back to "The Shadows" Weeks Hall remarked that he never suspected his friend could be so eloquent. "He's been living alone so long," he said, "that he's grown taciturn. Your visit had an extraordinary effect upon him." I smiled, knowing well that I had nothing to do with it. The experience was simply another proof, to my mind, of the fact that men can always be deeply aroused either by hatred or by touching upon the sense of mystery.

As I was about to go to my room Weeks called me from the studio, the only room he had not yet shown me. "Are you very tired?" he asked. "No, not too tired," I answered. "I've been wanting to show you something," he went on, "I think this is the moment for it." He ushered me into a room that appeared to be hermetically sealed, a room without windows or ventilation of any kind, illuminated only by artificial light. He moved his easel into the center of the room, placed a blank canvas on it, and from what looked like a magic lantern he shot a beam of light on it which threw the projection on the walls. By maneuvering the easel, by expanding and diminishing the frame of the canvas, the colored photograph was made to assume the most astonishing variety of forms and tones. It was like a private séance with Dr. Caligari himself. An ordinary landscape, or a harmless still life, when subjected to these whimsical manipulations, could express the most diversified, the most incongruous and incredible patterns and themes. The walls became a riot of changing color patterns, a sort of colored organ recital, which alternately soothed and stimulated the senses.

"Why should any one paint," he said, "when they can perform these miracles? Perhaps painting isn't all it should be in my life—I don't know. But these things give me pleasure. I can do in five minutes here what it would take me ten years to do in paint. You see, I stopped painting deliberately. It wasn't this arm at all—I smashed that up afterwards, to make sure, as it were—just as people go deaf or blind or insane when they can't stand it any more. I'm not a bad painter, take my word for it. I can still paint with my bad arm—if I really want to. I could have my paintings exhibited, and could probably sell them too, now and then, to museums and private collectors. It's not such a difficult thing, if you have a little talent. In fact, it's too easy, and also too futile. Pictures in an exhibition hall are like wares on a bargain counter. Pictures, if they are to be displayed, should be shown one at a time, at the right time, under the proper conditions. Pictures have no place to-day in the home—the houses are not right. I have the idea that I will never paint again with conviction unless the painting is for some purpose, and the easel picture is for no purpose except to collect a bunch of vapid compliments. It's like an artificial bait with which to catch a tarpon. In itself the easel picture is nil: it doesn't feed one. Just a bait for complacency . . . Listen, I think I said something there—remember that, will you?

"Of course," he went on, "a fellow like Rattner is different. He just had to paint—he was born to it. But for one like him there are a thousand who might just as well be carpentering or driving a truck. The difference, I suppose, is between procreation and creation—a difference of nine months. In the case of the creator it means a life's work—unceasing labor, study, observation—not just to make *a* picture, or even a hundred pictures, but to understand the relation between painting, between all arts, I might say, and living. To put your whole life into a canvas, into every canvas you do. It's the highest form of consecration, and our good friend Abe has it. Whether he's happy or not, I don't know. I don't suppose happiness means as much to an artist as to ordinary folk. . . ."

He lit a fresh cigarette. Paced nervously back and forth. He wanted to say something . . . he wanted to say a lot of things . . . *everything*, if I would only be patient and not run away. He began again, haltingly, clumsily, feeling his way like a man groping through a dark and winding passage.

"Look, this arm!" and he held it out for me to look at intently. "Smashed. Smashed for good. A terrible thing. One moment you have an arm there, the next moment it's a pulpy mess. I suppose the truth is that it was only good for the derrick-use which other arms are good for. This arm was perhaps too slick, too clever; it made me paint like a gambler deals and shuffles the cards. Perhaps my mind is too slick and too brittle. Not disciplined enough. And I know I won't improve it by my mania for research. That's just a pretext to forestall the day when I must really begin to paint. I know all that—but what are you going to do? Here I am living alone in a big house, a place which overwhelms me. The house is too much for me. I want to live in one room somewhere, without all these cares and responsibilities which I seem to have assumed from my forbears. How am I going to do it? Shutting myself up in this room is no solution. Even if I can't see them or hear them I know there are people outside clamoring to get in. And perhaps I *ought* to see them, talk to them, listen to them, worry about what they're worrying about. How should I know? After all they're not all fools. Maybe if I were the man I'd like to be I wouldn't have to set foot outside this door—the world would come to me. Maybe I'd paint under the worst conditions— perhaps right out there in the garden with all the sightseers crowding around me and asking me a thousand and one irrele- vant questions. Who knows but that, if I were deadly in earnest, they would let me alone, leave me in peace, without saying a word to them? Somehow people always recognize value. Take Swedenborg, for example. He never locked his door. People came and when they saw him they went away quietly, rever- ently, unwilling to disturb him though they had traveled, some of them, thousands of miles to ask him for help and guidance." With his good hand he took hold of the smashed arm and gazed at it, as though it belonged to some other person. "Can one change one's own nature—that's the question? Well, eventually this arm may act as the pole does for the tight-rope walker. *The balance*—if we don't have it within we've got to find it without.

I'm glad you came here . . . you've done me a world of good. God, when I was listening to you all talk about Paris I realized all I had missed these years. You won't find anything much in New Orleans, except the past. We've got *one* painter—that's Dr. Souchon. I want you to meet him. . . . I guess it's pretty late. You want to go to bed, don't you? I could talk all night, of course. I don't need much sleep. And since you all came here I can't sleep at all. I have a thousand questions to ask. I want to make up for all the time I've lost."

I had difficulty myself in going to sleep. It seemed cruel to leave a man stranded like that on a peak of exaltation. Rattner had prepared me for his exuberance and vitality, but not for his inexhaustible hunger. This hunger of his touched me deeply. He was a man who knew no stint. He gave just as recklessly and abundantly as he demanded. He was an artist to the finger-tips, no doubt about that. And his problems were no ordinary ones. He had probed too deeply. Fame and success would mean nothing to a man like that. He was in search of something which eluded all definition. Already, in certain domains, he had amassed the knowledge of a savant. And what was more, he saw the relatedness of all things. Naturally he could not be content in executing a masterful painting. He wanted to revolutionize things. He wanted to bring painting back to its original estate— painting for painting's sake. In a sense it might be said of him that he had already completed his great work. He had transformed the house and grounds, through his passion for creation, into one of the most distinctive pieces of art which America can boast of. He was living and breathing in his own masterpiece, not know- ing it, not realizing the extent and sufficiency of it. By his enthusiasm and generosity he had inspired other painters to do their work—had given birth to them, one might say. And still he was restless, longing to express himself surely and completely. I admired him and pitied him, both. I felt his presence all through the house, flooding it like some powerful magic fluid. He had created that which in turn would recreate him. That hermetically sealed studio—what was it in fact if not a symbolic expression of his own locked-in self? The studio could never contain him, any more than the house itself; he had outgrown the place, overflowed the bounds. He was a self-convicted prisoner inhabiting the aura of his own creation. Some day he would awaken, free himself of the snares and delusions which had gathered in the wake of creation. Some day he would look around and realize that he was free; then he would be able to decide calmly and quietly whether to remain or to go. I hoped that he would remain, that as the last link in the ancestral chain he would close the circle and by realizing the significance of his act expand the circle and circumference of his life to infinite dimensions.

When I took leave of him a day or two later I had the impression, from the look he gave me, that he had come to this conclusion himself. I left knowing that I would always find him at a moment's notice anywhere any time.

"No need to telephone me in the middle of the night, Weeks. As long as you remain centered I am at your side eternally. No need to say good-bye or good luck! Just continue being what you are. May peace be with you!"

REMEMBER TO REMEMBER

From Remember to Remember, *"Murder the Murderer" and "Obscenity and the Law of Reflection." Since this is a heterogeneous gathering of previously published materials, one would not expect* Remember *to have a real thematic core. Yet it does, for in these sprawling essays on artists, bread, memory, war, and obscenity we can see Miller at work on a definition of a healthy culture. Though his focus is on America (and what makes its culture unhealthy), Miller speaks here as a citizen of the world and as a writer who owes allegiance to human life rather than to any state. This is the informing stance of his long, two-part letter to Alfred Perlès. The first portion was written in 1941, the second in 1944 (the part included here). "Obscenity and the Law of Reflection" is one of the major twentieth-century statements on this subject and is obviously thematically related to Miller's letter on war.*

PART II: MURDER THE MURDERER

A period of darkness has set in. The world seems determined to resolve its problems by force. No single individual can stem the tide of hate. We are in the grip of cosmic forces and each one does what he can, or must.

To each man the conflict assumes a different face. Millions of men and women will sacrifice their lives; millions more will be maimed and mutilated. The innocent will suffer with the guilty, the wise with the foolish. It is beyond control now; we are in the hands of Fate.

Useless to say now that it need not have happened. It is not for us to question what happens; it is for us to accept. But there are a thousand ways of accepting the inevitable. In the way we accept lies our ability to transform a situation. No disaster is irremediable. The whole meaning of life is contained in the word suffering. That all the world can be suffering at one time is a fact of tremendous significance.[1] It never has happened before. It is an opportunity which we can reject or use to advantage.

Since I am having my say, I want to reveal what I sincerely believe this opportunity may be. We, the American people, having resisted war to the very last, have now thrown ourselves into the universal conflict. Whether we admit it to ourselves or not, whether or not we have lived up to that faith which the other peoples of the world have in us, *we are the hope of the world.* That is the rock on which America was founded. Let it be our rock now!

Are we at war to extend our empire, to increase our possessions, to gain ascendancy over the other nations of this earth? I believe the great body of American people would answer NO! Like other peoples, we have been misguided. Above all, we had grown callous and indifferent. That was our crime. Today we are ready to accept our share of suffering, along with the righteous and the unrighteous. Moreover, we are determined to endure what we have never endured before. That was evident the day war was declared.

What can we as a people do beyond anything our allies may expect of us? We can be magnanimous and far-sighted, we can be patient and full of understanding; we can be hard as steel, yet wise and full of tenderness when the time is ripe. We can be all these things because we are the favored people of the earth. Our forefathers, when first they came to this country, were hailed as gods. To our disgrace they behaved as demons. They asked for gold instead of grace. Today their sins are visited upon us. We are paying now for the crimes committed by our ancestors. They fled their self-imposed prisons because they had a vision of Paradise. Had they acted as the gods they were mistaken for by the aborigines of this continent they could have realized the Paradise which they were seeking. But they were only men and they were weak, and because they were weak the dream of Paradise was forgotten. Dreams are hard to kill; they linger on even when the memory of them is faded. The dream of golden

---

[1] Not quite the whole world!—the "civilized" peoples mostly.

opportunity still clings to the name America no matter what part of the world you may go to. It is regrettable that we, the American people, have fostered a false interpretation of that dream and thereby helped to further poison the world. We have given the impression that America was a place in which to grow rich. We have emphasized gold instead of opportunity. Out of greed we killed the goose that laid the golden egg. Yet, despite the tragic error, we all know that there *was* a golden goose. We are now at the point where we are obliged to interpret the fable intelligently.

What *was* the golden opportunity which was offered the American pilgrim? The opportunity to serve the world, the opportunity to bring about enlightenment and justice. Since the inception of this republic we had no enemies save the mother country, England. We were surrounded by friends. The only great struggle we had was an internal one. Then, in the last war, we were dragged into a world-wide conflict whose significance we only partially understood. The war over, we tried to take refuge again in our comfortable shell, unwilling to accept the responsibilities we had assumed as participants of that great conflict. We refused to sit at the Hague Tribunal and assist in the first crude attempt to establish some kind of international law and order. We refused for years to recognize the one government which had taken the lesson of the war to heart and was endeavoring to bring about a more intelligent and equitable order of human society. With the emergence of the dictators we sat by and watched one little nation after the other swallowed up and enslaved. When France fell we were full of bitterness. We cried "Shame!" though we hadn't lifted a finger to help her. We would have suffered England to undergo the same fate, but the English were made of different stuff. Until the treacherous attack by Japan, which we should have anticipated, considering all the lessons we had been given, we were undecided what course to pursue. Now suddenly we are united and, as in the last war, we are pretending that we are fighting to free the world. The newspapers are doing their best to make the American people believe this beautiful legend, knowing well that the psychology of the American people is based on a sense of utter unreality, that only when we visualize ourselves as saviours and crusaders can we kill with fury and efficiency. "Now at last," I read in today's paper, "a single devotion inspires the nation, a great moment has touched us and America has fallen in step to heroic music. We have renounced triviality, indifference and fear, we have taken up the responsibilities of our position in the world, we have turned as one man toward a shining star."[1] It goes on like that, soaring, skyrocketing, to end with the phrase "without compromise—to win."

It is unthinkable that we shall lose. But what do we hope to win? Or better, what do we hope to win to? That is the question which the editorial gentry cleverly evade by grandiloquent phrases such as "ridding the world forever of the Nazi pestilence," and so on. Are we microbe hunters and bug exterminators? Are we merely going to preserve the *tomb* of Christ from the desecrating paw of the infidel? For two thousand years the world has been squabbling over the dead body of Christ. The Christians themselves will admit that God sent his son, a *living* Christ, to redeem the world. He didn't send us a corpse to fight over. In effect, however, that is what the Christian world has done: it has welcomed every excuse to fight in the name of Christ who came to bring peace on earth. There can be no end to this repetitious pattern until each and every one of us become as Christ, until belief and devotion transform our words into deeds and thus make of myth reality.

"To War—and Beyond" reads the caption of the editorial I just cited. We are all interested in what lies beyond the war. Nobody is any longer interested in war for the sake of war. But what comes after the war depends altogether on the spirit in which we wage war. We will accomplish exactly what we aim to accomplish, and no more. In this respect war is no different from peace. The fact that we are desperate instead of lethargic means nothing, if we are not clear as to what we wish to attain. To defeat Hitler and his gang is not a particularly brilliant goal to set oneself. Hitler and his gang could have been defeated without war had we possessed the intelligence, the will, and the purity to undertake the task. Wherever there is indecision, confusion, dalliance and

[1] *New York Post,* December 13, 1941.

an atmosphere of unreality, you have Hitler. Just as Judas was necessary in order for Christ to enact the drama which was ordained, so Hitler was necessary for this age in order that the world might enact the drama of unification and regeneration. Christ chose Judas to betray him; we have chosen Hitler. All the intermediary figures, the supernumeraries, so to speak, good, honest gentlemen though they be, are dwarfed by this Satanic figure which looms across the horizon. Churchill, Roosevelt, Stalin, none of these is big enough to cope with the monster alone. It is fortunate that they are not, for now it devolves upon the little men, the poor anonymous figures who make up the great mass of humanity, to answer the challenge. Christ chose twelve little men to do his work—not great world figures.

I come back to that idea which America has always inspired in the minds of other peoples, the idea that the lowest man may rise and "make his place" in the world. (It would have been better had we inspired the idea of "finding one's place" in the world.) I repeat that the behavior of the American people has brought about a distortion of that idea. We have shown in ways too numerous to specify that we have reduced the conception of freedom and service to mankind to a poverty-stricken notion of power and riches. Power and riches, not for *all* Americans—that would be bad enough!—but for the few. Our democracy has been the worst democracy that has ever been tried out. It has never had anything to do with freedom, has never been anything more than a name. Put to the test, it explodes, as was demonstrated in the War between the States. It will explode again when the pressure becomes great enough, because it is not founded upon a respect for the individual, for the sacred human individual who in aggregate makes a democracy and in the ultimate will make divinity. We have been democratic in the crassest political way, but at bottom we have never been deceived about it. Our jokesters, our cartoonists, our caricaturists reveal only too clearly the conscious and unconscious disillusionment of the people.

What can the people of America do then in this great world crisis—beyond the intention of their dubiously disinterested leaders? How can they win a war which they had no desire to participate in and which very conceivably the peoples they oppose had no desire to initiate? I think of the film called *Juarez*, of that moment when Juarez confronts the assembled representatives of the European governments and tells them what the people of Mexico suffered from the "civilization" of the Europeans. How like jackals they looked, the assembled plenipotentiaries of Europe, in their pomp and persiflage! From time immemorial the dignitaries of Church and State have looked this way. And from time immemorial the people have looked on dumb and impassive, always shackled and manacled by their own spokesmen. We see the same thing happening today in the Labor movement. A Lincoln, a Lenin, a Juarez are not to be had every day. We have had only one Buddha, one Christ, one Mohammed, one Ramakrishna. We have had only one American who was capable of saying: "While there is a lower class I am in it; while there is a criminal element I am of it; while there is a soul in prison, I am not free." Can the American people endorse these simple, Christ-like words? *Will* they? If not, then some other people will assume the leadership. The Russians are already far beyond us in the realization of their aims. Tomorrow it will be China and India perhaps. We no longer lead the procession; we are being dragged along by the scalp.

What is our role? How shall we act? What example can we give?

To begin with, let us begin at the beginning. Put on your hat and go into the street. Stroll quietly down the avenue and look into the shop windows. Take a pad and pencil and list all the objects—clothes, food, furniture, drugs, jewelry, gadgets, knickknacks—which you consider unnecessary to produce now that we are at war. Send the list to President Roosevelt and mark it "Personal."

That's the first step. The second is to go home, sit down quietly and meditate. Try to picture what the world would look like if these useless things were eliminated. Ask yourself if you could get along with the bare necessities of life. Assume that the President will give serious attention to your suggestions.

The next step is to think about wages. Do you think you are entitled to more than the man in uniform who no longer has the right to vote and who is asked to sacrifice his life in order to protect you? Can you see any logical reason why a sergeant should receive higher pay than a private or a second lieutenant more than a sergeant? Can you see any reason why the president of the United States should receive *money* for the privilege of leading his people to victory? Can you see any reason why anybody should think about money when the government which represents us has in its power the means to provide us with the necessities of life? We are no longer on the gold standard; we buried our gold in the earth, where it belongs. But we have bright coins such as would please a savage, and little bits of paper expressing our confidence in God and in one another. To-morrow, if the government chooses, these objects can be made meaningless. There is nothing sacred about these monetary symbols. In themselves they have no value: they are merely relics of an ancient way of thinking.

What is a panic? Is it anything but a manifestation of loss of confidence? A panic is engendered by the realization that something we thought was there is gone. Today there is a panic on all fronts. *This is what war means: a complete loss of confidence on all sides.* Lacking faith, intelligence, good-will, we move in with big guns, tanks, battleships, bombers, high explosives and try to fill the breach. Even a child can understand the futility of trying to instill faith and confidence with bullets and poison gas. The theory behind the philosophy of war is that the enemy must be made to come to terms—*our terms.* Then and only then can we talk turkey.

Today this idea, like other atavistic notions, is very much in question. People are getting fed up with the idea of talking turkey only after wasteful slaughter and destruction. If there weren't such a strict taboo on the eating of human flesh it might not be so bad; one could eat a fresh corpse and live to fight another day. But making manure of human flesh and blood is a rather expensive method of fertilizing the earth. There are better things to be accomplished with the human body—at least some people think so.

Let's go back a bit. We were questioning the practicability of retaining little round pieces of metal and little oblong pieces of paper. Metals are scarce now and so is paper. And since they are only symbols of our mutual confidence, these relics of the past, why not scrap them and convert them into war materials?

And how will I buy a ham sandwich tomorrow?

Very simple. There will be no buying or selling tomorrow; there will be only give and take. If you have a bigger stomach than I you will eat three ham sandwiches to my one. And if you want twenty ham sandwiches at one sitting why you will have to take the consequences imposed by the laws of nature. The man who insists on having three overcoats, five hats and seven pairs of shoes will have to wear them all at once, otherwise he forfeits them. Whatever superfluous possessions you have will be redistributed among the needy. In war-time we can't have people bothering about needless possessions—it's too distracting. What we want, if we are going to rid the world of useless vermin (that's to say Germans, Japs, Italians, Hungarians, Roumanians—the inventory isn't quite made up yet), are men and women united in a single purpose: *to exterminate the enemy.* We can't have fighters who are thinking of stocks and bonds, high or low wages, profits and losses, perfumes, patent medicines, toilet water, platinum settings, monkey furs, silk bathrobes, collars, ties and alarm clocks. Especially not alarm clocks! We want an army of men and women, soldiers and workers, killers and producers, who will wake up without an alarm—people who can't sleep any more because they're itching to rid the world of human lice. People so restless, so wild with excitement, so full of ardor and devotion, that when they get through exterminating the foreign vermin they will go after their own. People who will exterminate one another, until there are no vermin left in the world. Isn't that it? Or have I exaggerated the case?

A people wild with excitement . . .

For example: supposing that tomorrow, owing to the most expert propaganda, there would be such a fever to enlist in all branches of the service that every able-bodied worker from ten to seventy-five years of age, including the eight or nine million unemployed, would descend upon the recruiting bureaus and demand the right to fight. A grand chaos ensues, with the result that everybody is ordered back to work. Good. They return to their jobs, still feverish, still rearing to go, still itching to serve in some vital, splendorous way. Then a wave of disgust, as they realize more and more each day that they are being asked to produce non-essentials. Supposing they take it into their heads to stop wasting time. Supposing they go on strike, fired with the exalted idea of producing only what will keep the war machine humming. They win, let us say. Nothing being produced now but the vital necessities. A new thing happens: the workingman becomes delirious with enthusiasm. He asks nothing better than to work and work and work. And so, instead of six or eight hours a day, the workers of America work twelve, sixteen, twenty hours a day; they drag the children out of school and the criminals out of jail and the insane out of the asylums. Everybody is put to work, without exception. They work night and day, day in and day out; no Sundays, no holidays, no rest periods. They work themselves to the bone, obsessed with a single idea: to bring about a speedy victory. In the meantime they ransack the patent offices and the secret archives of those whose interest it serves to withhold new inventions. They create new machines which provide an incalculable release of energies natural, human and divine. They invent, create and produce in five months what formerly it required five years to accomplish. And still they refuse to rest. They form suicide brigades of workers and producers. They drive their former slave-drivers to a quick death; they drive the sick and the aged to the grave; they force the children to mature, as blossoms are forced in the hot-house. "Work! More work!" they cry. The President is for caution, but the pace increases. Faster, faster. Fast and furiously, without let, without cess. A mania for work such as was never heard of on any planet in the memory of God. The President, bewildered by this inexplicable access of zeal, continues feebly to abjure and protest. "I beg you, my good fellow-citizens, don't work yourselves to death!" But it's in the blood now, they can't stop. God Almighty couldn't put a stop to it, so virulent and deep-seated has the mania become.

It becomes necessary to remove the President from office—he is regarded as a slacker. The Vice President takes over. In forty-eight hours he's demoted too. A new party arises, calling themselves "The Bees and Ants." There is no opposition—just one unanimous Party now. A new President is chosen, the hardest, fastest worker in the United States. He is to serve until he drops from exhaustion.

In the midst of this incredible toil and bubble new inventions are being turned out by the hour. Finally the great invention of the ages is ushered in—a sort of human Flit. A device which destroys the enemy everywhere instantaneously. Something so ingenious, so simple too, that it needs only to be stamped with a single word, such as *Japanese, German, Bulgarian, Italian,* and it goes directly to the mark, annihilating its victim. Total annihilation of the enemy everywhere! Think of the effect which this produces! At last the ideal victory. Something indeed which the men of this scientific age might well be proud of! Power! Absolute power! No need for Peace Conferences henceforth. No need to ball things up through compromise, chicanery and intrigue, as in the past. All our enemies are dead. Annihilated. The power to rule the world in our own hands. Who now will dare to rise up against us? Magnificent, *what?*

There are those, of course, who will immediately cry "Absurd! Fantastic! Impossible!" A *human Flit? . . .* tsch, tsch, tsch! How many years ago is it that the same was said against the steamboat, the railroad, the aeroplane, the telegraph, the telephone, the electric light, the X-ray? Is it necessary to reel off the whole list of what was once absurd, impossible and fantastic, to say nothing of impracticable, unprofitable, demonic and diabolical? *Whatever man sets his mind on accomplishing he accomplishes.* That is the beautiful and terrible thing about man, that he has within himself the power and the ability to make his dreams come true.

Nature too has certain powers which man, despite his superiority, is sometimes helpless to combat. Now and then man has to acknowledge that there are powers beyond his. For four long centuries there raged in Europe, and even beyond the confines of Europe, the plague known as the Black Death. Not one man living in that dark period was capable of finding a means to stem the avalanche of death. Death ruled like a demented monarch, turning everything topsy-turvy, including legal and moral codes. It seems almost incredible today. But it was so. It did happen. Only when Nature herself grew weary, and provided the antidote, did the Black Death cease to be the Supreme Master of Europe.

Will we take the cue from Nature? Will we, weary of shedding blood, create an anti-toxin to self-destruction? Perhaps, when we have had our fill of slaughter. Not before. We must kill and kill until we hit upon the means of killing without effort and without limit. We must exhaust this lust to kill at the risk of total annihilation. We must be able to visualize the ultimate effect of murder before we can hope to eradicate the instinct. We must become the black magicians before we can become the white. We must possess power absolutely, not worship it merely, before we can understand the use of it.

There is an old story about a man who had committed fifty-two murders. It bears repeating . . .

As the story goes, it was after the fifty-second crime that the murderer became conscience-stricken and decided to seek out a holy man in order to mend his ways. He lived with the holy man a few years, doing everything that he was prescribed to do and striving with all his heart to get the better of his vicious nature. Then one day the holy man told him that he was free to resume his life in the world, that he need have no more fear of committing murder again. At first the man was overjoyed, but elation soon gave way to fear and doubt. How could he be certain he would sin no more? He begged the holy man for some sign, some tangible proof that he was really liberated. And so the holy man gave him a black cloth, telling him that when the cloth turned white he could be absolutely certain of his innocence. The man departed and resumed his life in the world. A dozen times a day he looked at the black cloth to see if it had turned white. He could think of nothing else—he was obsessed. Little by little he began to inquire of others what he could do to bring the miracle about. Each one suggested something else. He followed out every suggestion, but to no avail. The cloth remained black. Finally he made a long pilgrimage to the Ganges, having been told that the holy waters of that sacred river would surely make the black cloth white. But as with all his efforts this one too proved unsuccessful. Finally, in despair, he decided to return to the holy man and live out the rest of his days in his presence. At least, he thought, by living with the holy man he would be able to avoid temptation. So he set out on the long journey. As he was nearing his destination he came upon a man attacking a woman. The screams which the woman gave out were heart-rending. He caught hold of the man and implored him to desist. But the man paid no heed to him. On the contrary, he redoubled his blows. There was no doubt that he intended to kill the woman. Something had to be done, and quickly, if the woman was not to be murdered before his very eyes. In a flash the ancient murderer reviewed the situation. Fifty-two murders he had committed. One more could make no great difference. Since he would have to atone for the others he could just as well make it fifty-three. Even if he were to stay in hell forever he could not stand by and see this woman murdered. And so he set upon the man and killed him. When he came to the holy man he told him what had happened, whereupon the holy man smiled and said: "Have you looked at the black cloth I gave you?" He had forgotten all about the black cloth since the fifty-third murder. Trembling he took it out and gazed upon it. It had turned white. . . .

There are murders and *murders* then. There is the kind that enslaves and the kind that liberates. But the final objective is to murder the murderer. The last act in the drama of "the ego and his own" is to murder one's own murderous self. The man who with the fifty-third murder renounces all hope of salvation is saved. To commit murder in full consciousness of the enormity of the crime is an act of liberation. It is heroic, and only those are capable of it who have purified their hearts of murder. Murder sanctioned by the Church, the State, or the community is murder just the same. Authority is the voice of confusion. The only authority is the individual conscience. To murder through fear, or love of country, is as bad as to murder from anger or greed. *To murder murder one has to have clean hands and a pure heart.*

If the Creator be all-powerful, all-wise, all beneficent why, it is often asked, does He permit us to murder one another? There are many answers to this conundrum, but the man who cherishes freedom realizes that the way to heaven is through hell. How can we eliminate what through lack of experience we do not understand? Murder is conflict on the lowest level, no more excusable when perpetrated en masse than when perpetrated by the individual. The man who attains to power and mastery, real power, real mastery, never makes use of his godhood for selfish reasons. The magician always breaks his magic wand eventually. Shakespeare understood that when he wrote *The Tempest*. Whitman demonstrated it when he elected to live the life of the common man. The Bodhisattva realizes it in renouncing the bliss of Nirvana. The whole world will understand and realize this simple truth eventually, slowly, one by one, through endless trial and error. The miraculous nature of power is made clear to us by those who renounced it. Power is in the being, not the having. Power is everywhere, in the tiniest atom as much as the dynamo. Those who know the secret of it are those who realize that it is free and that it destroys those who would possess it and use it for their own glorification. Murder is the crudest manifestation of power. Murder is fear in the service of a ghost.

Since the democratic wars, which began with Napoleon, the passion for making war has dwindled. The manner in which America went to war in 1917 is significant. Never before in the history of the world had there been coined the slogan—*"a war to end war."* We failed in our high purpose because we were unwilling to accept the responsibility which this magnificent gesture entailed. We were *not* without selfish motives, as we pretended. Hand in hand with the desire to bring about the end of all war was the desire to "make the world safe for democracy." Not real democracy, but the American brand. We did not open the way to debate and experiment. We only enabled our allies, who were full of fear and greed, to reestablish dominion over the defeated. We stood by and watched them shackle and manacle their victims. We did everything possible to abort the one promising experiment which the war brought about.

Now the task has to be performed all over again, this time at greater cost, greater risk, greater sacrifice. During the twenty years of moral stagnation which followed upon the last war the great body of Americans became more than ever disillusioned about making war. We waited to be attacked. We knew we would be attacked. We invited it. It was the only way to salve our conscience. We gained nothing from the last war, not even the gratitude of those whom we saved from destruction. We start out even more confused this time, avowedly to save our own skins and rather shamefacedly to save the world. *We will not save the world*—let us admit that immediately. If God could not do it, by sending his only begotton Son, how can we, a people swollen with pride and self-satisfaction? It doesn't matter whether you believe in the Christ story or not. The legend is profound and tragically beautiful. It has truth in it. The Son of God came to awaken the world by his example. *How he lived* is the important thing, not how he died. We are all crucified, whether we know it or not.

Nations reflect the cowardice and selfishness of the peoples which constitute them. It may have been possible once to serve God and country simultaneously. That is no longer true. The peoples of the earth have a great and compelling urge to unite. The boundaries established by nationalism are no longer valid. People are now murdering one another in a confused effort to break down these boundaries. Those who realize the true nature of the issue are at peace, even though they wield the sword.

Freedom without self-mastery is a snare and a delusion. Do we want power over others, or do we want liberation? The true liberators want to establish a world in which there is neither master nor slave, the democracy which Lincoln advocated. The warrior of the future will murder freely, without orders from above. He will murder whatever is murderous in human nature. He will not be an avenger but a liberator. He will not fight to destroy an "ism" but to destroy the destroyers, *whoever* they be and *wherever* they be. He will go on fighting even after peace is declared. He will make war until war becomes the lifeless thing which at heart it is.

Murder, murder! It's a fascinating subject. No end to it, seemingly. You know what it's like to kill a spider, an ant, a fly, a mosquito. You do it automatically, without the least compunction. Somehow it's not so easy to adopt that attitude with regard to human beings, even when the latter are annoying or dangerous, as the case may be. In a war such as the present one human beings are being polished off like fleas. To imagine the possibilities ahead, should we really discover that human Flit I spoke of, is almost unthinkable. Right now, at this point in the game, it is difficult to say whether the discoverer would be hailed as a saviour or an enemy to human society. If he springs from *our* side of the fence he will probably be looked upon as the saviour of mankind; if from the other side then as the Devil incarnate. *Is that so, or isn't it?* It's a moral dilemma of the first water. The so-called honest citizen who, in casting his vote for Tweedledum or Tweedledee feels that he has done his duty by the State, will of course refuse to occupy his mind with such a moral problem. It's too fantastic, too remote. He went to the polls last election, both sides promising to keep him out of the war, and he cast a mighty vote. Then the dirty Japs came and stabbed us in the back. Of course neither Tweedledum nor Tweedledee had expected such a dénouement. They were aghast, both of them, at such perfidy. And so war was solemnly declared. We were attacked by a treacherous enemy, our honor was violated. Just yesterday I saw Roosevelt and Churchill posing for the photographers. They were sitting side by side, and Roosevelt was beaming all over. Churchill looked a ringer for Schweik the good soldier. These are the heavenly twins who are going to save the world for us. Angelic creatures, I must say. Mind you, there'll be a bit of hard sledding first. We may have to sacrifice twenty-five or thirty million men, to say nothing of the enemy's losses. But when it's over there'll be an end of Hitler and Mussolini—and perhaps of that feeble-minded yellow-bellied Emperor Hirohito. It'll be worth it, what! A year from now, or two years or five or ten or twenty, we may have the pleasure of again seeing our two leaders arm in arm—when it comes time to inspect the graves of the dead. They will have to go places to bless all the dead this time. But with new inventions coming along they will probably be able to visit all the dead this time. But with new inventions coming along they will probably be able to visit all the graves in jig time. If any one reading these lines imagines for one moment that it wasn't necessary to sacrifice all these lives I advise him to keep his mouth closed. There *was* no other way out, you understand. Over 200,000,000 people, hypnotized by their insane leaders, refused to see that the democratic way of life is the best. Somehow, possibly because of the bad example we gave them, they remained unconvinced. Or perhaps they were just lazy-minded and decided that, if they had to fight, they might as well fight for their own way of life. That's a possibility too. Anyway, under the divine tutelage of Roosevelt and Churchill, we are now going to convince them—by extirpating them. Stalin will have something to say about it too, don't forget, because for the moment he's a democrat too. Good old Stalin! Only a few months ago he was an assassin, a fiend who was putting to death a helpless little country like Finland.[1] Some say that Stalin is even more democratic than Roosevelt or Churchill, believe it or not. They say he doesn't trust his democratic partners completely. I don't know why, because our hands are clean, we always act above board, as they say. We never help the little countries unless they're on the right side of the fence. *Strictly neutral*—until we're attacked and our own rights placed in jeopardy! Spain, Greece, Holland, Denmark, Belgium, Norway—we've always given them fine words of encouragement, haven't we? Gentleman-like, you know. Even with a big country like China we were behaving strictly according to Hoyle—until the Pearl Harbor fiasco. No more scrap-iron now for the dirty Japs—we're through with them. China, you will be rescued too—just wait a bit! *And India?* Well now, that's a horse of another color. Don't be so impatient, dear India. You will be freed, in time. Roosevelt and Churchill will arrange everything—when the proper moment comes. First we must get Hitler—he's the one who's responsible for this terrible mess. Impossible even to think straight until he's eliminated. You see how it is, don't you? *Be reasonable!*

Suppose we win the war, as we undoubtedly will, because we *must*, don't you know. Every one will get a square deal, including Hitler, Mussolini and Hirohito the feeble-minded yellow-belly. Austria will become Austrian again; Czechoslovakia Czechoslovakian; Poland Polish; Denmark Danish; France French; Hungary Hungarian; Greece Greek; China Chinese; Finland Finnish; Latvia Latvian; Spain Spanish. Et cetera, et cetera, et cetera. Everything will be put in place again, just as it was before Hitler.

[1] Now he's putting her to death again, but this time its O.K.—she deserved it.

It will be a new A.D. for the world, only this time everybody will have to be satisfied. We won't stand for any grousing. Wilhelmina must be put back on her throne. Haakon must be put back on *his* throne. (That is, if they're still alive and hankering for the job.) Hirohito of course must die, and so must Hitler and Mussolini. We've had enough of these bastards—they damned near ruined the world. And when we polish these maniacs off we don't want any revolution to spring up either. None of that nonsense this time. Revolutions are not democratic—they're disturbing, that's what. The Russian revolution, of course, was different. They made a good job of it, as we see now twenty years later. There *are* exceptions, naturally. But all that is in the past. Russia has been doing magnificently recently—just like any other democratic country. In fact, almost too good. We want her to act discreetly when this affair is over. Stalin, no monkey business! Yes, we've got to go cautiously when it comes to re-arranging the world. A little country like Bosnia or Croatia—an "enclave," we call it—can cause a lot of trouble. And then there's France, don't forget. Now she's half Vichy and half Pluto. We've got to fuse or weld the irreconcilables—gently, skillfully, of course. With an acetylene torch, if necessary. Can't allow France to slip back into a monarchical form of government. That would be disastrous. The monarchy is all right for Norway, Belgium, Holland and such like—or for England. But not for France. Why? Well *because* . . .

You see, there are going to be little problems coming up. We must be patient and willing to cooperate. That is, *they* must, the other fellows. We wouldn't be sacrificing the lives and fortunes of our good honest citizens did we not know what we were about. We honestly avoided the issue as long as possible, did we not? We had been worried about the world, what it was coming to, ever since Hitler began his crazy antics. But it wasn't our place to interfere—until we were ourselves attacked and dishonored—and by a half-witted yellow-belly of all things. That really was unforgivable. And yet, if he hadn't spat in our face, who knows—perhaps we wouldn't yet be ready to assume the task of putting the world in order. We have nothing to gain from this conflict. That's clear to every one, I hope. All we want is to see the restoration of the old status quo. We've kept all maps of the ancient world; we know just what belongs to whom, and we're going to see to it that what's his name gets his what not. And this time, dear fellow-Europeans, dear Chinese, dear Hindus, dear Patagonians, dear Eskimos, dear Zulus, dear Zombies, we want to be spared the humiliation of receiving a kick in the slats for our pains. Though we had to wait until we were treacherously attacked by that degenerate son of the Sun, we do not intend to stop fighting once we have driven the invader from our colonial outposts. We took a terrible slap in the face, but it was good for us, it enabled us to get properly worked up about the plight of the world. To be "the arsenal of the world" was all right as political propaganda—because at bottom, you know, we just loathe and abhor war—but now that we can use the arsenal ourselves we feel better. War is a nasty thing to watch, but once you're in it you feel differently about it. If you want to see an all-out war, boy, just keep your eye on us! We'll fry them alive, every man, woman and child that opposes us. Yes sir, no holding us back once we get our dander up. Nagasaki will look like a flaming rum omelette once we concentrate our attention on it. Berlin too, I'm telling you. And if it weren't for the Pope and his dear Vatican, I'd say the same for Rome. But that's a ticklish proposition, the Vatican. We don't want to blow up his Holiness the Pope accidentally. That's understandable, is it not? The Pope stands for peace—almost at any price. We all do, as a matter of fact—it's only in this matter of the price that we differ from one another. Even the Crusaders were peaceable souls. But they wanted Christ's bones to be left untouched, to lie in Christian soil. And so they fought tooth and nail to destroy the infidels. Some of them returned with the most amazing booty—but that's another story. I was almost on the point of saying that the civilization of Europe began with the return of the victorious Crusaders—you know, Chartres, Amiens, Beauvais, Notre Dame. It would be strange now, wouldn't it, if our Crusaders came back from Moscow and Leningrad, after signing the Peace Treaty, and found themselves afire with the spirit of collective government. That *would* give a queer twist to the situation. Let's hope that the good democratic spirit will survive all temptation. After all, it's a Christian world that we want to save, isn't it? Tomorrow is Christmas day and we

Christians all over the world will unite in prayer, as we have been doing for nigh on to two thousand years. It seems a little discouraging, perhaps, that after two thousand years we are praying for peace in full uniform, but that's not our fault. If it hadn't been for Hitler and that yellow-faced pagan Hirohito, we'd probably be at peace, isn't that so? It's amazing how, just when we get set for the millennium, some warmonger comes along and upsets our equilibrium. Fortunately we have our own dialectic. That instructs us how to build a permanent peace while being realistically on the alert to make war whenever and wherever necessary. We know what the goal is, which is more, I suppose, than one can say for Hitler and his satellites. The goal is Peace—but to get there you would be a damned fool if you didn't keep a revolver, or at least a hand grenade, in your hip pocket. There have always been, and there still are apparently, two kinds of people in the world: those who want peace and those who want war. Logic dictates that the peaceable ones must extinguish the war-like ones. That is to say, in order to be peaceful you must be a better fighter than the warrior. It sounds like a conundrum at first, but then the history of the world has demonstrated that it is very clear and simple. Wars are getting less and less frequent. We've had about six or eight wars in my life-time, but that's nothing compared to years ago. Before Napoleon's day only professional armies waged war. Nowadays everybody fights—to bring about peace. The last fight will be a splendid one, I'm sure of it. We've only begun to fight, as the saying goes. You see, the more peaceful we get the better we fight. If we were just fighting to fight we might grow slack, because even fighting can grow dull and monotonous if you think only of fighting. But to fight for peace—that's marvelous. That puts iron in you. When the millennium comes we'll all be tough as steel. We'll know how to enjoy peace, just as a murderer learns to enjoy the electric chair. In his zeal to kill, the murderer forgets about the electric chair—but it's always there, always waiting for him. That's his bliss, and when he sizzles and fries he realizes it and thanks the Creator for having made him a murderer. So it is with us. In our zeal to destroy the enemies of peace we forget that war brings about the death and destruction of all that is human and sacred. Peace awaits us, yes—but it is the peace of the grave.

The only peace we seem capable of understanding is the peace of death. We make one grand crusade after another in order to rescue the tomb of Christ from the hands of the infidel. We preserve the dead Christ, never the living one. Merry Christmas, I say, and peace on earth! I will not step into St. Patrick's Cathedral to offer up a prayer. I will not appeal to an impotent God to stop the carnage. I will not stand like a savage before the altar of superstition with a javelin in my hand and a mumbo-jumbo incantation on my lips. I will not ask the Creator to bless America without including Japan, Germany, Italy, Roumania, Bulgaria, Hungary and the other countries of the world. I cannot consider myself as innocent and the other fellow guilty. I am not a hypocrite, neither am I an ignoramus, though the society in which I was reared has done its best to make me behave like both. I say that peace can be brought about any time—*when we want it!* We have found the cunning and the ingenuity to invent the most diabolical weapons of destruction. We are versed in the art of war as no people before us has ever been. War is what we wanted—not peace! And now we have it, I say once again: "Merry Christmas! And a happy New Year!"

The above is scarcely off the typewriter when, on my way to lunch (it is the day before Christmas), I pick up the *N.Y. Post*. At the Italian restaurant, where I usually eat, I spread it open and lo! I come upon the following:

"CHRISTMAS IN MOSCOW"

by

A. T. Steele

It's not about Christmas at all because, as the correspondent explains in his special radio to *The Post*, December 25th will be just another working day to the Russian people. Christmas will come on January 7th in Moscow. No, it's about the failure of the Germans to celebrate Christmas in Moscow this year. There are two items in this message which have a little of the Christmas spirit in them. The first is this:

"I keep thinking of that callow boy with silky growth of down on his cheeks who lay under a snow-burdened fir tree on the battlefield at Klin, which I visited the other day. He was one of many German dead, but I noticed him especially because of his youth, the bandage half wrapped around his head and the way his frozen eyes looked unseeingly upward. He had apparently been wounded and had died of cold.

"Young Otto Seiter is probably listed on Hitler's casualty rolls as 'missing.' But I know he is dead. He won't be home this Christmas or any other Christmas. There are a lot like him."

He goes on to speak of the letters which he retrieved from the battlefield, letters of German wives and mothers to their men and boys. "They make appropriate reading for Christmas Eve," he cables, "because they remind you of something you are prone to forget in the heat of the war—that enemy soldiers are not beasts or monsters but human beings who have been hypnotized into blind allegiance to the mad idea of a half-mad leader. Scarcely any of these letters mentioned politics and only one of them closed with the salutation 'Heil Hitler' . . . In all the letters I examined . . . I found no words of bitterness against the Russians."

Yes, I agree—it sure does make appropriate reading for Christmas Eve. It's rather edifying, if I may say so. *Read it again, please.*

On the front page of this same journal the Pope gives his Five Points for Peace. Also very edifying. The trouble is nobody pays a damned bit of attention to the Pope. He's just a symbol of spiritual power. Anyway, among the other things he says: "True respect for treaties must be observed, and the principles of freedom and equality of rights for all people must underlie the new day." It's obvious that His Holiness is also a forward looker. There's such a gentle, passive, civilized note to his plea—might have been written by Woodrow Wilson himself. I'm making a note to have the Viking Press send him a copy of *The Bertrand Russell Case.* In praying for peace so assiduously this little drama of spiritual sabotage by the good Catholics of America may have escaped his attention.

If some one should give us Germany and Japan this minute, we would be so embarrassed we would hardly know what to do or say . . . We do not have the smallest notion of what we are going to do when we win. We are hopelessly unprepared for victory . . . We must face the truth. The hardest blow that could strike us at the moment would be victory. We would pass it from hand to hand as if it were hot, and would not know where to set it down. Our Congress once did conduct some rather magnificent debates as to what to do with new territories as they came into the democratic system. We even discussed whether there should be slavery or freedom in the new States. Both houses now sit tight, with nothing to say. Not to be able to put into specific, hard words the things the Colin Kellys are dying for is a confession of ineptness.

These are not my words, dear, gentle reader. These come to you through the courtesy of the *N.Y. Post* on Christmas Eve. They were written by Samuel Grafton in his column called "I'd Rather Be Right." And most of the time, to do him justice, he is right. Sometimes he's so damned right that it almost sounds treasonable. But everybody knows that Sam is on the right side; he can get away with murder.

I wish I had a little joke to tell now. It's such a solemn moment, and we've been through so many like it before. "Now is the time," as Dorothy Thompson says, "for the United States to wage the most brilliant psychological warfare against Germany and Italy and amongst the people of Europe." (Why leave out the Japs, I wonder?) "But," she adds, "no strategy of psychological warfare has been developed, and no command and staff capable of waging it have been created."

Yes, as Dorothy says—"it is a negligence which will prolong the war, and it should be remedied immediately." But then, if you follow Sam Grafton's reasoning, on the same page, you will see that we need a little time—because we haven't the least idea yet what our victory program should be. It's a bit confusing, to say the least.

A little joke, as I was saying a minute ago. Yes, Lincoln had his little joke just before reading the Emancipation Proclamation. Incidentally, you would think, if you were not a student of history, that the Emancipation Proclamation came first, and then the attack on Fort Sumter. But no, it was the other way round. It's like the Pope again. He talks about good, honest to God peace treaties, about non-persecution of the Church et cetera, before he knows what the outcome of the war will be. Anyway, the story goes that Lincoln had called his cabinet members together on a very important matter. The war was on some time already and the dead were rather numerous, to say nothing of the halt, the blind, the maimed, the mutilated. Lincoln has a book in front of him—by Artemas Ward. He reads a passage aloud to the assembled scarecrows and he laughs heartily in doing so. Nobody else laughs. So he tries it again. And again he laughs fit to burst his sides. But the grave-diggers look askance. They are at a loss to understand this ill-timed hilarity. Has he gone off his nut, they wonder? Lincoln feels sorry for them—for their lack of humor. It's a good book, he tells them, and you ought to sit down and read it. It would do you a world of good. Something like that. Then he quietly reaches into the tail pocket of his flap-doodle walking coat and, extracting the Emancipation Proclamation, he reads it to them quietly and solemnly . . . Whether it be true or not, it's a damned good story. Lincoln had his feet on the ground, as we would say. But his head was in the clouds. He had a quiet, sure confidence that right would prevail—in the end. He was ready to sacrifice any number of lives, his own included, to bring about that end. "As I would not be a *slave*, so I would not be a *master*. This expresses my idea of democracy. Whatever differs from this, to the extent of the difference, is no democracy." Those are Lincoln's words. It's a pity we never gave heed to them. We freed the black slaves, or we thought we had, but we forgot to free the white slaves. We freed the Filipinos and the Cubans and the Porto Ricans, but we didn't free ourselves. We rescued France and Belgium from the heels of the German military clique but then we put the Germans in the clink. So now, while Russia deals the death-blow to the Germans, we're getting ready to wipe out Hitlerism and all the other isms, as well as that degenerate yellow-bellied Hirohito.

Nobody can deny that we're the most philanthropic-minded people in the world. A few months ago there were eight or nine million people unemployed in this wonder-working land. Now it's down to about a million, an irreducible minimum, I believe it's called. We work fast, I'll say. And all because that half-witted Hirohito stabbed us in the back. Some say we had no right to be taken by surprise—criminal negligence they call it. Others seem pleased that it turned out so—it proved that we were angels, that we had no intention of going to war with Japan, that our fleet and our fortifications were created only to *frighten* the enemy away. It's six one way and a half dozen the other. I was always of the opinion that if you make cannon you've got to use them some time or other. I'm never surprised when a gun goes off unexpectedly. I expect the unexpected. What does surprise me is that people who believe in making cannon should be aggrieved to see them used so effectively. "In time of peace prepare for war," said the Father of this beloved country. He was a realist, just as Stalin is today. He didn't get himself elected a third time by promising to keep his people out of war. He was no half-wit. No sir, he was an aristocrat, a great land-holder with slaves and port and sherry in the cellar. The people were so grateful to him for making this country a democracy that they almost made him a king. About seventy years later there appeared in the State of Massachusetts, noted even then for its hypocrisy, repression and iniquity, a troublesome character who sensed that all was not well with the government of these United States. What's more, he had the courage to say so. He wrote a paper called "Civil Disobedience" which we look upon today as a monument to the democratic spirit. Here is a citation from this beautifully embalmed document:

"The progress from an absolute to a limited monarchy, from a limited monarchy to a democracy, is a progress towards a true respect for the individual. Even the Chinese philosopher was wise enough to regard the individual as the basis of the empire. Is a democracy, such as we know it, the last improvement possible in government? Is it not possible to take a step further towards recognizing and organizing the rights of man? There will never be a really free and enlightened State until the State comes to recognize the individual as a higher and independent power, from which all its own power and authority are derived, and treats him accordingly. I please myself with imagining a State at last which can afford to be just to all men, and to treat the individual with respect as a neighbor; which even would not think it inconsistent with its own repose if a few were to live aloof from it, not meddling with it, nor embraced by it, who fulfilled all the duties of neighbors and fellow-men. A State which bore this kind of fruit, and suffered it to drop off as fast as it ripened, would prepare the way for a still more perfect and glorious State, which also I have imagined, but not yet anywhere seen."

That was Henry David Thoreau, author of *Walden* and defender of John Brown, speaking. No doubt the only excuse we can make today for such a treasonable anarchistic utterance is to palm him off as a half-witted graduate of the then Transcendentalist School of Philosophy. About the only person I can think of who would have dared to defend him, in our time, had he openly expressed his desire to live a life apart from the most holy and sacrosanct State, is the recently defunct Justice of the Supreme Court, Louis D. Brandeis. In the case of Whitney versus the State of California, Brandeis, whose vote was overruled, wrote a brief in which there appeared these words:

"Those who won our independence by revolution were not cowards. They did not fear political change. They did not exalt order at the cost of liberty. To courageous, self-reliant men, with confidence in the power of free and fearless reasoning applied through the processes of popular government, no danger flowing from speech can be deemed clear and present, unless the incidence of evil apprehended is so imminent that it may befall before there is opportunity for full discussion. If there be time to expose through discussion the falsehood and fallacies, to avert the evil by the processes of education, the remedy to be applied is more speech, not enforced silence. Only an emergency can justify repression. Such must be the rule if authority is to be reconciled with freedom. Such, in my opinion, is the command of the Constitution. It is, therefore, always open to Americans to challenge a law abridging free speech and assembly by showing that there was no emergency justifying it."

Nevertheless, when the good shoe-maker and the poor fish-peddler found themselves at the bar of justice in the benighted State of Massachusetts some few years ago, they were unable to get a fair, honest hearing. Despite all the noble words handed down by the upstanding members of the judiciary, and they are the wordiest people on God's green earth, Sacco and Vanzetti were foully murdered. But just before he went to the chair Vanzetti gave birth to a few lines which are destined to be as immortal as any of Lincoln's or Jefferson's . . .

"If it had not been for these thing, I might have live out my life talking at street corners to scorning men. I might have died, unmarked, unknown, a failure. Now we are not a failure. This is our career and our triumph. Never in our full life could we hope to do such work for tolerance, for joostice, for man's understanding of man as now we do by accident. Our words—our lives—our pains—nothing! The taking of our lives—lives of a good shoe-maker and a poor fish-peddler—all! That last moment belongs to us—that agony is our triumph."

A few days ago, moved by the President's declaration of war, the newspapers gave some space to the remarks made by John Haynes Holmes, Minister of the Community Church, N.Y., in tendering his resignation. He had just finished a sermon, it seems, on the 150th anniversary of the Bill of Rights. Mr. Holmes is quoted as saying that "neither as clergyman nor as citizen would he participate in the war," adding however that "neither would he oppose, obstruct or interfere with officials, soldiers or citizens in the performance of what they regard as their patriotic duty."

Then he threw this bombshell:

"I will be loyal and obedient to my government, and loyal and obedient to my God; and when these loyalties conflict, I will choose, as did the Apostles, to 'obey God rather than men.'"

I wait to see if Mr. Holmes will be condemned to prison. In the last world war there were three great figures who, because they openly announced their opposition to war, suffered dire persecution. They were Romain Rolland, Bertrand Russell and Eugene V. Debs. Unimpeachable characters, all three. I'm going to give you Debs' speech on being condemned to prison, but before I do so I want to mention the Very Reverend Dean Inge's statement about a German theologian named Harnack. "War," writes the gloomy Dean, "is a very horrible thing, an unmixed evil, a reversion to barbarism no less than cannibalism, human sacrifice and judicial torture. Most of us think that we were obliged to resist German aggression, which threatens to extinguish liberty, and with liberty all that makes life worth living, over the whole continent of Europe. But no good can ever come out of war. It is a flat negation of Christianity. Even Harnack, a Prussian and the most learned theologian in Europe, said that it is futile to deny that Christ condemned war absolutely." He adds that the Quakers believe they are the only consistent Christians. And what is the history of the Quaker movement? According to recent authority on the subject, the Quaker movement was met with terrific persecution, first from mob violence and later from organized legal procedure. George Fox himself endured eight imprisonments, and more than fifteen thousand Quakers were imprisoned in England before the period of toleration, of whom three hundred and sixty-six died under their sufferings. Four Quakers were hanged on Boston Common and a great number in the American Colonies endured beatings and mutilation.

Today the Quakers are exempt from military service, in these United States. But what a battle! A man who is not a Quaker, like Eugene V. Debs for example, gets it in the neck. Yet no Quaker could have made a more simple, honest, dignified statement of his views than did Eugene V. Debs. Here are his beautiful, moving words:

"Gentleman of the Jury, I am accused of having obstructed the war. I admit it. Gentlemen, I abhor war. I would oppose the war if I stood alone. When I think of a cold, glittering steel bayonet being plunged in the white, quivering flesh of a human being, I recoil with horror.

"Men talk about holy wars. There are none. War is the trade of unholy savages and barbarians . . .

"Gentlemen of the Jury, I am accused of being unpatriotic. I object to that accusation. It is not true. I believe in patriotism. I have never uttered a word against the flag. I love the flag as a symbol of freedom . . .

"I believe, however, in a wider patriotism. Thomas Paine said, 'My country is the world. To do good is my religion.' That is the sort of patriotism I believe in. I am an Internationalist. I believe that nations have been pitted against nations long enough in hatred, in strife, in warfare. I believe there ought to be a bond of unity between all of these nations. I believe that the human race consists of one great family. I love the people of this country, but I don't hate a human being because he happens to be born in some other country. Why should I? Like myself, he is the image of his Creator. I would infinitely rather serve him and love him than to hate him and kill him . . .

"Yes, I am opposed to killing him. I am opposed to war. I am perfectly willing on that account to be branded as a traitor. And if it is a crime under the American law to be opposed to human bloodshed, I am perfectly willing to be branded as a criminal and to end my days in a prison cell . . .

"And now, Gentlemen of the Jury, I am prepared for the sentence. I will accept your verdict. What you will do to me does not matter much. Years ago I recognized my kinship with all living beings, and I made up my mind that I was not one whit better than the meanest of earth. I said then, and I say now, that while there is a lower class, I am in it; while there is a criminal element, I am of it; while there is a soul in prison, I am not free."

"Unless from us the future takes place, we are death only," said D. H. Lawrence. A monumental statement. Meanwhile death is piling up all around us. The political and military leaders, if they do not actually make light of it, discount it as they would a promptly paid bill. The bill is victory, they say, and they are willing to pay in advance no matter how many millions of lives it costs. They are even ready to sacrifice their own lives, but fortunately for them most of them are so placed that the risk is slight. When the war is ended the victory will be theirs, no gainsaying it. The dead won't count, nor the millions of maimed and mutilated ones who will go on living until death robs them of the fruits of victory.

Death, especially on a wholesale scale, can raise an awful stench. On the battle-fronts now and then a truce is declared to give the opposing forces an opportunity to bury their dead. It has never occurred to the political and military cliques that it might be an excellent innovation to incorporate among the polite rules of civilized warfare a clause stipulating that every thirty or sixty days a truce shall be declared (for twenty-four hours, let us say) to reconsider the supposed basis of the erstwhile conflict. What would happen, I wonder, if the armies waging war all over the earth, and the friends and relatives supporting these armies, could pause every so often in the process of blood-letting and honestly examine their conscience? Supposing further—and now we get really fantastic—that during these let-ups a vote could be taken on both sides of the fence to see whether the fight should be continued or not. It is not altogether impossible to imagine that perhaps only the higher officers of the armies and navies, together with the congressmen and of course the various dictators, would be in favor of continuing with the slaughter. The great body of men and women, the ones of whom the great sacrifice is being demanded, would most likely yell for peace. Perhaps even "peace at any price"! *If they were given an honest chance!*

The stench of death . . . One day we read that 4,000 Germans were killed on the Russian front. Another day it may be 16,000 or 23,000. Fine! *Progress*, we say. Or, if we wipe out a nest of dirty Japs, still better . . . *bully!* According to this logic, the most magnificent step forward that we could make would be to annihilate them utterly. (Let's get busy and trot out that human Flit I was talking about earlier!) Now the military man will tell you, and utterly sincerely too, that annihilation of the enemy is not the goal at all. The objective, according to the military expert, is merely to render *hors de combat* the enemy's army or navy, as the case may be. That accomplished, the war is won. If it can be done without loss of life, so much the better. The most brilliant defeat that could be inflicted, from the standpoint of these experts, would be a bloodless one. That would indeed be something to record in the annals of history! That would make war look quite jolly, for a change. It would be most superlatively magnificent: a super-duper sort of victory, if you get what I mean. Some people credit Hitler with having had some such idea. He had it all figured out— it was to be a push-over, as we say.

However, to get back to war as we know it, nothing like this is going to happen in our time. War now means just as it did in the past, "blood, sweat and tears"—oodles of it. Not blood, sweat and tears for those who launch it, but for those who have to go through with it. And that means practically everybody, except, as I said before, the favored few who direct the show. The latter are just as eager to give their lives as the little fellows, don't make any mistake about that. Only, because of the peculiar set-up involved in these fracases, they are somehow never privileged to enjoy this supreme sacrifice. They must be protected in order that the others can be most efficiently sacrificed. You can understand what anguish this causes the political and military leaders of any war. (Yet few of them ever pine away because of it. On the contrary, they seem to grow tough as steel.) However, if it were possible to take them by surprise, assure them that nothing they said would be held against them, it's just possible you'd discover that they were fed up with it too. A moment later, to be sure, they would be ready to deny such weak sentiments. "What would people think?" they'd say. Always that to fall back on. *The people!* It was the people who wanted the war. Of course. Yes, when they're stabbed in the back the people may cry for war, *but*—how does it happen that they get stabbed in the back, and at just the right moment? And so, right or wrong, willing or unwilling, "the war must be fought to a just and victorious conclusion!" From time immemorial every leader has proclaimed that high and mighty truth. That's why the future is always so full of death. Right or wrong, the war must be continued, always. No looking back. No looking forward. *Head down and charge!* That's the order of the day. Victory? Just around the corner. And if not victory, death. Death, death, death. Always death. Or, if you're lucky, your old job back in the mines. The future? It never begins. You had your future yesterday, don't you remember? There is only the present, and the present is never pleasant. Only the future is bright. But then, the future never takes place. The future always recedes, that's the law. When the original Fascists have been vanquished, or exterminated, we'll all be Fascists—that's what the future, if there is to be any future, promises. And that means more death, more blood, sweat and tears, more Churchills, more Roosevelts, more Hitlers, more Stalins. There won't be any more Mussolinis, probably, because he for one has been thoroughly exploded. But there may be another Hirohito, and mark my words, he'll be a yellow-belly too.

It's going to be a lovely world tomorrow, when everything is properly organized and running smoothly. It may take a hundred years, but what's that (Man lives in the eternal—*when he lives*.) There may even be another war—or several—between times, but that shouldn't disturb us any. We got through this one, didn't we? You see the logic . . . it runs as smooth as tooth-paste from an old-fashioned tube. Incidentally, you won't have to worry about toothpaste when the New Day is ushered in; we'll all be fitted with Dr. Cowen's beautiful lightweight platinum teeth. Only cows will chew with their own teeth in the future. Everything's going to be under control, you'll see. Should a new enemy arise (though it's hard to see why he should, with Utopia just in the offing), we'll know how to deal with him. Nothing must or shall hinder our plans for the worldwide improvement of the human race. The human race, of course, will not be understood to include such inferior peoples as the Zulus and the Hottentots, for example. No sir, let's not fall into that sublime error. Only people walking around in pants, with Bibles in their hands and platinum teeth in their mouths, and preferably only those speaking the English language, will be regarded as belonging to the human race.

Utopia, then, will be a world in which the white race (half Slav, half Anglo-Saxon) will know no enemies and will have as neighbors such harmless peoples as the Javanese, the Hindus, the Malays, and perhaps the Arabs too—if they behave. On the fringe of our tremendous colonial possessions there will be the not-quite-human species, who are no longer a menace . . . in other words, the primitives. These will gradually be absorbed into the blood-stream by the process of higher education. They will be "our little brown brothers," so to speak, and will work for us (willingly, of course) like bees and ants. For how otherwise will they be able to make themselves fit to enjoy the fruits of civilization?

There will be only two languages to begin with: Russian and English. After a time the Russians will give up their mother tongue and speak English only. What the Chinese and Hindus will speak will hardly concern us since, though numerically superior, perhaps even morally and spiritually superior, they will be of no consequence in the management of a Utopian world. As for the primitives, they have survived these last fifty to a hundred thousand years without the knowledge of English, so why worry?

There will be no money, of course. Not even the hat money of the Penangs. As it used to say on the silver dollar: *e pluribus unum!* The bookkeeper will be eliminated, and the breed of lawyers too, since most litigation arises over money transactions. The absence of money will also solve the debt problem which arises after every war to end war. No money, no debts! *All for one and one for all,* just like it said once on the silver dollar. The New Deal will go into effect throughout the whole pluralistic universe. Naturally there will have to be a new flag: the flag of Utopia. I should imagine it will be pure white, signifying "peace, purity, and forgiveness of our sins." No emblem will be needed, not even the hammer and sickle . . . not even a *plastic* hammer and sickle. Nothing but a white piece of cloth—of the finest material. Under this banner, for the first time in the history of mankind, everybody will get a break, perhaps even the Zulus and the Hottentots. War will be a thing of the past; all our enemies will be dead or incapacitated. Should any new ones threaten to arise, get out the Flit! Simple, what! No need for standing armies any longer. Just oodles of Flit—and a big squirt gun. To be sure, it may be necessary to do a bit of wholesale murdering—clean house, so to speak—before all the enemy are eliminated. It may take ten to twenty years to eradicate the last Jap, German, Bulgarian, Roumanian, Hungarian, Finn or other human pest, but we'll do it, we'll weed them out like vipers. The problem will be what to do with those of mixed blood. It will take a Solomon to decide that issue. However, with the education and training heretofore wasted in turning out admirals, generals and field marshals, we shall undoubtedly pave the way for the emergence of several Solomons. If necessary we can import a few from India or China.

With war eliminated and money eliminated, with the breed of lawyers and bookkeepers wiped out, with politics converted to management, with Solomons sitting in judgment upon all grave matters of dispute, can any intelligent person visualize even the possibility of a miscarriage? Under the slogan "all for one and one for all" the earth will slowly but surely be transformed into a Paradise. There will be no more struggle, except to surpass one another in virtue. There will be no more pain, except that which doctors and dentists impose. We will love one another to death.

Truly, if people would only realize what a glorious future is about to unroll, would they not this instant get down on their knees and devoutly offer up thanks to those great benefactors— Stalin, Churchill, Roosevelt and Madame Chiang Kai-shek? If they were to think about the matter profoundly, would they not also bless Hitler and Mussolini, and above all that yellow-bellied Hirohito, because, if these angelic monsters had not unleashed this grim catastrophe, we would never have thought to usher in the millennium. How true the saying: "It's an ill wind that blows no one some good!" In glory and significance all other wars pale before this one. That Ireland, Sweden, Spain, Portugal, Switzerland, India, Argentina have not evinced the spirit of the crusader is regrettable, but they will doubtless see the wisdom of this heroic strife when we make life more comfortable for them. With the Utopia to follow upon the close of this war the neutral countries will enjoy the same privileges and advantages as the ones that went to war.

The question may arise: what will become of the instinct to kill, which is so deep-rooted in the human being? Can an instinct be wholly extirpated? The answer is Yes and No, which is the answer to all fundamental questions. Men will still kill animals, birds of the air, and ground birds too, as well as insects, snakes and microbes. By the time a hundred years have rolled around there will be new, more intangible, still more invisible, creatures—if we may call them such—to kill. Don't worry, there are more millennia to come before killing is killed off altogether. But, if we stop killing one another, that is a big step forward. And that is all we are concerned about on the threshold of this Utopia. Just to stop killing one another en masse. It's taken us a long time to reach this point. Cannibalism has died out, at least among the civilized peoples of the earth. That took quite a long time to disappear, but it disappeared. Incest is no longer in vogue either, nor the practice of suttee, thanks to the humane conquerors of India. No, we should never despair. Every two or three hundred thousand years we make a real step forward. The point is not to take one step forward and three steps backward, which is what human beings usually do. With the facilities offered us by the higher education and all that rigamarole, however, there appears to be little danger that we shall go on repeating our old habit patterns.

If we were there now in that Utopia we all long to establish, and which none of us now living shall ever see, if we were there for just one moment, could take one swift backward glance at that old murderous self which made history so exciting, how odd everything would look to us! See, there stands a man with a javelin in his hand, ready to plunge it into the breast of a fellow man. There is another, with a hand grenade which he is making ready to hurl; when it hits the mark it will explode, and another fellow being, an "enemy," will be blown to bits. Why are they carrying on this way? Because they believe that by killing their fellow men they will make the world a better place to live in. And why are they so afraid of one another, why do they hate each other so? Because they all believe in a god of love. Do they not sense the inconsistent in their behavior? Yes, but they have a logic which accounts for all inconsistencies. By this logic they prove to themselves that to usher in the new life, to bring about the kingdom of heaven on earth, it is first necessary to slaughter all the enemies of mankind. And who are the enemy? You, me, anybody, according to how the wind blows . . .

If we could see it from over the line, this period of ten to twenty thousand years, which has been called civilization, would seem like a night of utter confusion. By comparison the savage lived in clear daylight. Civilization, compared with other periods the human race has lived through, will be like a parenthesis in the preamble to a new way of life. For there *will* be a new way of life, no matter how many wars have to be fought, no matter how many lives are destroyed.

With the conclusion of this war it is not even probable that we shall see the dissolution of national boundaries. To eliminate race prejudice no one can say how many more wars it will require. There are thousands of problems for which men will find no solution but war. No system of government now in vogue offers the slightest hope of a future free of war. The remedy for dissent is still, as it was in the past, subjugation or extirpation. The government has never existed which recognizes the freedom and equality of all men. As for freedom of thought, freedom to express one's ideas—not to speak of living them out—where is the government which ever permitted this? Conformity is the rule, and conformity will be the rule as long as men believe in governing one another.

Men of good-will need no government to regulate their affairs. In every age there is a very small minority which lives without thought of, or desire for, government. These men never brought about a war. So long as civilization lasts it is quite possible that this minority will never be substantially increased. Such men are not the products of our religious organizations or our educational systems; they live outside the cultural pattern of the times. The most we can say, in explanation of their appearance and existence, is that they are evolved beings. And here we must needs touch on the drawback to all schemes, Utopian or otherwise, for the improvement of human society: the failure inherent in all of them to recognize that the human race does not evolve at the same speed nor with the same rhythm. Where there is dream and wish fulfillment merely—and what else can there be if one focuses on society instead of the individual?—there is confusion and disillusionment. Even with red-hot bayonets up their rear, men cannot be prodded all at the same time into Paradise. It is this fact, of course, which the so-called realists, who are always defeatists, seize upon with grim relish in order to excuse and perpetuate the business of murder. With each war they pretend that they are preserving society from a dire fate, or that they are protecting the weak and the helpless. The men of wisdom, who are really the men of good-will, and who are found in every stratum of society and not in any particular class, never make such pretenses. They are often accused of being aloof, remote, out of touch with the world. Yet it is to them that all men turn for comfort and guidance in their hour of need. For, even the clod seems to sense that genuine disinterestedness is a source of strength.

If any particular set of men were destined to rule the world it would seem logical that it should be ruled by the men of wisdom. But that is not the case, and there is good reason for it. No one man, no set of men, is capable of ruling the world. The world is ruled by its own inner, mysterious laws. It evolves according to a logic which defies our man-made logic. The higher the type of man, moreover, the less inclined he feels to rule others; he lives in harmony with the world despite the fact that he is in total disagreement with the vast majority, as well as with the leaders of the world. Were there good reason to kill, he could find a thousand justifications to the ordinary man's one. The principal reason, however, for his failure to become embroiled in the world conflicts is his absence of fear. Accustomed as he is to live habitually in the world of ideas, he is not frightened when he learns that his neighbor thinks differently from him. Indeed, he might really become alarmed if he found that his neighbors were in agreement with him. The average man, on the contrary, is more frightened of alien ideas than of cold steel or flame throwers. He has spent most of his empty life getting adjusted to the few simple ideas which were thrust on him by his elders or superiors. Anything which menaces this precarious adjustment, which he calls his liberty, throws him into a panic. Let an alien idea become active, and the transition from fear to hate proceeds like clockwork. Trot out the word "enemy," and the whole bloody race behaves as if it had the blind staggers. The nit-wits who never showed the least ability to govern themselves suddenly get the idea that their last mission on earth is to teach the enemy good government. It makes no difference whether this nit-wit be a Communist, Fascist, or Democrat: the reaction is always the same. Just tell him that the other fellow is threatening his liberty, and he reaches for his gun—*automatically*.

And what is the little bundle of ideas around which this precious notion of liberty is formed? Private property, the sanctity of the home, the church he belongs to, the preservation of the political party, or the system, which gives him the privilege of being a drudge all his life. If he could but take one sweeping view of the planet, see what different things the same words mean everywhere, see how all men, including the primitives, believe that whatever they believe is right and just, and of course supremely intelligent, would he be so quick to reach for the sword or the gun? Yes, he would, because he has been educated to understand with his head but not with the rest of his being. As a civilized creature, a man can study and know the ways and customs of a thousand different peoples, yet insist on defending the ways of his own, even though he knows them to be stupid, inadequate or wrong. He will describe with irony and subtle discrimination the reasons why other peoples make war, but he will go to war himself when the time comes, even though he does not believe in killing. He will kill rather than be humiliated by his own people.

In how many wars have people killed who had no desire to kill? Many who killed one another had more in common with their own compatriots. Were men to seek their real enemies they would have only to turn round and examine the ranks behind them. If men were to realize who their true enemies were, what a scrimmage would ensue! But again, one of the disadvantages of living under civilized rule is that only those may be considered as enemies, and therefore killed or enslaved, whom the governments designate as such. To kill your commanding officer, for example, even though he be the bitterest enemy you have, is strictly taboo. So it goes . . . scholars killing scholars, poets killing poets, workers killing workers, teachers killing teachers, and no one killing the munitions makers, the politicians, the priests, the military idiots or any of the other criminals who sanction war and egg one on to kill one another off.

Just to take one element, the munitions makers, for example: who could be more international-minded than they? Come war and they will sell to any side that has the money to buy. Strictly neutral, these birds, until they see which way the wind blows. No amount of taxation impoverishes them; the longer the war lasts, the more the dead pile up, the fatter they grow. Imagine the colossal absurdity of supporting a body of men whose mission in life it is to supply us with the means of self-destruction. (Whereas it is a crime to attempt to take one's own life by one's own means, no matter how unbearable life becomes!) Nobody considers the munitions maker—not even the Communist, mind you—as an enemy. Yet he is the greatest enemy man has. He sits like a vulture and waits and prays for the day to come when we shall lose our reason and beg him to furnish us with his most expensive lethal products. Instead of being looked upon as a leper he is given a place of honor in human society; often he is knighted for his indubitably dubious services. On the other hand, Monsieur le Paris, who really performs a service for society, albeit a most disagreeable one, is shunned like a pariah. Strange paradox. If there is any logic to it it is thus: the man who by our own sanction justly removes a murderer from the ranks of society is a worthless wretch, whereas the man who provides the means of killing en masse, for no matter what reason good or bad, deserves a place of honor in our midst. Corollary logic: murder on a wholesale scale is always justifiable, as well as profitable and honorable, but ordinary murder, whether for passion or greed, is so disgraceful that even the man whose duty it is to make way with the culprit appears to us as tainted.

And what of all the plans fond parents make for their children's sake? Why bother to make plans when we know for a certainty that in each generation there will be one or more wars? Why not plan to make no plans at all, to just vegetate until the bugle calls? What a waste of time, money and effort to prepare your son for the ministry or the law, or any other pursuit, when you know that the army or navy will get him, and if not the army or navy, then the marines. Why think of training your boy to go into business when the only important business of every new generation is to make war? Talk about common sense . . . what sense is there in pretending that one will engage in peaceful pursuits when the only pursuit we ever enter wholeheartedly, and with vim and vigor, is the pursuit of war? Why not train your son from the beginning to be a killer, an expert killer? Why delude yourself and him too? Sooner or later your boy must learn to kill; the quicker he learns the less pain and disillusionment he will suffer. Don't teach him how to live, teach him how to die! Prepare him not for the pleasures of this world, for the chances are he will never taste them; prepare him for the pleasures of the afterworld. If you find that he is hypersensitive, kill him while he is still young. Better to kill him with your own hands than to let him die at the hands of a ruthless enemy. Kill off all the males, if possible, and let only the females survive. And if the females begin warring with one another, kill them off at birth too. In any case, believe no one who promises you peace and prosperity unless all the munitions makers have been killed off and the machines they employ destroyed.

If the idea that your son must become a killer as well as a provider is abhorrent to you, if you believe that death-dealing weapons should not continue to be manufactured, even if never used, then make a new world in which killing will be unnecessary. Concentrate all your energies upon that, and that alone. If you had a home which you were fond of, and it were suddenly invaded by rats, would you not set everything aside to eliminate the pest? War is the greatest plague that civilized man has had to contend with. And what has he done in all these thousands of years to grapple with the problem? Nothing, really. With the passage of time he has devoted increasing effort, ingenuity and money towards aggrandizing the horrors of war, as though pretending to himself that if war became too horrible it might cease of itself. The greatest nations have ruined themselves in preparing for and making war. Nevertheless the whole civilized world deludes itself into believing (by what amazing self-hypnosis!) that men are becoming better, more humane, more intelligent, more considerate of one another. The truth is that the farther along the path of civilization we go the more diabolical men seem to become. The torture inflicted upon one another by savages is nothing compared to the torture which civilized beings inflict upon one another. (This is true even in times of peace.) Add to this, that in taking over the so-called inferior peoples of the earth, in adapting them to our ways, the price we demand of them is that they become good auxiliary fighters. When there is a particularly dirty job of butchering to be done, we throw in the colonial troops. Progress! Progress!

Moreover, and above all, and to add to the illogical, the inconsistent and the paradoxical—does any serious-minded person believe for one moment that a victorious China, Russia, America, England will not become more militant, more ready and prepared for war, more suited to find fresh problems to quarrel over? Germany and Japan *may* be put out of harm's way. Agreed. But what then? Are they the only enemies man will ever have or could have? Since when have Big Powers agreed with one another, or laid down their arms and become as lambs? Since when have the Big Powers treated Little Powers with equal tact and consideration? And what of the Little Powers, when we have liberated them by our victorious but ruinous campaigns? Will they be grateful and ready to fall in line with our way of life when their people return to the desolate, ruined lands which we turned into a stupendous proving ground? Will they perhaps differ with us as to how life and liberty is to be maintained in the future?

Who will rule the coming world? The strong ones. And who are the strong? America, Russia, England, China. (We have not yet finished with Japan. It remains to be seen if she will be thoroughly subjugated and castrated, or if one of the present Big Powers will form an unholy alliance with her, in order to be better prepared for the next conflict, which already impends.) England, we know, will not give up her Empire willingly. France will demand the restoration of her colonies. So will Holland. Perhaps Italy too. Germany of course will never be allowed to have anything but the air to breathe. As for America, she will relinquish everything, that goes without question. The one great Empire which will remain, and which should long ago have fallen to pieces, is the British Empire. This is only fair and just, because the Four Freedoms, being an Anglo-Saxon conception of justice, does not exclude Empires. France will be allowed to grow strong again, because France is a freedom-loving nation, though also an Empire. But France musn't grow too strong, for then she might become a menace to England's freedom and security, which is based upon a greed for possessions almost unheard of. Everything will have to be maintained in an equilibrium as delicate as the workings of a Swiss watch. The master minds of the new Entente Cordiale, however, will solve all these intricate problems with ease and dispatch. There is no danger of their quarreling among themselves. Oh no, not the slightest! Russia will remain Communist, England an Empire, America a benevolent Democracy (with Roosevelt at the helm until death), and France Republican. China, of course, will remain a complete chaos, as always. The directors of the great show will see eye to eye on all future major problems; as for the minor problems, the future will take care of these.

The great question, to be sure, which will come up as soon as the war ends, is: who will buy whose goods and how? As for the debt problem, that is easily solved. The people will pay off the debts. The people always pay. Though the people never start a war, nor even a revolution, the government somehow always convinces the people that they must pay for these adventures, both before and after. A war is fought for the benefit of the people. By the time the war is over, however, there are no benefits, just debts, death and desolation. All of which has to be paid for.

This time the peoples who make up the victorious nations won't mind the cost because they will have the Four Freedoms. They will also have all sorts of new machines, new labor-saving devices, which will make work a pleasure. (And the harder they work the faster the debts will be paid off; the more ready they will be, too, for the next war.) Yes, there will be all sorts of new inventions, which, if they are not used destructively, will bring untold bliss. There will be, among other things, new airplanes capable of taking us back and forth to China in twenty-four hours—and for a song! Weekends the workers of the world will be flying around the globe greeting their fellow-workers in Java, Borneo, Mozambique, Saskatchewan, Tierra del Fuego and such places. No need to go to Coney Island any more, or Deauville, or Brighton—there will be far more interesting places at which to spend the weekend. There will be television, too, don't forget. If you don't care to fly around the world in your spare time you can sit quietly by the hearth and watch the Eskimos climbing up and down the slippery icebergs, or look at the primitive peoples in the jungle busy gathering rice, ivory, coffee, tea, rubber, chicle and other useful commodities for our delectation. Every one will be working blissfully, even the Chinese coolies. For, by that time the vast and all-powerful Chiang Kai-shek dynasty will be operating with the smoothness of a high-powered dynamo. The opium traffic will be wiped out, and the heretofore ignorant coolies will be able to understand and appreciate American movies, which are an excellent substitute for opium. We will probably make special Grade D pictures for them at a figure so absurd that even the lowest coolie will be able to afford the price of admission. We will have Grade K or J pictures for "our little brown brothers" too. We will make chewing gum in greater quantities, and Eskimo pies, and malted milk shakes, to say nothing of can openers and other gadgets, so that the little people everywhere may enjoy some of the luxuries of our economic millennium.

The thing to guard against, however, is that the little peoples of the world should not be infected with Communism. Russia will have to be content to communize Siberia, Mongolia, and possibly Japan. But not China! And not the Malay archipelago, nor Africa, nor South America. South America will be somewhat of a problem, especially as miscegenation assumes increasing proportions. It won't do for the peoples of North America, "the melting pot," to begin intermarrying with the black, brown, and yellow races. Marrying red-skins is quite another matter; the Indian, it seems is a hundred percent American, and we don't mind any more if they have a touch of color. But don't let any one think, especially south of the Mason-Dixon line, that the Four Freedoms means freedom for blacks and whites to intermarry! That belongs to the fifth or sixth freedom, and will probably demand another war.

With a plethora of new labor-saving devices flooding the market there will no longer be any question of who is to do the dirty work of the world. *The machine will do it!* No one will need to soil his hands. The machines will work with such efficiency, in fact, that there may be danger of the workers growing bored. Unless the master minds introduce new forms of creative activity. It is quite possible that in the next few hundred years we shall see everybody turning artist. An hour or two at the machine each day, and the rest of the day for art! Perhaps that will be the new order in the world to come. How glorious! *The joy of creation:* something man has never known before, at least not the civilized races. Suddenly, thanks to the ubiquity and the domination of the machine, we will become again as the primitives, only wiser, happier, conscious at last of our blessedness. Everybody dancing, singing, painting, carving, fiddling, drumming, strumming . . . so marvelous! All due to the machine. How simple!

Finally, when every one has become a genius, when genius becomes the norm, there will be no room for envy or rivalry. Art will be truly universal. There will be no need for critics or interpreters; the dealers and middle men will perish, and with them the publishers and editors, the lawyers, the bookkeepers, the politicians, perhaps even the police. Every one will have the kind of home he chooses to live in, and with it a frigidaire, a radio, a telephone, a vacuum cleaner, a washing machine, an automobile, an airplane, a parachute, *and*—a full set of Dr. Cowen's light-weight platinum teeth. The cripples will all have the most wonderful, the most extraordinary, light-weight artificial limbs, which will enable them to run, skip, dance, jump or walk with perfect ease. The insane will have better lunatic asylums, and more humane, more intelligent keepers. The prisons will be more spacious, more sanitary, more comfortable in every way. There will be hospitals in abundance, on every street, and ambulances fitted up like Pullmans. There will be such a variety of pain removers that no one need ever suffer any more, not even the throes of death. Add to this, that when all the world learns English, which will happen inevitably, there won't be the least possibility of a misunderstanding any more. One language, one flag, one way of life. The machine doing all the dirty work, the master minds doing all the thinking: an Entente Cordiale with a vengeance.

That's how it looks for the next five hundred years or so. *Or doesn't it?* Anyway, that's how it *could* look, you must admit. And what's to hinder? Well, we don't know yet, but undoubtedly there will arise some idiot, some fanatic, who will have a better idea to foist upon us. And that will cause trouble. Trouble always starts with "a better idea." It's too soon to predict the nature of the monkey wrench which will wreck the Utopian machine we have just described, but that there will be such a joy-killer we have no doubt. It's in the cards.

So, just to play safe, hold on to your battleships and battle wagons, your tanks, your flame-throwers, your bombing machines and everything super-duper in the way of destructive devices—we may have need for them again. One day, out of a clear sky—always a clear sky, mind you!—some fanatic will make an issue of some unforeseeable little incident, magnify it to the proportions of a calamity, and then a fresh catastrophe will be at our door. But if we are armed to the teeth, if we are better prepared than we were this last time, perhaps we shall get it over with more quickly. We must never relinquish the Four Freedoms, remember that! If possible, we must pave the way for a fifth and sixth freedom. Because, the more freedoms we pile up, the nearer we will be to freedom in the abstract.

Each new freedom, to be sure, will entail a few million deaths, as well as the destruction of our principal cities. But, if we achieve ten or twelve freedoms, we won't mind how many millions of lives are sacrificed, nor will we care how many cities are destroyed. After all, we can always make babies, and we can always build new cities—better babies, better cities. If we were able to discover a way to homogenize and irradiate cow's milk we surely will find the way to homogenize and irradiate the minds of our children. If we have to destroy everything now standing, including the Vatican, it will be worth it. What we want is a world in which war will be unthinkable. And, by God, if we have to wipe out the human race in order to achieve it, we will. *Mieux vaut revenir en fantôme que jamais,* as the French say.

So, until that blessed day looms upon the horizon, do please go on murdering one another. Murder as you have never murdered before. Murder the murderers, murder murder, but murder! murder! murder! Murder for God and country! Murder for peace! Murder for sweet murder's sake. Don't stop murdering ever! Murder! Murder! Murder! Murder your mother! Murder your brother! Murder the animals of the field, murder the insects, the birds, the flowers, the grass! Murder the microbes! Murder the molecule and the atom! Murder the electron! Murder the stars, and the sun and moon, if you can get at them! Murder everything off, so that we shall have at last a bright, pure, clean world in which to live in peace, bliss and security until the end of time!

OBSCENITY AND THE LAW OF REFLECTION

To discuss the nature and meaning of obscenity is almost as difficult as to talk about God. Until I began delving into the literature which has grown up about the subject I never realized what a morass I was wading into. If one begins with etymology one is immediately aware that lexicographers are bamboozlers every bit as much as jurists, moralists and politicians. To begin with, those who have seriously attempted to track down the meaning of the term are obliged to confess that they have arrived nowhere. In their book, *To the Pure,* Ernst and Seagle state that "no two persons agree on the definitions of the six deadly adjectives: obscene, lewd, lascivious, filthy, indecent, disgusting." The League of Nations was also stumped when it attempted to define what constituted obscenity. D. H. Lawrence was probably right when he said that "nobody knows what the word obscene means." As for Theodore Schroeder, who has devoted his whole life to fighting for freedom of speech,[1] his opinion is that "obscenity does not exist in any book or picture, but is wholly a quality of the reading or viewing mind." "No argument for the suppression of obscene literature," he states, "has ever been offered which by unavoidable implications will not justify, and which has not already justified, every other limitation that has ever been put upon mental freedom."

As someone has well said, to name all the masterpieces which have been labeled obscene would make a tedious catalogue. Most of our choice writers, from Plato to Havelock Ellis, from Aristophanes to Shaw, from Catullus and Ovid to Shakespeare, Shelley and Swinburne, together with the Bible, to be sure, have been the target of those who are forever in search of what is impure, indecent and immoral. In an artice called "Freedom of Expression in Literature,"[2] Huntington Cairns, one of the most broadminded and clear-sighted of all the censors, stresses the need for the re-education of officials charged with law enforce-

[1] See his *A Challenge to Sex Censors* and other works.
[2] From the *Annals of the American Academy of Political and Social Science,* Philadelphia, November, 1938.

ment. "In general," he states, "such men have had little or no contact with science or art, have had no knowledge of the liberty of expression tacitly granted to men of letters since the beginnings of English literature, and have been, from the point of view of expert opinion, altogether imcompetent to handle the subject. Administrative officials, not the populace who in the main have only a negligible contact with art, stand first in need of re-education."

Perhaps it should be noted here, in passing, that though our Federal government exercises no censorship over works of art originating in the country, it does permit the Treasury Department to pass judgments upon importations from abroad. In 1930, the Tariff Act was revised to permit the Secretary of the Treasury, in his discretion, to admit the classics or books of recognized and established literary or scientific merit, even if obscene. What is meant by "books of recognized and established literary merit?" Mr. Cairns gives us the following interpretation: "books which have behind them a substantial and reputable body of American critical opinion indicating that the works are of meritorious quality." This would seem to represent a fairly liberal attitude, but when it comes to a test, when a book or other work of art is capable of creating a furor, this seeming liberality collapses. It has been said with regard to the Sonnets of Aretino that they were condemned for four hundred years. How long we shall have to wait for the ban to be lifted on certain famous contemporary works no one can predict. In the article alluded to above, Mr. Cairns admits that "there is no likelihood whatever that the present obscenity statutes will be repealed." "None of the statutes," he goes on to say, "defines the word 'obscenity' and there is thus a wide latitude of discretion in the meaning to be attributed to the term." Those who imagine that the *Ulysses* decision established a precedent should realize by now that they were over-optimistic. Nothing has been established where books of a disturbing nature are concerned. After years of wrestling with prudes, bigots and other psychopaths who determine what we may or may not read, Theodore Schroeder is of the opinion that "it is not the inherent quality of the book which counts, but its hypothetical influence upon some hypothetical person, who at some problematical time in the future may hypothetically read the book."

In his book called *A Challenge to the Sex Censors,* Mr. Schroeder quotes an anonymous clergyman of a century ago to the effect that "obscenity exists only in the minds that discover it and charge others with it." This obscure work contains most illuminating passages; in it the author attempts to show that, by a law of reflection in nature, everyone is the performer of acts similar to those he attributes to others; that self-preservation is self-destruction, etc. This wholesome and enlightened viewpoint, attainable, it would seem, only by the rare few, comes nearer to dissipating the fogs which envelop the subject than all the learned treatises of educators, moralists, scholars and jurists combined. In Romans XIV: 14 we have it presented to us axiomatically for all time: "I know and am persuaded by the Lord Jesus that there is nothing unclean of itself, but to him that esteemeth anything to be unclean, to him it is unclean." How far one would get in the courts with this attitude, or what the postal authorities would make of it, surely no sane individual has any doubts about.

A totally different point of view, and one which deserves attention, since it is not only honest and forthright but expressive of the innate conviction of many, is that voiced by Havelock Ellis, that obscenity is a "permanent element of human social life and corresponds to a deep need of the human mind."[1] Ellis goes so far as to say that "adults need obscene literature, as much as children need fairy tales, as a relief from the oppressive force of convention." This is the attitude of a cultured individual whose purity and wisdom has been acknowledged by eminent critics everywhere. It is the worldly view which we profess to admire in the Mediterranean peoples. Ellis, being an Englishman, was of course persecuted for his opinions and ideas upon the subject of sex. From the nineteenth century on all English authors who dared to treat the subject honestly and realistically have been persecuted and humiliated. The prevalent attitude of the English people is, I believe, fairly well presented in such a piece of

[1] *More Essays of Love and Virtue.*

polished inanity as Viscount Brentford's righteous self-defense—
"*Do We Need a Censor?*" Viscount Brentford is the gentleman who
tried to protect the English public from such iniquitous works as
Ulysses and *The Well of Loneliness*. He is the type, so rampant in the
Anglo-Saxon world, to which the words of Dr. Ernest Jones
would seem to apply: "It is the people with secret attractions to
various temptations who busy themselves with removing these
temptations from other people; really they are defending themselves under the pretext of defending others, because at heart
they fear their own weakness."

As one accused of employing obscene language more freely
and abundantly than any other living writer in the English
language, it may be of interest to present my own views on the
subject. Since the *Tropic of Cancer* first appeared in Paris, in 1934, I
have received many hundreds of letters from readers all over the
world; they are from men and women of all ages and all walks of
life, and in the main they are congratulatory messages. Many of
those who denounced the book because of its gutter language
professed admiration for it otherwise; very, very few ever remarked that it was a dull book, or badly written. The book
continues to sell steadily "under the counter" and is still written
about at intervals although it made its appearance thirteen years
ago and was promptly banned in all the Anglo-Saxon countries.
The only effect which censorship has had upon its circulation is to
drive it underground, thus limiting the sales but at the same time
insuring for it the best of all publicity—word of mouth recom-
mendation. It is to be found in the libraries of nearly all our
important colleges, is often recommended to students by their
professors, and has gradually come to take its place beside other
celebrated literary works which, once similarly banned and sup-
pressed, are now accepted as classics. It is a book which appeals
especially to young people and which, from all that I gather
directly and indirectly, not only does not ruin their lives, but
increases their morale. The book is a living proof that censorship
defeats itself. It also proves once again that the only ones who
may be said to be protected by censorship are the censors
themselves, and this only because of a law of nature known to all
who over-indulge. In this connection I feel impelled to mention a

curious fact often brought to my attention by booksellers, namely, that the two classes of books which enjoy a steady and ever-increasing sale are the so-called pornographic, or obscene, and the occult. This would seem to corroborate Havelock Ellis's view which I mentioned earlier. Certainly all attempts to regulate the traffic in obscene books, just as all attempts to regulate the traffic in drugs or prostitution, is doomed to failure wherever civilization rears its head. Whether these things are a definite evil or not, whether or not they are definite and ineradicable elements of our social life, it seems indisputable that they are synonymous with what is called civilization. Despite all that has been said and written for and against, it is evident that with regard to these factors of social life men have never come to that agreement which they have about slavery. It is possible, of course, that one day these things may disappear, but it is also possible, despite the now seemingly universal disapproval of it, that slavery may once again be practiced by human beings.

The most insistent question put to the writer of "obscene" literature is: why did you have to use such language? The implication is, of course, that with conventional terms or means the same effect might have been obtained. Nothing, of course, could be further from the truth. Whatever the language employed, no matter how objectionable—I am here thinking of the most extreme examples—one may be certain that there was no other idiom possible. Effects are bound up with intentions, and these in turn are governed by laws of compulsion as rigid as nature's own. That is something which non-creative individuals seldom ever understand. Someone has said that "the literary artist, having attained understanding, communicates that understanding to his readers. That understanding, whether of sexual or other matters, is certain to come into conflict with popular beliefs, fears and taboos, because these are, for the most part, based on error." Whatever extenuating reasons are adduced for the erroneous opinions of the populace, such as lack of education, lack of contact with the arts, and so on, the fact is that there will always be a gulf between the creative artist and the public because the latter is immune to the mystery inherent in and surrounding all creation. The struggle which the artist wages, consciously or unconsciously, with the public, centers almost exclusively about the problem of a necessitous choice. Putting to one side all questions of ego and temperament, and taking the broadest view of the creative process, which makes of the artist nothing more than an instrument, we are nevertheless forced to conclude that the spirit of an age is the crucible in which, through one means or another, certain vital and mysterious forces seek expression. If there is something mysterious about the manifestation of deep and unsuspected forces, which find expression in disturbing movements and ideas from one period to another, there is nevertheless nothing accidental or bizarre about it. The laws governing the spirit are just as readable as those governing nature. But the readings must come from those who are steeped in the mysteries. The very depth of these interpretations naturally make them unpalatable and unacceptable to the vast body which constitutes the unthinking public.

Parenthetically it is curious to observe that painters, however unapproachable their work may be, are seldom subjected to the same meddling interference as writers. Language, because it also serves as a means of communication, tends to bring about weird obfuscations. Men of high intelligence often display execrable taste when it comes to the arts. Yet even these freaks whom we all recognize, because we are always amazed by their obtuseness, seldom have the cheek to say what elements of a picture had been better left out or what substitutions might have been effected. Take, for example, the early works of George Grosz. Compare the reactions of the intelligent public in his case to the reactions provoked by Joyce when his *Ulysses* appeared. Compare these again with the reactions which Schoenberg's later music inspired. In the case of all three the revulsion which their work first induced was equally strong, but in the case of Joyce the public was more articulate, more voluble, more arrogant in its pseudo-certitude. With books even the butcher and the plumber seem to feel that they have a right to an opinion, especially if the book happens to be what is called a filthy or disgusting one.

I have noticed, moreover, that the attitude of the public alters perceptibly when it is the work of primitive peoples which they must grapple with. Here for some obscure reason the element of the "obscene" is treated with more deference. People who would be revolted by the drawings in *Ecce Homo* will gaze unblushingly at African pottery or sculpture no matter how much their taste or morals may be offended. In the same spirit they are inclined to be more tolerant of the obscene works of ancient authors. Why? Because even the dullest are capable of admitting to themselves that other epochs might, justifiably or not, have enjoyed other customs, other morals. As for the creative spirits of their own epoch, however, freedom of expression is always interpreted as license. The artist must conform to the current, and usually hypocritical, attitude of the majority. He must be original, courageous, inspiring and all that—but never too disturbing. He must say Yes while saying No. The larger the art public, the more tyrannical, complex and perverse does this irrational pressure become. There are always exceptions, to be sure, and Picasso is one of them, one of the few artists in our time table to command the respect and attention of a bewildered and largely hostile public. It is the greatest tribute that could be made to his genius.

*   *   *

The chances are that during this transition period of global wars, lasting perhaps a century or two, art will become less and less important. A world torn by indescribable upheavals, a world preoccupied with social and political transformations, will have less time and energy to spare for the creation and appreciation of works of art. The politician, the soldier, the industrialist, the technician, all those in short who cater to immediate needs, to creature comforts, to transitory and illusory passions and prejudices, will take precedence over the artist. The most poetic inventions will be those capable of serving the most destructive ends. Poetry itself will be expressed in terms of blockbusters and lethal gases. The obscene will find expression in the most unthinkable techniques of self-destruction which the inventive genius of man will be forced to adopt. The revolt and disgust which the prophetic spirits in the realm of art have inspired, through their vision of a world in the making will find justification in the years to come as these dreams are acted out.

The growing void between art and life, art becoming ever more sensational and unintelligible, life becoming more dull and hopeless, has been commented on almost ad nauseum. The war, colossal and portentous as it is, has failed to arouse a passion commensurate with its scope or significance. The fervor of the Greeks and the Spaniards was something which astounded the modern world. The admiration and the horror which their ferocious struggles evoked was revelatory. We regarded them as mad and heroic, and we had almost been on the point of believing that such madness, such as heroism, no longer existed. But what strikes one as "obscene" and insane rather than mad is the stupendous machine-like character of the war which the big nations are carrying on. It is a war of materiel, a war of statistical preponderance, a war in which victory is coldly and patiently calculated on the basis of bigger and better resources. In the war which the Spaniards and the Greeks waged there was not only a hopelessness about the immediate outcome but a hopelessness as to the eternal outcome, so to speak. Yet they fought, and with tooth and nail, and they will fight again and again, always hopelessly and always gloriously because always passionately. As for the big powers now locked in a death struggle, one feels that they are only grooming themselves for another chance at it, for a chance to win here and now in a victory that will be everlasting, which is an utter delusion. Whatever the outcome, one senses that life will not be altered radically but to a degree which will only make it more like what it was before the conflict started. This war has all the masturbative qualities of a combat between hopeless recidivists.

If I stress the obscene aspect of modern warfare it is not simply because I am against war but because there is something about the ambivalent emotions it inspires which enables me better to grapple with the nature of the obscene. Nothing would be regarded as obscene, I feel, if men were living out their inmost desires. What man dreads most is to be faced with the manifestation, in word or deed, of that which he has refused to live out, that which he has throttled or stifled, buried, as we say now, in his subconscious mind. The sordid qualities imputed to the enemy are always those which we recognize as our own and therefore rise to slay, because only through projection do we realize the enormity and horror of them. Man tries as in a dream to kill the enemy in himself. This enemy, both within and without, is just as, but no more, real than the phantoms in his dreams. When awake he is apathetic about this dream self, but asleep he is filled with terror. I say "when awake," but the question is, *when is he awake, if ever?* To those who no longer need to kill, the man who indulges in murder is a sleep walker. He is a man trying to kill himself in his dreams. He is a man who comes face to face with himself *only in the dream.* This man is the man of the modern world, everyman, as much a myth and a legend as the Everyman of the allegory. Our life today is what we dreamed it would be aeons ago. Always it has a double thread running through it, just as in the age-old dream. Always fear and wish, fear and wish. Never the pure fountain of desire. And so we have and we have not, we are and we are not.

In the realm of sex there is a similar kind of sleepwalking and self-delusion at work; here the bifurcation of pure desire into fear and wish has resulted in the creation of a phantasmagorical world in which love plays the role of a chameleon-like scapegoat. Passion is conspicuous by its absence or by monstrous deformations which render it practically unrecognizable. To trace the history of man's attitude towards sex is like threading a labyrinth whose heart is situated in an unknown planet. There has been so much distortion and suppression, even among primitive peoples, that today it is virtually impossible to say what constitutes a free and healthy attitude. Certainly the glorification of sex, in pagan times, represented no solution of the problem. And, though Christianity ushered in a conception of love superior to any known before, it did not succeed in freeing man sexually. Perhaps we might say that the tyranny of sex was broken through sublimation in love, but the nature of this greater love has been understood and experienced only by a rare few.

Only where strict bodily discipline is observed, for the purpose of union or communion with God, has the subject of sex ever been faced squarely. Those who have achieved emancipation by this route have, of course, not only liberated themselves from the tyranny of sex but from all other tyrannies of the flesh. With such individuals, the whole body of desire has become so transfigured that the results obtained have had practically no meaning for the man of the world. Spiritual triumphs, even though they affect the man in the street immediately, concern him little, if at all. He is seeking for a solution of life's problems on the plane of mirage and delusion; his notions of reality have nothing to do with ultimate effects; he is blind to the permanent changes which take place above and beneath his level of understanding. If we take such a type of being as the Yogi, whose sole concern is with reality, as opposed to the world of illusion, we are bound to concede that he has faced every human problem with the utmost courage and lucidity. Whether he incorporates the sexual or transmutes it to the point of transcendence and obliteration, he is at least one who has attained to the vast open spaces of love. If he does not reproduce his kind, he at least gives new meaning to the word birth. In lieu of copulating he creates; in the circle of his influence conflict is stilled and the harmony of a profound peace established. He is able to love not only individuals of the opposite sex but all individuals, everything that breathes, in fact. This quiet sort of triumph strikes a chill in the heart of the ordinary man, for not only does it make him visualize the loss of his meagre sex life but the loss of passion itself, passion as he knows it. This sort of liberation, which smashes his thermometrical gauge of feeling, represents itself to him as a living death. The attainment of a love which is boundless and unfettered terrifies him for the very good reason that means the dissolution of his ego. He does not want to be freed for service, dedication and devotion to all mankind; he wants comfort, assurance and security, the enjoyment of his very limited powers. Incapable of surrender, he can never know the healing power of faith; and lacking faith he can never begin to know the meaning of love. He seeks release but not liberation, which is like saying that he prefers death instead of life.

As civilization progresses it becomes more and more apparent that war is the greatest release which life offers the ordinary man. Here he can let go to his heart's content for here crime no longer has any meaning. Guilt is abolished when the whole planet swims in blood. The lulls of peacetime seem only to permit him to sink deeper into the bogs of the sadistic-masochistic complex which has fastened itself into the heart of our civilized life like a cancer. Fear, guilt and murder—these constitute the real triumvirate which rules our lives. *What is obscene then?* The whole fabric of life as we know it today. To speak only of what is indecent, foul, lewd, filthy, disgusting, etc., in connection with sex, is to deny ourselves the luxury of the great gamut of revulsion-repulsion which modern life puts at our service. Every department of life is vitiated and corroded with what is so unthinkingly labeled "obscene." One wonders if perhaps the insane could not invent a more fitting, more inclusive term for the polluting elements of life which we create and shun and never identify with our behavior. We think of the insane as inhabiting a world completely divorced from reality, but our own everyday behavior, whether in war or peace, if examined from only a slightly higher standpoint, bears all the earmarks of insanity. "I have said," writes a well-known psychologist, "that this is a mad world, that man is most of the time mad; and I believe that in a way what we call morality is merely a form of madness, which happens to be a working adaptation to existing circumstances."

* * *

When obscenity crops out in art, in literature more particularly, it usually functions as a technical device; the element of the deliberate which is there has nothing to do with sexual excitation, as in pornography. If there is an ulterior motive at work it is one which goes far beyond sex. Its purpose is to awaken, to usher in a sense of reality. In a sense, its use by the artist may be compared to the use of the miraculous by the Masters. This last minute quality, so closely allied to desperation, has been the subject of endless debate. Nothing connected with Christ's life, for example, has been exposed to such withering scrutiny as the miracles attributed to him. The great question is: should the Master indulge himself or should he refrain from employing his extraordinary powers? Of the great Zen masters it has been observed that they never hestitate to resort to any means in order to awaken their disciples; they will even perform what we would call sacrilegious acts. And, according to some familiar interpretations of the Flood, it has been acknowledged that even God grows desperate at times and wipes the slate clean in order to continue the human experiment on another level.

It should be recognized, however, with regard to these questionable displays of power, that only a Master may hazard them. As a matter of fact, the element of risk exists only in the eyes of the uninitiated. The Master is always certain of the result; he never plays his trump card, as it were, except at the psychological moment. His behavior, in such instances, might be compared to that of the chemist pouring a last tiny drop into a prepared solution in order to precipitate certain salts. If it is a push it is also a supreme exhortation which the Master indulges in. Once the moment is passed, moreover, the witness is altered forever. In another sense, the situation might be described as the transition from belief to faith. Once faith has been established, there is no regression; whereas with belief everything is in suspense and capable of fluctuation.

It should also be recognized that those who have real power have no need to demonstrate it for themselves; it is never in their own interests, or for their own glorification, that these performances are made. In fact, there is nothing miraculous, in the vulgar sense, about these acts, unless it be the ability to raise the consciousness of the onlooker to that mysterious level of illumination which is natural to the Master. Men who are ignorant of the source of their powers, on the other hand, men who are regarded as the powers that move the world, usually come to a disastrous end. Of their efforts it is truly said that all comes to nought. On the worldly level nothing endures, because on this level, which is the level of dream and delusion, all is fear and wish vainly cemented by will.

To revert to the artist again . . . Once he has made use of his extraordinary powers, and I am thinking of the use of obscenity in just such magical terms, he is inevitably caught up in the stream of forces beyond him. He may have begun by assuming that he could awaken his readers, but in the end he himself passes into another dimension of reality wherein he no longer feels the need of forcing an awakening. His rebellion over the prevalent inertia about him becomes transmuted, as his vision increases, into an acceptance and understanding of an order and harmony which is beyond man's conception and approachable only through faith. His vision expands with the growth of his own powers, because creation has its roots in vision and admits of only one realm, the realm of imagination. Ultimately, then, he stands among his own obscene objurgations like the conqueror midst the ruins of a devastated city. He realizes that the real nature of the obscene resides in the lust to convert. He knocked to awaken, but it was himself he awakened. And once awake, he is no longer concerned with the world of sleep; he walks in the light and, like a mirror, reflects his illumination in every act.

Once this vantage point is reached, how trifling and remote seem the accusations of moralists! How senseless the debate as to whether the work in question was of high literary merit or not! How absurd the wrangling over the moral or immoral nature of his creation! Concerning every bold act one may raise the reproach of vulgarity. Everything dramatic is in the nature of an appeal, a frantic appeal for communion. Violence, whether in deed or speech, is an inverted sort of prayer. Initiation itself is a violent process of purification and union. Whatever demands radical treatment demands God, and always through some form of death or annihilation. Whenever the obscene crops out one can smell the imminent death of a form. Those who possess the highest clue are not impatient, even in the presence of death; the artist in words, however, is not of this order, he is only at the vestibule, as it were, of the palace of wisdom. Dealing with the spirit, he nevertheless has recourse to forms. When he fully understands his role as creator he substitutes his own being for the medium of words. But in that process there comes the "dark night of the soul" when, exalted by his vision of things to come and not yet fully conscious of his powers, he resorts to violence. He becomes desperate over his inability to transmit his vision. He resorts to any and every means in his power; this agony, in which creation itself is parodied, prepares him for the solution of his dilemma, but a solution wholly unforeseen and mysterious as creation itself.

All violent manifestations of radiant power have an obscene glow when visualized through the refractive lens of the ego. All conversions occur in the speed of a split second. Liberation implies the sloughing off of chains, the bursting of the cocoon. What is obscene are the preliminary or anticipatory movements of birth, the preconscious writhing in the face of a life to be. It is in the agony of death that the nature of birth is apprehended. For in what consists the struggle if it is not between form and being, between that which was and that which is about to be? In such moments creation itself is at the bar; whoever seeks to unveil the mystery becomes himself a part of the mystery and thus helps to perpetuate it. Thus the lifting of the veil may be interpreted as the ultimate expression of the obscene. It is an attempt to spy on the secret processes of the universe. In this sense the guilt attaching to Prometheus symbolizes the guilt of man-the-creator, of man-the-arrogant-one who ventures to create before being crowned with wisdom.

The pangs of birth relate not to the body but to the spirit. It was demanded of us to know love, experience union and communion, and thus achieve liberation from the wheel of life and death. But we have chosen to remain this side of Paradise and to create through art the illusory substance of our dreams. In a profound sense we are forever delaying the act. We flirt with destiny and lull ourselves to sleep with myth. We die in the throes of our own tragic legends, like spiders caught in their own webs. If there is anything which deserves to be called "obscene" it is this oblique, glancing confrontation with the mysteries, this walking up to the edge of the abyss, enjoying all the ecstasies of vertigo and yet refusing to yield to the spell of the unknown. The obscene has all the qualities of the hidden interval. It is as vast as the Unconscious itself and as amorphous and fluid as the very stuff of the Unconscious. It is what comes to the surface as strange, intoxicating and forbidden, and which therefore arrests and paralyzes, when in the form of Narcissus we bend over our own image in the mirror of our own iniquity. Acknowledged by all, it is nevertheless despised and rejected, wherefore it is constantly emerging in Protean guise at the most unexpected moments. When it is recognized and accepted, whether as a figment of the imagination or as an integral part of human reality, it inspires no more dread or revulsion than could be ascribed to the flowering lotus which sends its roots down into the mud of the stream on which it is borne.

STAND STILL LIKE THE HUMMINGBIRD

From Stand Still Like the Hummingbird, *"Walt Whitman" and "Henry David Thoreau." The sketches of Whitman and Thoreau are further examples of Miller's skills as a literary portraitist. But more significantly, they are sharp tributes to two nineteenth-century Americans who defined themselves against the grain of their culture and so blazed the trail for subsequent writers and artists who would find themselves obliged to march to different drummers. Here Miller is interested in what makes these writers continually and radically relevant; he is not interested in merely dusting the icons.*

WALT WHITMAN

I have never understood why he should be called "the good gray poet." The color of his language, his temperament, his whole being is electric blue. I hardly think of him as poet. Bard, yes. The bard of the future.

America has never really understood Whitman, or accepted him. America has exalted Lincoln, a lesser figure.

Whitman did not address the masses. He was as far removed from the people as a saint is from the members of a church. He reviled the whole trend of American life, which he characterized as mean and vulgar. Yet only an American could have written what he did. He was not interested in culture, tradition, religion or Democracy. He was what Lawrence called "an aristocrat of the spirit."

I know of no writer whose vision is as inclusive, as all-embracing as Whitman's. It is precisely this cosmic view of things which has prevented Whitman's message from being accepted.

He is all affirmation. He is completely outgoing. He recognizes no barriers of any kind, not even evil.

Everyone can quote from Whitman in justification of his own point of view. No one has arisen since Whitman who can include his thought and go beyond it. The "Song of the Open Road" remains an absolute. It transcends the human view, obliges man to include the universe in his own being.

The poet in Whitman interests me far less than the seer. Perhaps the only poet with whom he can be compared is Dante. More than any other single figure, Dante symbolizes the medieval world. Whitman is the incarnation of the modern man, of whom thus far we have only had intimations. Modern life has not yet begun. Here and there men have arisen who have given us glimpses of this world to come. Whitman not only voiced the keynote of this new life in process of creation but behaved as if it already existed. The wonder is that he was not crucified. But here we touch the mystery which shrouds his seemingly open life.

Whoever has studied Whitman's life must be amazed at the skill with which he steered his bark through troubled waters. He never relinquishes his grasp of the oar, never flinches, never wavers, never compromises. From the moment of his awakening —for it was truly an awakening and not a mere development of creative talent—he marches on, calm, steady, sure of himself, certain of ultimate victory. Without effort he enlists the aid of willing disciples who serve as buffers to the blows of fate. He concentrates entirely upon the deliverance of his message. He talks little, reads little, but speculates much. It is not, however, the life of a contemplative which he leads. He is very definitely in and of the world. He is worldly through and through, yet serene, detached, the enemy of no man, the friend of all. He posesses a magic armor against wanton intrusion, against violation of his being. In many ways he reminds one of the "resurrected" Christ.

I stress this aspect of the man deliberately because Whitman himself gave expression to it most eloquently—it is one of his most revelatory utterances—in a prose work. The passage runs as follows: "A fitly born and bred race, growing up in right conditions of outdoor as much as indoor harmony, activity and development, would probably, from and in those conditions, find it enough merely *to live*—and would, in their relations to the sky, air, water, trees, etc., and to the countless common shows, and in the fact of *life* itself, discover and achieve happiness—with Being suffused night and day by wholesome ecstasy, surpassing all the pleasures that wealth, amusement, and even gratified intellect, erudition, or the sense of art, can give." This view, so utterly alien to the so-called modern world, is thoroughly Polynesian. And that is where Whitman belongs, out beyond the last frontiers of the Western world, neither of the West nor of the East but of an intermediary realm, a floating archipelago dedicated to the attainment of peace, happiness and well-being here and now.

I maintain most stoutly that Whitman's outlook is not American, any more than it is Chinese, Hindu or European. It is the unique view of an emancipated individual, expressed in the broadest American idiom, understandable to men of all languages. The flavor of his language, though altogether American, is a rare one. It has never been captured again. It probably never will. Its universality springs from its uniqueness. In this sense it has all tradition behind it. Yet, I repeat, Whitman had no respect for tradition; that he forged a new language is due entirely to the singularity of his vision, to the fact that he felt himself to be a new being. Between the early Whitman and the "awakened" Whitman there is no resemblance whatever. No one, scanning his early writings, could possibly detect the germ of the future genius. Whitman remade himself from head to foot.

I have used the word *message* several times in connection with his writings. Yes, the message is explicit as well as implicit in his work. It is the message which informs of his work. Remove the message and his poetry falls apart. Like Tolstoy, he may be said to have made of art propaganda. But is this not merely to say that unless used for life, put at the service of life, art is meaningless? Whitman is never a moralist or a religionist. His concern is to open men's vision, to lead them to the center of nowhere in order that they may find their true orientation. He does not preach, he exhorts. He is not content merely to speak his view, he sings it, shouts it triumphantly. If he looks backward it is to show that past and future are one. He sees no evil anywhere. He sees through and beyond, always.

He has been called a pantheist. Many have referred to him as the great democrat. Some have asserted that he possessed a cosmic consciousness. All attempts to label and categorize him eventually break down. Why not accept him as a pure phenomenon? Why not admit that he is without a peer? I am not attempting to divinize him. How could I, since he was so strikingly human? If I insist on the uniqueness of his being, is it not to suggest the clue which will unravel the mysterious claims of democracy?

"Make Room for Man" is the title of a poem by his faithful friend and biographer, Horace Traubel. What is it that has stood in the way of man? *Only man*. Whitman demolishes every flimsy barrier behind which man has sought to take refuge. He expresses utter confidence in man. He is not a democrat, he is an anarchist. He has the faith born of love. He does not know the meaning of hate, fear, envy, jealousy, rivalry. Born on Long Island, moving to Brooklyn at the commencement of his career, serving first as carpenter and builder, later as reporter, typesetter, editor, nursing the wounded during the bloody Civil War, he finally settles in Camden, a most inconspicuous spot. He journeyed over a good part of America and in his poems he has recorded his impressions, hopes and dreams.

It is a grandiose dream indeed. In his prose works he issues warnings to his countrymen, unheeded, of course. What would he say if he could see America today? I think his utterances would be still more impassioned. I believe he would write a still greater *Leaves of Grass*. He would see potentialities "immenser far" than those he had originally visioned. He would see "the cradle endlessly rocking."

Since his departure we have had the "great poems of death" which he spoke of, and they have been *living* poems of death. The poem of life has still to be lived.

Meanwhile the cradle is endlessly rocking. . . .

HENRY DAVID THOREAU*

There are barely a half-dozen names in the history of America which have meaning for me. Thoreau's is one of them. I think of him as a true representative of America, a type, alas, which we have ceased to coin. He is not a democrat at all, in the sense we give to the word today. He is what Lawrence would call "an aristocrat of the spirit," which is to say, that rarest thing on earth: an individual. He is nearer to being an anarchist than a democrat, socialist or communist. However, he was not interested in politics; he was the sort of person who, if there were more of his kind, would soon cause governments to become nonexistent. This, to my mind, is the highest type of man a community can produce. And that is why I have an unbounded respect and admiration for Thoreau.

The secret of his influence, which is still alive, still active, is a very simple one. He was a man of principle whose thought and behavior were in complete agreement. He assumed responsibility for his deeds as well as his utterances. Compromise was not in his vocabulary. America, for all her advantages, has produced only a handful of men of this caliber. The reason for it is obvious: men like Thoreau were never in agreement with the trend of the times. They symbolized that America which is as far from being born today as it was in 1776 or before. They took the hard road instead of the easy one. They believed in themselves first and foremost, they did not worry about what their neighbors thought of them, nor did they hesitate to defy the government when justice was at stake. There was never anything supine about their acquiescence: they could be wooed or seduced but not intimidated.

The essays gathered together in this little volume were all speeches, a fact of some importance if one reflects how impossible it would be today to give public utterance to such sentiments. The very notion of "civil disobedience," for example, is now unthinkable. (Except in India, perhaps, where in his campaign of passive resistance Gandhi used this speech as a textbook.) In our

* Originally a Preface to *Life without Principle*, three essays by Thoreau, hand-printed in 1946 for James Ladd Delkin.

country a man who dared to imitate Thoreau's behavior with regard to any crucial issue of the day would undoubtedly be sent to prison for life. Moreover, there would be none to defend him— as Thoreau once defended the name and reputation of John Brown. As always happens with bold, original utterances, these essays have now become classic. Which means that, though they still have the power to mold character, they no longer influence the men who govern our destiny. They are prescribed reading for students and a perpetual source of inspiration to the thinker and the rebel, but as for the reading public in general they carry no weight, no message any longer. The image of Thoreau has been fixed for the public by educators and "men of taste": it is that of a hermit, a crank, a nature faker. It is the caricature which has been preserved, as is usually the case with our eminent men.

The important thing about Thoreau, in my mind, is that he appeared at a time when we had, so to speak, a choice as to the direction we, the American people, would take. Like Emerson and Whitman, he pointed out the right road—the hard road, as I said before. As a people we chose differently. And we are now reaping the fruits of our choice. Thoreau, Whitman, Emerson— these men are now vindicated. In the gloom of current events these names stand out like beacons. We pay eloquent lip service to their memory, but we continue to flout their wisdom. We have become victims of the times, we look backward with longing and regret. It is too late now to change, we think. But it is not. As individuals, as *men*, it is never too late to change. That is precisely what these sturdy forerunners of ours were emphasizing all their lives.

With the creation of the atom bomb, the whole world suddenly realizes that man is faced with a dilemma whose gravity is incommensurable. In the essay called "Life without Principle," Thoreau anticipated that very possibility which shook the world when it received the news of the atom bomb. "Of what consequence," says Thoreau, "though our planet explode, if there is no character involved in the explosion? . . . I would not run around a corner to see the world blow up."

I feel certain Thoreau would have kept his word, had the planet suddenly exploded of its own accord. But I also feel certain that, had he been told of the atom bomb, of the good and bad that it was capable of producing, he would have had something memorable to say about its use. And he would have said it in defiance of the prevalent attitude. He would not have rejoiced that the secret of its manufacture was in the hands of the righteous ones. He would have asked immediately: "Who is righteous enough to employ such a diabolical instrument destructively?" He would have had no more faith in the wisdom and sanctity of this present government of the United States than he had of our government in the days of slavery. He died, let us not forget, in the midst of the Civil War, when the issue which should have been decided instantly by the conscience of every good citizen was at last being resolved in blood. No, Thoreau would have been the first to say that no government on earth is good enough or wise enough to be entrusted with such powers for good and evil. He would have predicted that we would use this new force in the same manner that we have used other natural forces, that the peace and security of the world lie not in inventions but in men's hearts, men's souls. His whole life bore testimony to the obvious fact which men are constantly overlooking, that to sustain life we need less rather than more, that to protect life we need courage and integrity, not weapons, not coalitions. In everything he said and did he was at the farthest remove from the man of today. I said earlier that his influence is still alive and active. It is, but only because truth and wisdom are incontrovertible and must eventually prevail. Consciously and unconsciously we are doing the very opposite of all that he advocated. But we are not happy about it, nor are we at all convinced that we are right. We are, in fact, more bewildered, more despairing, than we ever were in the course of our brief history. And that is most curious, most disturbing, since we are now acknowledged to be the most powerful, the most wealthy, the most secure of all the nations of the earth. We are at the top, but have we the vision to maintain this vantage point? We have a vague suspicion that we have been saddled with a responsibility which is too great for us. We know that we are not superior, in any real sense, to the other peoples of this earth. We are just waking up to the fact that morally we are far behind ourselves, so to speak. Some blissfully imagine that the threat of extinction—cosmic suicide—will rout us out of our lethargy. I am afraid that such dreams are doomed to be smashed even more effectively than the atom itself. Great things are not accomplished through fear of extinction. The deeds which move the world, which sustain life and give life, have a different motivation entirely.

The problem of power, an obsessive one with Americans, is now at the crux. Instead of *working* for peace, men ought to be urged to relax, to stop work, to take it easy, to dream and idle away their time for a change. Retire to the woods! if you can find any nearby. Think your own thoughts for a while! Examine your conscience, but only after you have thoroughly enjoyed yourself. What is your job worth, after all, if tomorrow you and yours can all be blown to smithereens by some reckless fool? Do you suppose that a government can be depended on any more than the separate individuals who compose it? Who are these individuals to whom the destiny of the planet itself now seems to be entrusted? Do you believe in them utterly, every one of them? What would *you* do if you had the control of this unheard-of power. Would you use it for the benefit of all mankind, or just for your own people, or your own little group? Do you think that men can keep such a weighty secret to themselves? Do you think it *ought* to be kept secret?

These are the sort of questions I can imagine a Thoreau firing away. They are questions which, if one has just a bit of common sense, answer themselves. But governments never seem to possess this modicum of common sense. Nor do they trust those who are in possession of it.

This American government—what is it but a tradition, though a recent one, endeavoring to transmit itself unimpaired to posterity, but each instant losing some of its integrity? It has not the vitality and force of a single living man; for a single man can bend it to his will. It is a sort of wooden gun to the people themselves. But it is not the less necessary for this, for the people must have some complicated machinery or other, and hear its din, to satisfy that idea of government which they have. Governments show thus how successfully men can be imposed on, even impose on themselves, for their own advantage. It is excellent, we must all allow. Yet this government never of itself furthered any enterprise, but by the alacrity with which it got out of its way. *It* does not keep the country free. *It* does not settle the West. *It* does not educate. The character inherent in the American people has done all that has been accomplished; and it would have done somewhat more, if the government had not sometimes got in its way. . . .

That is the way Thoreau spoke a hundred years ago. He would speak still more unflatteringly if he were alive now. In these last hundred years the State has come to be a Frankenstein. We have never had less need of the State than now when we are most tyrannized by it. The ordinary citizen everywhere has a code of ethics far above that of the government to which he owes allegiance. The fiction that the State exists for our protection has been exploded a thousand times. However, as long as men lack self-assurance and self-reliance, the State will thrive; it depends for its existence on the fear and uncertainty of its individual members.

By living his own life in his own "eccentric" way Thoreau demonstrated the futility and absurdity of the life of the (so-called) masses. It was a deep, rich life which yielded him the maximum of contentment. In the bare necessities he found adequate means for the enjoyment of life. "The opportunities of living," he pointed out, "are diminished in proportion as what are called the 'means' are increased." He was at home in Nature, where man belongs. He held communion with bird and beast, with plant and flower, with star and stream. He was not an unsocial being, far from it. He had friends, among women as well as men. No American has written more eloquently and truthfully of friendship than he. If his life seems a restricted one, it was a thousand times wider and deeper than the life of the ordinary American today. He lost nothing by not mingling with the crowd, by not devouring the newspapers, by not enjoying the radio or the movies, by not having an automobile, a refrigerator, a vacuum cleaner. He not only did not lose anything through the lack of these things, but he actually enriched himself in a way far beyond the ability of the man of today who is glutted with these dubious comforts and conveniences. Thoreau lived, whereas we may be said to barely exist. In power and depth his thought not only matches that of our contemporaries, but usually surpasses it. In courage and virtue there are none among our leading spirits today to match him. As a writer, he is among the first three or four we can boast of. Viewed now from the heights of our decadence, he seems almost like an early Roman. The word *virtue* has meaning again, when connected with his name.

It is the young people of America who may profit from his homely wisdom, from his example even more. They need to be reassured that what was possible then is still possible today. America is still a vastly unpopulated country, a land abounding in forests, streams, lakes, deserts, mountains, prairies, rivers, where a man of good-will with a little effort and belief in his own powers can enjoy a deep, tranquil, rich life—provided he go his own way. He need not and should not think of making a good living, but rather of creating a good life for himself. The wise men always return to the soil; one has only to think of the great men of India, China and France, their poets, sages, artists, to realize how deep is this need in every man. I am thinking, naturally, of creative types, for the others will gravitate to their own unimaginative levels, never suspecting that life holds any better promise. I think of the budding American poets, sages and artists because they appear so appallingly helpless in this present-day American world. They all wonder so naïvely how they will live if they do not hire themselves out to some taskmaster; they wonder still more how, after doing that, they will ever find time to do what they were called to do. They never think any more of going into the desert or the wilderness, of wresting a living from the soil, of doing odd jobs, of living on as little as possible. They remain in the towns and cities, flitting from one thing to another, restless, miserable, frustrated, searching in vain for a way out. They ought to be told at the outset that society, as it is now constituted, provides no way out, that the solution is in their own hands and that it can be won only by the use of their own two hands. One has to hack his way out with the ax. The real wilderness is not out there somewhere, but in the towns and cities, in that complicated web which we have made of life and which serves no purpose but to thwart, cramp and inhibit the free spirits. Let a man believe in himself and he will find a way to exist despite the barriers and traditions which hem him in. The America of Thoreau's day was just as contemptuous of, just as hostile to, his experiment as we are today to anyone who essays it. Undeveloped as the country was then, men were lured from all regions, all walks of life, by the discovery of gold in California. Thoreau stayed at home, where he cultivated his own mine. He had only to go a few miles to be deep in the heart of Nature. For most of us, no matter where we live in this great country, it is still possible to travel but a few miles and find oneself in nature. I have traveled the length and breadth of the land, and if I was impressed by one thing it was by this—that America is empty. It is also true, to be sure, that nearly all this empty space is owned by someone or other—banks, railroads, insurance companies and so on. It is almost impossible to wander off the beaten path without "trespassing" on private property. But that nonsense would soon cease if people began to get up on their hind legs and desert the towns and cities. John Brown and a bare handful of men virtually defeated the entire population of America. It was the Abolitionists who freed the slaves, not the armies of Grant and Sherman, not Abraham Lincoln. There is no ideal condition of life to step into anywhere at any time. Everything is difficult, and everything becomes more difficult still when you choose to live your own life. But, to live one's own life is still the best way of life, always was, and always will be. The greatest snare and delusion is to postpone living your own life until an ideal form of government is created which will permit everyone to lead the good life. Lead the good life now, this instant, every instant, to the best of your ability and you will bring about indirectly and unconsciously a form of government nearer to the ideal.

Because Thoreau laid such emphasis on conscience and on active resistance, one is apt to think of his life as bare and grim. One forgets that he was a man who shunned work as much as possible, who knew how to idle his time away. Stern moralist that he was, he had nothing in common with the professional moralists. He was too deeply religious to have anything to do with the Church, just as he was too much the man of action to bother with politics. Similarly he was too rich in spirit to think of amassing wealth, too courageous, too self-reliant, to worry about security and protection. He found, by opening his eyes, that life provides everything necessary for man's peace and enjoyment—one has only to make use of what is there, ready to hand, as it were. "Life is bountiful," he seems to be saying all the time. *"Relax!* Life is here, all about you, not there, not over the hill."

He found Walden. But Walden is everywhere, if the man himself is there. Walden has become a symbol. It should become a reality. Thoreau himself has beome a symbol. But he was only a man, let us not forget that. By making him a symbol, by raising memorials to him, we defeat the very purpose of his life. Only by living our lives to the full can we honor his memory. We should not try to imitate him but to surpass him. Each one of us has a totally different life to lead. We should not strive to become like Thoreau, or even like Jesus Christ, but to become what we are in truth and in essence. That is the message of every great individual and the whole meaning of being an individual. To be anything less is to move nearer to nullity.

BIG SUR AND THE ORANGES
OF HIERONYMUS BOSCH

From Big Sur and the Oranges of Hieronymus Bosch. *By the time Miller arrived at Big Sur in the spring of 1944, he was far removed from the Paris years. He now had achieved a reputation as a "legitimate" writer, and he had a steadily lengthening list of publications to his credit. But his novels were still banned, he was still living hand-to-mouth, and he still lacked a fixed residence, a place where he could set up his typewriter and his books. These were conditions more easily borne by a younger man, and perhaps for the first time, Miller found himself longing for a place of rest and retreat. And even an outlaw writer may dream of writing in peace and modest security, surrounded by a few kindred spirits. But, as Miller well knew, it was what was in the person, not what was in the place, that made the crucial difference.*

The little community of one, begun by the fabulous "outlander," Jaime de Angulo, has multiplied into a dozen families. The hill (Partington Ridge) is now nearing the saturation point, as things go in this part of the world. The one big difference between the Big Sur I encountered eleven years ago and that of today is the advent of so many new children. The mothers here seem to be as fecund as the soil. The little country school, situated not far from the State Park, has almost reached its capacity. It is the sort of school which, most unfortunately for our children, is rapidly disappearing from the American scene.

In another ten years we know not what may happen. If uranium or some other metal vital to the warmongers is discovered in these parts, Big Sur will be nothing but a legend.

Today Big Sur is no longer an outpost. The number of sight-seers and visitors increases yearly. Emil White's "Big Sur Guide" alone brings swarms of tourists to our front door. What was inaugurated with virginal modesty threatens to end as a bonanza. The early settlers are dying off. Should their huge tracts of land be broken up into small holdings, Big Sur may rapidly develop into a suburb (of Monterey), with bus service, barbecue stands, gas stations, chain stores and all the odious claptrap that makes Suburbia horrendous.

This is a bleak view. It may be that we will be spared the usual horrors which accompany the tides of progress. Perhaps the millenium will be ushered in before we are taken over!

I like to think back to my early days on Partington Ridge, when there was no electricity, no butane tanks, no refrigeration—and the mail came only three times a week. In those days, and even later when I returned to the Ridge, I managed to get along without a car. To be sure, I did have a little cart (such as children play with), which Emil White had knocked together for me. Hitching myself to it, like an old billy goat, I would patiently haul the mail and groceries up the hill, a fairly steep climb of about a mile and a half. On reaching the turn near the Roosevelts' driveway, I would divest myself of everything but a jock-strap. What was to hinder?

The callers in those days were mostly youngsters just entering or just leaving the service. (They're doing the same today, though the war ended in '45.) The majority of these lads were artists or would-be artists. Some stayed on, eking out the weirdest sort of existence; some came back later to have a serious go at it. They were all filled with a desire to escape the horrors of the present and willing to live like rats if only they might be left alone and in peace. What a strange lot they were, when I think on it! Judson Crews of Waco, Texas, one of the first to muscle in, reminded one—because of his shaggy beard and manner of speech—of a latter-day prophet. He lived almost exclusively on peanut butter and wild mustard greens, and neither smoked nor drank. Norman Mini, who had already had an unusual career, starting as in Poe's case with his dismissal from West Point, stayed on (with wife and child) long enough to finish a first novel—the best first novel I have ever read and, as yet, unpublished. Norman was "different" in that, though poor as a church mouse, he clung to his cellar, which contained some of the finest wines (native and foreign) anyone could wish for. And then there was Walker Winslow, who was then writing *If a Man Be Mad*, which turned out to be a best seller. Walker wrote at top speed, and seemingly without interruption, in a tiny shack by the roadside which Emil White had built to house the steady stream of stragglers who were forever busting in on him for a day, a week, a month or a year.

In all, almost a hundred painters, writers, dancers, sculptors and musicians have come and gone since I first arrived. At least a dozen possessed genuine talent and may leave their mark on the world. The one who was an unquestionable genius and the most spectacular of all, aside from Varda, who belongs to an earlier period, was Gerhart Muench of Dresden. Gerhart belongs in a category all by himself. As a pianist he is phenomenal, if not incomparable. He is also a composer. And in addition, a scholar, erudite to the finger tips. If he had done no more for us than to interpret Scriabin—and he did vastly more, all without result, alas!—we of Big Sur ought be forever indebted to him.

Speaking of artists, the curious thing is that few of this stripe ever last it out here. Is something lacking? Or is there too much . . . too much sunshine, too much fog, too much peace and contentment?

Almost every art colony owes its inception to the longing of a mature artist who felt the need to break with the clique surrounding him. The location chosen was usually an ideal one, particularly to the discoverer who had spent the better years of his life in dingy holes and garrets. The would-be artists, for whom place and atmosphere are all important, always contrive to convert these havens of retreat into boisterous, merry-making colonies. Whether this will happen to Big Sur remains to be seen. Fortunately there are certain deterrents.

It is my belief that the immature artist seldom thrives in idyllic surroundings. What he seems to need, though I am the last to advocate it, is more first-hand experience of life—more bitter experience, in other words. In short, more struggle, more privation, more anguish, more disillusionment. These goads or stimulants he may not always hope to find here in Big Sur. Here, unless he is on his guard, unless he is ready to wrestle with phantoms as well as bitter realities, he is apt to go to sleep mentally and spiritually. If an art colony is established here it will go the way of all the others. Artists never thrive in colonies. Ants do. What the budding artist needs is the privilege of wrestling with his problems in solitude—and now and then a piece of red meat.

The chief problem for the man who endeavors to live apart is the idle visitor. One can never decide whether he is a curse or a blessing. With all the experience which these last few years have provided, I still do not know how, or whether, to protect myself against the unwarranted intrusion, the steady invasion, of that prying, curious-minded species of "homo fatuoso" endowed with the annoying faculty of dropping in at the wrong moment. To seek a hide-out more difficult of access is futile. The fan who wants to meet you, who is *determined* to meet you, if only to shake your hand, will not stop at climbing the Himalayas.

In America, I have long observed, one lives exposed to all comers. One is expected to live thus or be regarded as a crank. Only in Europe do writers live behind garden walls and locked doors.

In addition to all the other problems he has to cope with, the artist has to wage a perpetual struggle to fight free. I mean, find a way out of the senseless grind which daily threatens to annihilate all incentive. Even more than other mortals, he has need of harmonious surroundings. As writer or painter, he can do his work most anywhere. The rub is that wherever living is cheap, wherever nature is inviting, it is almost impossible to find the means of acquiring that bare modicum which is needed to keep body and soul together. A man with talent has to make his living on the side or do his creative work on the side. A difficult choice!

If he has the luck to find an ideal spot, or an ideal community, it does not follow that his work will there receive the encouragement he so desperately needs. On the contrary, he will probably find that no one is interested in what he is doing. He will generally be looked upon as strange or different. And he *will* be, of course, since what makes him tick is that mysterious element "X" which his fellow-man seems so well able to do without. He is almost certain to eat, talk, dress in a fashion eccentric to his neighbors. Which is quite enough to mark him out for ridicule, contempt and isolation. If, by taking a humble job, he demonstrates that he is as good as the next man, the situation may be somewhat ameliorated. But not for long. To prove that he is "as good as the next man" means little or nothing to one who is an artist. It was his "otherness" which made him an artist and, given the chance, he will make his fellow-man other too. Sooner or later, in one way or another, he is bound to rub his neighbors the wrong way. Unlike the ordinary fellow, he will throw everything to the winds when the urge seizes him. Moreover, if he *is* an artist, he will be compelled to make sacrifices which worldly people find absurd and unnecessary. In following the inner light he will inevitably choose for his boon companion poverty. And, if he has in him the makings of a great artist, he may renounce everything, even his art. This, to the average citizen, particularly the good citizen, is preposterous and unthinkable. Thus it happens now and then that, failing to recognize the genius in a man, a most worthy, a most respected, member of society may be heard to say: "Beware of that chap, he's up to no good!"

The world being what it is, I give it as my candid opinion that anyone who knows how to work with his two hands, anyone who is willing to give a fair day's work for a fair day's pay, would be better off to abandon his art and settle down to a humdrum life in an out of the way place like this. It may indeed be the highest wisdom to elect to be a nobody in a relative paradise such as this rather than a celebrity in a world which has lost all sense of values. But this is a problem which is rarely settled in advance.

There is one young man in this community who seems to have espoused the kind of wisdom I refer to. He is a man with an independent income, a man of keen intelligence, well educated, sensitive, of excellent character, and capable not only with his hands but with brain and heart. In making a life for himself he has apparently chosen to do nothing more than raise a family, provide its members with what he can, and enjoy the life of day to day. He does everything single-handed, from erecting buildings to raising crops, making wines, and so on. At intervals he hunts or fishes, or just takes off into the wilderness to commune with nature. To the average man he would appear to be just another good citizen, except that he is of better physique than most, enjoys better health, has no vices and no trace of the usual neuroses. His library is an excellent one, and he is at home in it; he enjoys good music and listens to it frequently. He can hold his own at any sport or game, can vie with the toughest when it comes to hard work, and in general is what might be called "a good fellow," that is, a man who knows how to mix with others, how to get along with the world. But what he also knows and does, and what the average citizen can not or will not do, is to enjoy solitude, to live simply, to crave nothing, and to share what he has when called upon. I refrain from mentioning his name for fear of doing him a disservice. Let us leave him where he is, Mr. X, a master of the anonymous life and a wonderful example to his fellow-man.

While in Vienne (France) two years ago I had the privilege of making the acquaintance of Fernand Rude, the *sous-préfet* of Vienne, who possesses a remarkable collection of Utopian literature. On leaving, he presented me with a copy of his book, *Voyage en Icarie*,* which is the account of two workers from Vienne who came to America just a hundred years ago to join Étienne Cabet's experimental colony at Nauvoo, Illinois. The description given of American life, not only at Nauvoo but in the cities they passed through—they arrived at New Orleans and left by way of New York—is worth reading today, if only to observe how essentially unchanged is our American way of life. To be sure, Whitman was giving us about this same time (in his prose works) a similar picture of vulgarity, violence and corruption, in high and low places. One fact stands out, however, and that is the inborn urge of the American to experiment, to try out the most crack-brained schemes having to do with social, economic, religious and even sex relations. Where sex and religion were dominant, the most amazing results were achieved. The Oneida Community (New York), for example, is destined to remain as memorable an

---

* The title is taken from the book of the same name by Étienne Cabet wherein the latter describes his (imaginary) Utopia. A remarkable work in this, that though Communistic in the romantic sense, it is an accurate blueprint of the totalitarian governments we now have.

experiment as Robert Owen's in New Harmony (Indiana). As for the Mormons, nothing comparable to their efforts has ever been undertaken on this continent, and probably never will again.

In all these idealistic ventures, particularly those initiated by religious communities, the participants seemed to posssess a keen sense of reality, a practical wisdom, which in no way conflicted (as it does in the case of ordinary Christians) with their religious views. They were honest, law-abiding, industrious, self-sustaining, self-sufficient citizens with character, individuality and integrity, somewhat corroded (to our present way of thinking) by a Puritan sobriety and austerity, but never lacking in faith, courage and independence. Their influence on American thought, American behavior, has been most powerful.

Since living here in Big Sur I have become more and more aware of this tendency in my fellow-American to experiment. Today it is not communities or groups who seek to lead "the good life" but isolated individuals. The majority of these, at least from my observation, are young men who have already had a taste of professional life, who have already been married and divorced, who have already served in the armed forces and seen a bit of the world, as we say. Utterly disillusioned, this new breed of experimenter is resolutely turning his back on all that he once held true and viable, and is making a valiant effort to start anew. Starting anew, for this type, means leading a vagrant's life, tackling anything, clinging to nothing, reducing one's needs and one's desires, and eventually—out of a wisdom born of desperation—leading the life of an artist. Not, however, the type of artist we are familiar with. An artist, rather, whose sole interest is in creating, an artist who is indifferent to reward, fame, success. One, in short, who is reconciled from the outset to the fact that the better he is the less chance he has of being accepted at face value. These young men, usually in their late twenties or early thirties, are now roaming about in our midst like anonymous messengers from another planet. By force of example, by reason of their thoroughgoing nonconformity and, shall I say, "nonresistance," they are proving themselves a more potent, stimulating force than the most eloquent and vociferous of recognized artists.

The point to note is that these individuals are not concerned with undermining a vicious system but with leading their own lives—on the fringe of society. It is only natural to find them gravitating toward places like Big Sur, of which there are many replicas in this vast country. We are in the habit of speaking of "the last frontier," but wherever there are "individuals" there will always be new frontiers. For the man who wants to lead the good life, which is a way of saying *his own life*, there is always a spot where he can dig in and take root.

But what is it that these young men have discovered, and which, curiously enough, links them with their forebears who deserted Europe for America? That the American way of life is an illusory kind of existence, that the price demanded for the security and abundance it pretends to offer is too great. The presence of these "renegades," small in number though they be, is but another indication that the machine is breaking down. When the smashup comes, as now seems inevitable, they are more likely to survive the catastrophe than the rest of us. At least, they will know how to get along without cars, without refrigerators, without vacuum cleaners, electric razors and all the other "indispensables" . . . probably even without money. If ever we are to witness a new heaven and a new earth, it must surely be one in which money is absent, forgotten, wholly useless.

Here I should like to quote from a review of *Living the Good Life*, by Helen and Scott Nearing.* Says the editor: "What we are trying to suggest is that the solution for a cluttered, frustrated existence is not merely in moving to the country and attempting to practise 'the simple life.' The solution is in an attitude towards human experience which makes simple physical and economic arrangements almost a moral and esthetic necessity. It is the larger purpose in life which gives to its lesser enterprises—the obtaining of food, shelter and clothing—their essential harmony and balance. So often people dream of an ideal life "in community," forgetting that a "community" is not an end in itself, but a frame for higher qualities—the qualities of the mind and the heart. Making a community is not a magic formula for happiness and good; making a community is the result of the happiness and

* From *Manas*, Los Angeles, March 23, 1955.

the good which people already possess in principle, and the community, whether of one family or several, is the infinitely variable expression of the excellences of human beings, and not their cause. . . ."

Digging in at Big Sur eleven years ago, I must confess that I had not the least thought or concern about the life of the community. With a population of one hundred souls scattered over several hundred square miles, I was not even conscious of an existent "community." My community then comprised a dog, Pascal (so named because he had the sorrowful look of a thinker), a few trees, the buzzards, and a seeming jungle of poison oak. My only friend, Emil White, lived three miles down the road. The hot sulphur baths were three miles farther down the road. There the community ended, from my standpoint.

I soon found out how mistaken I was, of course. It was no time before neighbors began popping up from all sides—out of the brush, it seemed—and always laden with gifts, as well as the most discreet and sensible advice, for the "newcomer." Never have I known better neighbors! All of them were endowed with a tact and subtlety such as I never ceased to marvel at. They came only when they sensed you had need of them. As in France, it seemed to me that I was once again among people who knew how to let you be. And always there was a standing invitation to join them at table, should you have need of food or company.

Being one of those unfortunate "helpless" individuals who knew nothing but city ways, it wasn't long before I had to call upon my neighbors for aid of one kind or another. Something was always going amiss, something was always getting out of order. I hate to think what would have happened had I been left entirely to my own resources! Anyway, with the assistance that was always willingly and cheerfully extended, I received instruction in how to help myself, the most valuable gift that can be offered. I discovered all too quickly that my neighbors were not only extremely affable, helpful, generous in every way, but that they were far more intelligent, far wiser, far more self-sufficient than I had fatuously thought myself to be. The community, from being at first an invisible web, gradually became most tangible, most real. For the first time in my life I found myself surrounded by kind souls who were not thinking exclusively of their own welfare. A strange new sense of security began to develop in me, one I had never known before. In fact, I would boast to visitors that, once a resident of Big Sur, nothing evil could possibly happen to one. I would always add cautiously: "But one has first to prove himself a good neighbor!" Though they were addressed to my visitor, I meant these words for myself. And often, when the visitor had departed, I would repeat them to myself like a litany. It took time, you see, for one who had always lived the jungle life of the big city to realize that he too could be "a neighbor."

Here I must say flatly, and not without a bad conscience, that I am undoubtedly the worst neighbor any community could boast of. That I am still treated with more than mere tolerance is something which still surprises me.

Often I am so completely out of it all that the only way I can "get back" is to look at my world through the eyes of my children. I always begin by thinking back to the glorious childhood I enjoyed in that squalid section of Brooklyn known as Williamsburg. I try to relate those squalid streets and shabby houses to the vast expanse of sea and mountain of this region. I dwell on the birds I never saw except for the sparrow feasting on a fresh pile of manure, or a stray pigeon. Never a hawk, a buzzard, an eagle, never a robin or a hummingbird. I think of the sky which was always hacked to pieces by rooftops and hideous smoking chimneys. I breathe again the air that filled the sky, an atmosphere without fragrance, often leaden and oppressive, saturated with the reek of burning chemicals. I think of the games we played in the street, ignorant of the lure of stream and forest. I think, and with tenderness, of my little companions, some of whom later went to the penitentiary. Despite it all, it was a good life I led there. A wonderful life, I might say. It was the first "Paradise" I knew, there in that old neighborhood. And though forever gone, it is still accessible in memory.

But *now*, when I watch the youngsters playing in our front yard, when I see them silhouetted against the blue white-capped Pacific, when I stare at the huge, frightening buzzards swirling lazily above, circling, dipping, forever circling, when I observe the willow gently swaying, its long fragile branches drooping ever lower, ever greener and tenderer, when I hear the frog croaking in the pool or a bird calling from the bush, when I suddenly turn and espy a lemon ripening on a dwarfish tree or notice that the camellia has just begun to bloom, I see my children set against an eternal background. They are not even *my* children any longer, but just children, children of the earth . . . and I know they will never forget, never forsake, the place where they were born and raised. In my mind I am with them as they return from some distant shore to gaze upon the old homestead. My eyes are moist with tears as I watch them moving tenderly and reverently amid a swarm of golden memories. Will they notice, I wonder, the tree they were going to help me plant but were too busy then having fun? Will they stand in the little wing we built for them and wonder how on earth they ever fitted into such a cubicle? Will they pause outside the tiny workroom where I passed my days and tap again at the windowpane to ask if I will join them at play—*or must I work some more?* Will they find the marbles I gathered from the garden and hid so that they would not swallow them? Will they stand in reverie at the forest glade, where the little stream prattles on, and search for the pots and pans with which we made our make-believe breakfast before diving into the woods? Will they take the goat path along the flank of the mountain and look up in wonder and awe at the old Trotter house teetering in the wind? Will they run down to the Rosses, if only in memory, to see if Harrydick can mend the broken sword or Shanagolden lend us a pot of jam?

For every wonderful event in my golden childhood they must possess a dozen incomparably more wonderful. For not only did they have their little playmates, their games, their mysterious adventures, as did I, they had also skies of pure azure and walls of fog moving in and out of the canyons with invisible feet, hills in winter of emerald green and in summer mountain upon mountain of pure gold. They had even more, for there was ever the unfathomable silence of the forest, the blazing immensity of the Pacific, days drenched with sun and nights spangled with stars and—"Oh, Daddy, come quick, see the moon, it's lying in the pool!" And besides the adoration of the neighbors, a dolt of a father who preferred wasting his time playing with them to cultivating his mind or making himself a good neighbor. Lucky the father who is merely a writer, who can drop his work and return to childhood at will! Lucky the father who is pestered from morn till sundown by two healthy, insatiable youngsters! Lucky the father who learns to see again through the eyes of his children, even though he become the biggest fool that ever was!

"The Brothers and Sisters of the Free Spirit called their devotional community-life 'Paradise' and interpreted the word as signifying the quintessence of love."*

Looking at a fragment of "The Millennium" (by Hieronymus Bosch) the other day, I pointed out to our neighbor, Jack Morgenrath (formerly of Williamsburg, Brooklyn), how hallucinatingly real were the oranges that diapered the trees. I asked him why it was that these oranges, so preternaturally real in appearance, possessed something more than would oranges painted, say, by Cézanne (better known for his apples) or even by Van Gogh. To Jack it was simple. (Everything is quite simple to Jack, by the way. It's part of his charm.) Said Jack: "It's because of the ambiance." And he is right, absolutely right. The animals in this same triptych are equally mysterious, equally hallucinating, in their super-reality. A camel is always a camel and a leopard a leopard, yet they are altogether unlike any other camels, any other leopards. They can hardly even be said to be the camels and leopards of Hieronymus Bosch, magician though he was. They belong to another age, an age when man was one with all creation . . . "when the lion lay down with the lamb."

Bosch is one of the very few painters—he was indeed more than a painter!—who acquired a magic vision. He saw through the phenomenal world, rendered it transparent, and thus revealed its pristine aspect.† Seeing the world through his eyes it

---

* *The Millennium of Hieronymus Bosch*, by Wilhelm Fränger (Chicago: University of Chicago Press, 1951), page 104.

† "This human mind has drawn a net of logical relationships and practical ingenuity over the phenomenal world with which it is confronted; and so, by this intellectual and material domination of the world, it has removed itself to an infinite distance from the created world in which it once had a purely natural

appears to us once again as a world of indestructible order, beauty, harmony, which it is our privilege to accept as a paradise or convert into a purgatory.

The enchanting, and sometimes terrifying, thing is that the world can be so many things to so many different souls. That it can be, and is, all these at one and the same time.

I am led to speak of the "Millennium" because, receiving as many visitors as I do, and from all parts of the globe, I am constantly reminded that I am living in a virtual paradise. ("And how did you manage to find such a place?" is the usual exclamation. As if *I* had any part in it!) But what amazes me, and this is the point, is that so very few ever think on taking leave that they too might enjoy the fruits of paradise. Almost invariably the visitor will confess that he lacks the courage—imagination would be nearer the mark—to make the necessary break. "You're lucky," he will say—meaning, to be a writer—"you can do your work anywhere." He forgets what I have told him, and most pointedly, about the other members of the community—the ones who really support the show—who are not writers, painters or artists of any sort, except in spirit. "Too late," he probably murmurs to himself, as he takes a last wistful glance about.

How illustrative, this attitude, of the woeful resignation men and women succumb to! Surely every one realizes, at some point along the way, that he is capable of living a far better life than the one he has chosen. What stays him, usually, is the fear of the sacrifices involved. (Even to relinquish his chains seem like a sacrifice.) Yet everyone knows that nothing is accomplished without sacrifice.

The longing for paradise, whether here on earth or in the beyond, has almost ceased to be. Instead of an *idée-force* it has become an *idée fixe*. From a potent myth it has degenerated into a taboo. Men will sacrifice their lives to bring about a better world—whatever that may mean—but they will not budge an inch to attain paradise. Nor will they struggle to create a bit of paradise in

---

share. It was this natural world in which the Brethren of the Free Spirit saw the meaning of life." (*The Millennium of Hieronymus Bosch*, page 152.)

the hell they find themselves. It is so much easier, and gorier, to make revolution, which means, to put it simply, establishing another, a different, status quo. If paradise were realizable—this is the classic retort!—it would no longer be paradise.

What is one to say to a man who insists on making his own prison?

There is a type of individual who, after finding what he considers a paradise, proceeds to pick flaws in it. Eventually this man's paradise becomes even worse than the hell from which he had escaped.

Certainly paradise, whatever, wherever it be, contains flaws. (Paradisiacal flaws, if you like.) If it did not, it would be incapable of drawing the hearts of men *or* angels.

The windows of the soul are infinite, we are told. And it is through the eyes of the soul that paradise is visioned. If there are flaws in your paradise, open more windows! Vision is entirely a creative faculty: it uses the body and the mind as the navigator uses his instruments. Open and alert, it matters little whether one finds a supposed short cut to the Indies—or discovers a new world. Everything is begging to be discovered, not accidentally, but intuitively. Seeking intuitively, one's destination is never in a beyond of time or space but always here and now. If we are always arriving and departing, it is also true that we are eternally anchored. One's destination is never a place but rather a new way of looking at things. Which is to say that there are no limits to vision. Similarly, there are no limits to paradise. Any paradise worth the name can sustain all the flaws in creation and remain undiminished, untarnished.

If I have entered upon a vein which I must confess is one not frequently discussed here, I am nevertheless certain that it is one which secretly engages the minds of many members of the community.

Everyone who has come here in search of a new way of life had made a complete change-about in his daily routine. Nearly every one has come from afar, usually from a big city. It meant abandoning a job and a mode of life which was detestable and insufferable. To what degree each one has found "new life" can be estimated only by the efforts he or she put forth. Some, I suspect, would have found "it" even had they remained where they were.

The most important thing I have witnessed, since coming here, is the transformation people have wrought in their own being. Nowhere have I seen individuals work so earnestly and assiduously on themselves. Nor so successfully. Yet nothing is taught or preached here, at least overtly. Some have made the effort and failed. Happily for the rest of us, I should say. But even these who failed gained something. For one thing, their outlook on life was altered, enlarged if not "improved." And what could be better than for the teacher to become his own pupil, or the preacher his own convert?

In a paradise you don't preach or teach. You practice the perfect life—or you relapse.

There seems to be an unwritten law here which insists that you accept what you find and like it, profit by it, or you are cast out. Nobody does the rejecting, please understand. Nobody, no group here, would crave such authority. No, the place itself, the elements which make it, do that. It's the law, as I say. And it is a just law which works harm to no one. To the cynical-minded it may sound like the same old triumph of our dear status quo. But the enthusiast knows that it is precisely the fact that there is no status quo here which makes for its paradisiacal quality.

No, the law operates because that which makes for paradise can not and will not assimilate that which makes for hell. How often it is said that we make our own heaven and our own hell. And how little it is taken to heart! Yet the truth prevails, whether we believe in it or not.

Paradise or no paradise, I have the very definite impression that the people of this vicinity are striving to live up to the grandeur and nobility which is such an integral part of the setting. They behave as if it were a privilege to live here, as if it were by an act of grace they found themselves here. The place itself is so overwhelmingly bigger, greater, than anyone could hope to make it that it engenders a humility and reverence not frequently met with in Americans. There being nothing to improve on in the surroundings, the tendency is to set about improving oneself.

It is of course true that individuals have undergone tremendous changes, broadened their vision, altered their natures, in hideous, thwarting surroundings—prisons, ghettos, concentration camps, and so on. Only a very rare individual elects to *remain* in such places. The man who has seen the light follows the light. And the light usually leads him to the place where he can function most effectively, that is, where he will be of most use to his fellow-men. In this sense, it matters little whether it be darkest Africa or the Himalayan heights. God's work can be done anywhere, so to say.

We have all met the soldier who has been overseas. And we all know that each one has a different story to relate. We are all like returned soldiers. We have all been somewhere, spiritually speaking, and we have either benefited by the experience or been worsted by it. One man says: "Never again!" Another says: "Let it come! I'm ready for anything!" Only the fool hopes to repeat an experience; the wise man knows that *every* experience is to be viewed as a blessing. Whatever we try to deny or reject is precisely what we have need of; it is our very need which often paralyzes us, prevents us from welcoming a (good or bad) experience.

I come back once again to those individuals who came here full of needs and who fled after a time because "it" was not what they hoped to find, or because "they" were not what they thought themselves to be. None of them, from what I have learned, has yet found it or himself. Some returned to their former masters in the manner of slaves unable to support the privileges and responsibilities of freedom. Some found their way into mental retreats. Some became derelicts. Others simply surrendered to the villainous status quo.

I speak as if they had been marked by the whip. I do not mean to be cruel or vindictive. What I wish to say quite simply is that none of them, in my humble opinion, is a whit happier, a whit better off, an inch advanced in any respect. They will all continue to talk about their Big Sur adventure for the rest of their lives— wistfully, regretfully, or elatedly, as occasion dictates. In the hearts of some, I know, is the profound hope that their children will display more courage, more perseverance, more integrity than they themselves did. But do they not overlook something? Are not their children, as the product of self-confessed failures, already condemned? Have they not been contaminated by the virus of "security"?

The most difficult thing to adjust to, apparently, is peace and contentment. As long as there is something to fight, people seem able to brace all manner of hardships. Remove the element of struggle, and they are like fish out of water. Those who no longer have anything to worry about will, in desperation, often take on the burdens of the world. This not through idealism but because they must have something to do, or at least something to talk about. Were these empty souls truly concerned about the plight of their fellow-men they would consume themselves in the flames of devotion. One need hardly go beyond his own doorstep to discover a realm large enough to exhaust the energies of a giant, or better, a saint.

Naturally, the more attention one gives to the deplorable conditions outside the less one is able to enjoy what peace and liberty he possesses. Even if it be heaven we find ourselves in, we can render it suspect and dubious.

Some will say they do not wish to *dream* their lives away. As if life itself were not a dream, a very real dream from which there is no awakening! We pass from one state of dream to another: from the dream of sleep to the dream of waking, from the dream of life to the dream of death. Whoever has enjoyed a good dream never complains of having wasted his time. On the contrary, he is delighted to have partaken of a reality which serves to heighten and enhance the reality of everyday.

The oranges of Bosch's "Millennium," as I said before, exhale this dreamlike reality which constantly eludes us and which is the very substance of life. They are far more delectable, far more potent, than the Sunkist oranges we daily consume in the naive belief that they are laden with wonder-working vitamins. The millennial oranges which Bosch created restore the soul; the ambiance in which he suspended them is the everlasting one of spirit become real.

Every creature, every object, every place has its own ambiance.

Our world itself possesses an ambiance which is unique. But worlds, objects, creatures, places, all have this in common: they are ever in a state of transmutation. The supreme delight of dream lies in this transformative power. When the personality liquefies, so to speak, as it does so deliciously in dream, and the very nature of one's being is alchemized, when form and substance, time and space, become yielding and elastic, responsive and obedient to one's slightest wish, he who awakens from his dream knows beyond all doubt that the imperishable soul which he calls his own is but a vehicle of this eternal element of change.

In waking life, when all is well and cares fall away, when the intellect is silenced and we slip into reverie, do we not surrender blissfully to the eternal flux, float ecstatically on the still current of life? We have all experienced moments of utter forgetfulness when we knew ourselves as plant, animal, creature of the deep or denizen of the air. Some of us have even known moments when we were as the gods of old. Most every one has known *one* moment in his life when he felt so good, so thoroughly attuned, that he has been on the point of exclaiming: *"Ah, now is the time to die!"* What is it lurks here in the very heart of euphoria? The thought that it will not, can not last? The sense of an ultimate? Perhaps. But I think there is another, deeper aspect to it. I think that in such moments we are trying to tell ourselves what we have long known but ever refuse to accept—that living and dying are one, that all is one, and that it makes no difference whether we live a day or a thousand years.

Confucius put it this way: "If a man sees Truth in the morning, he may die in the evening without regret."

STAND STILL LIKE THE HUMMINGBIRD

From Stand Still Like the Hummingbird, *"My Life as an Echo." The Zen of having survived intact for seventy years.*

MY LIFE AS AN ECHO*

One of the chief complaints leveled at me by English critics is that I never write about anything but myself. By now, it is true, I must have written several million words, scattered throughout a dozen or more so-called autobiographical romances. I am sick of hearing about myself, even from my own lips. But since I am challenged to write a few thousand more words—about myself—I must acquiesce, and with good grace, even at the risk of boring the reader. So here goes. . . .

It is usual to commence these things with a few pertinent facts—date and place of birth, education, married or divorced, and so forth. Is it necessary, I wonder? Next year I shall be seventy years old. Old enough, in other words, for even the average reader to have gleaned a few salient facts about my life. That is, if I am what rumor always purports me to be: a nine-day wonder in the realm of obscenity, farce, mysticism and obscurantism.

Though I was born in Yorkville, Manhattan, a few hours too late to be a Christmas present, and though I claim as my country the 14th Ward of Brooklyn, actually I might just as well have been born in the Himalayas or on Easter Island. American through and through, I am less at home in my own country than anywhere. I

---

*Apologies to Moishe Nadir, the Yiddish writer whose title I have borrowed.

am an anomaly, a paradox and a misfit. Most of the time I live *en marge*. My ideal is to become thoroughly anonymous—a Mr. What's-his-name. Or just George, like the iceman. In short, I am at my best when nobody knows me, nobody recognizes me. When I am just another nobody, in other words.

It was about the middle of the 1930s, when I first read about Zen, that I began to perceive the delicious efficacity of being a nobody. Not that I had ever longed to be a somebody. No, all I had ever begged of the Creator was to permit me to become a writer. Not a sensational writer, or a celebrated one, either. Just a writer. I had tried, you see, to be most everything else—without success. Even as a garbage collector, even as gravedigger, I showed no marked signs of ability. The one position I did fill with some degree of success (though unrecognized by my masters) was that of personnel director in the Western Union Telegraph Company, in New York. The four years I spent hiring and firing the miserable creatures who made up the fluctuating force of messengers of this organization were the most important years of my life, from the standpoint of my future role as writer. It was here that I was in constant touch with Heaven and Hell. It was for me what Siberia was for Dostoevsky. And it was while serving as personnel director that I made my first attempts at writing. It was high time. I was already thirty-three years old and, as the title of my trilogy indicates, it was a rosy crucifixion which I was about to experience.

To be truthful, the ordeal commenced somewhat before entering the service of the Western Union. It commenced with my first marriage and hung over into my second. (The Italian reader should bear in mind, of course, that at thirty-three an American is still somewhat of an adolescent. Few indeed, even if they live to be a hundred, ever pass beyond the stage of adolescence.) Naturally, it was not the marriages which were the cause of my suffering. Not altogether, at any rate. The cause was myself, my own cussed nature. Never satisfied with anything, never willing to compromise, never getting *adjusted*—that abominable word which the Americans have taken over and raised to apotheosis.

It was only when I got to France, where I came to grips with myself, that I realized that I alone was responsible for all the misfortunes which had befallen me. The day that truth dawned on me—and it came like a flash—the burden of guilt and suffering fell away. What a tremendous relief it was to cease blaming society, or my parents, or my country. "Guilty, Your Honor! Guilty, Your Majesty! Guilty on all points!" I could exclaim. And feel good about it.

Of course I have suffered since, many times, and undoubtedly will continue to do so . . . but in a different way. I am now like those alcoholics who, after years of abstinence, finally learn how to take a drink without fear of becoming drunk. I mean that I have made my peace with suffering. Suffering belongs, just as much as laughter, joy, treachery or what have you. When one perceives its function, its value, its usefulness, one no longer dreads it, this endless suffering which all the world is so eager to dodge. When it is regarded in the light of understanding it becomes something else. I called this process of transmutation my "rosy crucifixion." Lawrence Durrell, who was then visiting me (at Villa Seurat), expressed it in another way; he dubbed me "as of henceforth" *The Happy Rock.*

To become a writer! Little did I dream, in begging the Creator to grant me this boon, what a price I would have to pay for the privilege. Never did I dream that I would be obliged to deal with so many idiots and blunderbusses as have crossed my path these last twenty years or more. I had imagined, in writing my books, that I was addressing myself to kindred spirits. Never did I realize that I would be accepted, and for the wrong reasons, by the unthinking mob which reads with equal relish the comic strips, the sports news and the financial reports of the *Wall Street Journal.* Everyone knows, who has read my book about Big Sur (where I have been living these last fourteen years), that my life in this remote, isolated spot is that of a squirrel in a cage: perpetually on view, perpetually at the mercy of any and every curiosity seeker, every autograph hound, every tuppenny newspaper reporter. Perhaps it was the premonition of just such an absurdity which led me to insert a long quotation from Papini's *Uomo Finito* in my very first book, *Tropic of Cancer.* Today, much like Einstein, I feel that if I were granted a second life I would elect to be a carpenter or fisherman, anything but a writer. The few whom one's words reach, to whom one's words make sense, give joy and comfort, will be what they are whether they read one's books or not. The whole damned business of book after book, line after line, boils down to a stroll in the park, a few doffs of the hat, and a "Good morning, Tom, how goes it?" "Just fine . . . *and you?*" Nobody is any the wiser, sadder or happier. *C'est un travail du chapeau, voilà tout!*

Then why do you continue? one may well ask. The answer is simple. I write now because I enjoy it; it gives me pleasure. I'm an addict, a happy addict. I no longer have any illusions about the importance of words. Lao-Tzu put all his wisdom into a few indestructible pages. Jesus never wrote a line. As for the Buddha, he is remembered for the wordless sermon he gave while holding a flower for his listeners to regard (or hear). Words, like other waste matter, eventually drift down the drain. Acts live on. The Acts of the Apostles, *bien entendu,* not the beehive activity which today passes for action.

Action. Often I think of it this way: I and my body. You fling your body around—here, there, everywhere—but *you* remain the same. You might as well have stood still. If what must happen, what must be learned, doesn't occur in this life, it will the next time around, or the third or the fourth time. We have all time on our hands. What we need to discover is eternity. The only life is the eternal life. I have no ready-made prescription as to how to obtain it.

No doubt some of the foregoing observations are highly unpalatable, particularly to those benighted souls who long to set the world on fire. Do they not realize, I wonder, that the world has ever been on fire, and always will be? Aren't they aware that the Hell we are living in is more real than the one to come—if one deals in that nonsense? They should at least take a little pride in the fact that they too have contributed to the making of this Hell. Life on earth will always be a Hell; the antidote is not a hereafter called Heaven but a new life here below—"the new heaven and the new earth"—born of the complete acceptance of life.

I see that I am forgetting my subject—myself. It is obvious that there are other subjects which are more enticing to me. Sometimes I even find theology absorbing. Believe me, it *can be,* if one is not tempted as a result to become a theologian. Even science can assume an interesting aspect, provided one does not take it seriously. Any theory, any idea, any speculation can augment the zest for life so long as one does not make the mistake of thinking that he is getting somewhere. We are getting nowhere, because (metaphysically speaking) there is nowhere to go. We are already there, have been since eternity. All we need do is wake up to the fact.

It took me some fifty-odd years to wake up. Even now I am not thoroughly awake, else I would not be writing these extraneous words. But then, one of the things one learns as one goes along is that nonsense also has its place. The real nonsense, of course, goes under such highfalutin names as science, religion, philosophy, history, culture, civilization, and so on and so forth. The Mad Hatter is not your miserable *clochard* lying in the gutter with a bottle clasped to his bosom but His Excellency, Sir Popinjay of His Majesty's Court, he who pretends to have us believe that, armed with the right words, the right portfolio, the right top hat and spats, he can placate, tame or subdue this or that monster who is making ready to gobble up the world on behalf of The Peepul, or in the name of Christ, or whatever the song happens to be.

Frankly, if we must play with this idea of saving the world, then I say that in making an aquarelle which pleases me—*me*, not *you* necessarily—I am doing my share better than any cabinet minister with or without portfolio. I believe that even His Holiness, the Pope, little as I believe in him, may be doing his part too. But then, if I include him I must also include such as Al Capone and Elvis Presley. Why not? Can you prove the contrary?

As I was saying, after I quit the Messenger Employment Department, after I had been a gravedigger and a scavenger, a librarian, a bookseller, an insurance agent, a ticket chopper, a ranch hand and a hundred other equally important things (spiritually speaking), I landed in Paris, soon was down and out—would have become a pimp or a prostitute had I had the makings for it—and ended up becoming a writer. *What more would you like to know?* Between times is what I can't fill in, because I have already used up my fillers in my "autobiographical romances," which, if I have not already warned the reader, should be taken with a grain of salt. There are times when I myself no longer know whether I said and did the things I report or whether I dreamed them up. Anyway, I always dream true. If I lie a bit now and then it is mainly in the interest of truth. What I mean to say is that I try to put together the broken parts of myself. The dreamer who rapes or murders in his sleep is the same person who sits in the bank all day counting somebody else's money or who officiates as president of a republic. Or isn't he? Are all the crooks of this world behind bars or are some of them masquerading as ministers of finance?

Maybe this is the moment to observe that I am at last approaching the end of my interminable autobiographical sleigh ride. The first half of *Nexus* has recently been issued by Editions du Chêne, Paris. The second half, which I should have written six months ago but may not begin for another five years to come, will bring to an end what I planned and projected in the year 1927. At that time I thought the story of my life (which is, in truth, only the record of seven years of my life, the crucial years before leaving for France), at that time, as I say, I thought one huge volume would do the trick. (*The Story of My Misfortunes*, by Henry Abélard Miller.) I would have my say, in short, and then bury myself. It was not that simple. Nothing is simple, except to the sage. I got caught in my own web, so to speak. What I have now to learn is whether I can break the web or not. "The Web and the Rock"—are they not one and the same?

Never shall I forget the impact which Otto Rank's *Art and Artist* made upon me. Particularly that part wherein he speaks of the type of writer who loses himself in his work: who makes his work his tomb, in other words. And who did it most effectively, according to Rank? *Shakespeare*. I would also include Hieronymus Bosch, of whose life we know almost as little as we do of Shakespeare's. Where artists are concerned, we are always desperately struggling—*itching* would be the better word—to put our fingers on the man. As if the man called Charles Dickens, for example, were quite another entity. It is not that we are so eager to have the complete being in our grasp as it is that we can never quite believe that the artist and the man are one and the same. In my own case there are friends, for example, who know me intimately, or at least who treat me as if they did, and who profess that they do not understand a word I have written. Or worse, who have the cheek to tell me that I invented it all. Fortunately I have a few friends, a mere handful, who know and accept me as a writer and as a man. Were it not so I might have grave doubts as to my true identity. To be a writer at all one must certainly have a split personality. But when it comes time to reach for your hat and take an airing, you've got to be certain that it's *your hat,* your own legs, and the name is Miller, not Mahatma Gandhi.

As for tomorrow, there just ain't any. I've lived all my yesterdays and all my tomorrows. *Pro tem* I am just treading water.

Should I write more books, books I never intended to write, I will excuse myself by calling it a stroll in the park. . . . "Good morning, Tom, how goes it?" "Fine . . . *and you?*" In other words, I now have my tail in my mouth. With your permission I'll just roll along. No need for anyone to give me a rap with a drumstick, if you get what I mean. Frankly, I don't quite get it myself, but that's the general idea, as we say in our American lingo.